P9-BII-416

"HILARIOUS AND SHOCKING . . .

Prose, one of the best and quirkiest fiction writers, has written a noir slapstick send-up of American hypocrisies and neuroses."

San Francisco Chronicle

"Prose is a relentless and scathingly perceptive observer of pretensions, and she has a fresh, smart ability to turn the familiar on its head with acute, vivid language."

Chicago Tribune

"Prose's deft comedy of manners goes beyond raillery to strike darker, more resonant chords. . . . A most engaging novel. The dialogue is droll, the pace smart. Francine Prose mingles domestic anguish and high comedy, the drabness of the mundane with the sparkle of badinage. . . . Wit, wisdom and rueful observation distinguish the well-made PRIMITIVE PEOPLE."

The Boston Globe

"Blood, tears, sweat, sacrifice. All human life is here plus the funniest lines, the saddest moments, the most vigorous, impossible, dreadful people you're ever likely to meet on the printed page. Life, in Francine Prose's fictional world, is almost too painful to live, yet you wouldn't want to lose a moment of it. This is her special art."

FAY WELDON

Please turn the page for more critical acclaim. . . .

PRIMITIVE PEOPLE

Francine Prose

IVY BOOKS • NEW YORK

Ivy Books
Published by Ballantine Books
Copyright © 1992 by Francine Prose

"I Can't Help It If I'm Still in Love With You" written by Hank Williams, © 1951, renewed 1979 Acuff-Rose Music, Inc. (BMI) and Hiriam Music (BMI). All rights reserved. International copyright secured. Used by permission. "Dark End of the Street" written by Dan Penn & Chips Moman, © 1967, 1977 Screen Gems-EMI Music Inc. All rights reserved. International copyright secured. Used by permission.

I would like to thank the John Simon Guggenheim Memorial Foundation for its generous support. F.P.

Library of Congress Catalog Card Number: 91-28692

ISBN 0-8041-1110-3

This edition published by arrangement with Farrar Straus & Giroux, Inc.

Manufactured in the United States of America

First Ballantine Books Edition: May 1993

For Howie, Bruno, and Leon

"AND THIS IS the attic," Mrs. Porter said, "where supposedly my husband's ancestors hid out during the Civil War. They'd heard rumors that the Confederate navy was sailing up the Hudson. Of course by then the Porters had already been inbreeding for several generations past the point of total genetic depletion."

Why was Mrs. Porter taking Simone on this needlessly thorough tour of her mansion, volunteering personal and historic details Simone would never need, visiting places her duties would never take her, such as, Simone hoped, the attic? You'd think Simone was buying the house instead of wanting to come and work there, applying for a job as a cook and caregiver for Mrs. Porter's two children—two bright little spirits, their mother said, who lately seemed slightly dejected.

Mrs. Porter took a dutiful breath—deep inside her antique fur coat, her fragile bird-skeleton seemed to rattle—and plunged ahead with the tiresome task of leading Simone through the attic, a labyrinth of gutted armchairs, fractured mirrors, curlicues of peeled veneer, lethal hairdryers, and toasters like mini-electric chairs. Simone stopped to stare—rudely, she feared—at some paintings stacked against a wall: portraits, caramelized by age, of pale ghostly men and women with ragged, empty, almond-shaped holes where their eyes should have been.

"Oh, the family portraits," Mrs. Porter said. "I suppose they do look *affreux*. When the children were tiny I used to let them cut out the eyes for their paper dolls. What could

1

I have been thinking of? Some marvelous early primitives. Well, they're Geoffrey's ancestors. Probably they deserve it. How do you say? *Les enfants*." She snipped the air. *"Pour les poupées de papier."*

And why was Mrs. Porter speaking French? Simone understood English and spoke with only a faint Haitian accent. In Haiti she'd studied with American nuns and then at the university, and though she worried that she sounded less intelligent in English than in French or Creole, it was difficult to tell, and in any case seemed appropriate; so many of the people to whom she spoke English expected her to be stupid. Certainly this had been true at the American embassy in Port-au-Prince, where Simone had been chief assistant to the U.S. Cultural Attaché, and also at the gallery where Simone worked weekends, persuading American tourists to buy her fiancé Joseph's paintings.

Joseph painted dancing couples, drummers, old women smoking cigars, black girls in white dresses carrying laundry on their heads—and told Simone he hated himself for painting the white tourist's dream of Haiti. That was why he drank so much and ran off with every woman he met, though of course he'd given up women as soon as he met Simone. How hard it had been to see in him the person who drew those carefree figures, so relaxed they looked poured into their chairs, spilled out across the dance floor. Joseph yelled and threw beer bottles when the slightest thing went wrong. Then Duvalier left and the violence surfaced and scared off all the tourists, so that they still had the army and the *tonton macoute* but no more buyers for Joseph's work. As soon as Joseph understood what had changed and what hadn't, he first grew chilly to Simone and then ran off with Simone's friend Inez.

Simone and Joseph used to laugh at Inez, with her rich society-dentist husband and her crazy love affairs. But of course Simome was the crazy one for thinking Joseph wouldn't be curious, or that it was in her interest to enlist him as an ally against crazy love like Inez's. Inez bought six of Joseph's paintings, the only sale that month. It was just a few nights later that Simone saw them together in a café, Joseph's arm draped casually around Inez's shoulders, as if they were the window frame of some hot flashy car he was driving.

"I know what you must be thinking!" Mrs. Porter said. "You're thinking it's some kind of voodoo! You're looking at these paintings and thinking the Porter family must be into some kind of black magic!"

"No, not at all," Simone said quickly, though the truth was: No, not exactly. Mutilating paintings was very different from, say, decapitating a rooster. But for a moment she'd thought Mrs. Porter might practice some strange religion. There were portraits of children and puppy dogs, and their eyes had been scissored out, too. Simone was Catholic, though it had been years since she'd gone to confession.

"Oh, Haiti," Mrs. Porter was saying. "People used to go there. That marvelous creepy Graham Greene hotel and all that great naïve art. But AIDS didn't do it a favor, exactly, and then there was all that violence, drowned boat people washing up on the beach all over the Florida Keys. I hear Port-au-Prince is a nightmare. Dead bodies on the street."

In fact, there had been a body on the sidewalk near Simone's house. One morning almost a year ago, on her way to work, she'd found a man sliced open from his collarbone to his waist. From a distance Simone thought the man was wearing a flower-printed shirt, but up close the print turned out to be dirt and hibiscus-colored bloodstains. Two fat crows hopped around, poking the corpse, interested and efficient.

Even so, even with the daily riots and killings and strikes, Simone might have stayed in Haiti. She wasn't the type of person to just move to another country. She was more likely to stay put and pray that nothing too awful happened to her. Inertia would have reconciled her to remaining where she was, insofar as you could be reconciled to gunfire rattling all night and the smoke of burning cars hanging over the morning.

But seeing Joseph with Inez had sent her into a kind of panic in which she acted on instinct and faith, stealthily and in secret—as if one part of her had to sneak past the part of her that would have stayed. She had to get away, show everyone, leave Joseph and Inez. In that way emigration was like suicide without having to actually die. Of course escape required money, and luckily Simone had some: the money Inez had given her to pay for Joseph's paintings.

Simone intercepted Inez's money, the fee for Joseph's work, and bought an illegal marriage certificate to a citizen of the United States. Though she knew technically what crime she had committed, she could never think of herself as a thief or even as guilty of theft. She believed that a person could do something so utterly uncharacteristic that this isolated act filled just one line on a page in the book of the rest of their lives.

She spent the plane flight from Haiti to New York practicing telling the officials that she'd come to join her husband, not a name she'd gotten from the travel agency in Port-au-Prince, but a man she had loved and lived with and missed since he'd been gone. But the husband of her dreams resisted imagination; the image that kept coming to mind was, inconveniently, Joseph's. At Immigration she produced her documents with a vaguely combative air, as if the officers should have been proud of her for having any papers at all.

The INS man took his time riffling suspiciously through Simone's papers. She was a head taller than he was, and when he asked if she'd had a job, it was from the regal top of her height that she replied, "In Haiti I was chief assistant to the U.S. Cultural Attaché at the embassy in Port-au-Prince." It was the kind of long sentence that insisted on being heard to the end, and Simone, who was by nature reserved, felt she had transcended herself in this extreme situation. The Immigration man goggled at her, then grew markedly distracted and seemed to fall under a spell of momentary indecision, from which he emerged bewildered to see Simone, and shrugged and waved her through.

Simone met her husband only once: a nervous, freckle-faced man named Emile. He picked her up at Kennedy in his cab and drove her out to Brooklyn. He couldn't decide whether to dance with the steering wheel or talk politics with Simone, and seemed afraid that the slightest friendliness might cause her to lose all control and confuse business with romance and throw herself into his arms. He kept popping in Haitian music tapes and bumping his chest against the wheel, then pressing the eject button and asking for news of home, then starting the music loud again before Simone could answer. This social torment should at least have absorbed Simone's full attention, but instead it stretched the minutes and gave her lots of time to consider her problems with men, her great awkwardness in talking to them and sustaining their interest, when ugly, stupid, nasty girls seemed to have no trouble at all.

Simone stared out Emile's windshield at the boxy, colorless buildings and the razory slivers of light glinting off the dusty plate glass. The angular streets were, by Haitian standards, tidy and deserted, washed clean of dust and fruit rinds and sleepy or menancing dogs. Here no one sold cigarettes or fried food, no one ate or smoked or milled around in bored, volatile crowds. No one squatted, everyone walked. Everyone had a job or somewhere to go and good clothes to wear there. The only thing reminiscent of home was all the writing on the walls. They passed a sprawling graveyard, jammed and bristling with tombstones. Even these crowded dead had more room than those in the National Cemetery, where Simone's parents lay in a marble crypt the width of a single bed.

While Emile's tape was reversing, Simone said in Creole, "I saw a body on the sidewalk. On a street near my house. All the time we used to see crowds, looking down at something, and we would know from the look of the crowd that someone was lying there dead. But this was different. Me and this dead man alone in the street with two crows, his body parts in the road . . ."

Long before she'd finished, Simone knew she'd made a

serious mistake. She sensed immediately that this was very
inappropriate, very unfeminine conversation. But wasn't it
relevant to Emile's asking how things were in Port-au-
Prince? In fact, he had not asked about body parts in the
road. How easy it was to say too much, how much wiser
to say nothing.

A silver crucifix on Emile's dashboard wore a wreath of
pink cloth roses. Emile gazed out the window and
drummed his fingers on the wheel. The front seat was up-
holstered with a blanket of wooden beads that rolled dis-
concertingly under Simone every time she moved. An
awful smell filled her nostrils—the smell of the corpse on
the street. What man would want a woman who had
smelled something like that? Relieved that Emile seemed
uninterested in exercising his conjugal rights, Simone nonetheless felt that he was judging her as a woman, rejecting
and divorcing her after forty-five minutes of marriage

Emile turned to Simone and whispered, "The CIA is
behind all the killing. Everybody knows that."

Then Simone thought sadly of the embassy in Port-au-
Prince, where she'd worked for Miss McCaffrey, the Cultural Attaché. Miss McCaffrey was thirty-five, ten years
older than Simone, a sweet, polite, pretty woman with the
voice of a two-year-old child. Simone liked and respected
Miss McCaffrey, despite her many naïve ideas. Miss
McCaffrey believed that world harmony could be achieved
through the arts and by following the rules of diplomatic
protocol with an almost religious devotion. Miss McCaffrey
told Simone that being an agnostic made it easier for her to
live in many countries for only three years at a time.

She was the only person Simone told about her plan to
leave Haiti. Miss McCaffrey offered to help Simone get a
job in New York and a green card, and when Simone politely refused, Miss McCaffrey looked hurt and bewildered.
But Simone was in a hurry, she knew how long those
things could take, and besides, Miss McCaffrey was about
to be rotated to another Caribbean post. Bill Webb, her re-
placement, had already toured the office. He was round and

pink and shook Simone's hand with miniature cocktail-sausage fingers as he gazed up at her, shading his eyes, as if she were taller than she was. Several times she heard him say, "I don't know why they gave me this post. I'm from South Carolina. My idea of culture is comic books and Elvis paintings on velvet."

For a long time Simone had felt that she and Miss McCaffrey were descending a staircase while a continuous procession of men streamed up the other side—good old boys in shirt-sleeves and psychotics in stay-pressed suits. She could tell Emile these men were CIA; probably it was true.

She could also tell Emile that on the plane from Haiti she'd opened the lavatory door and walked in on an American man urinating into the toilet. He wore a gray suit and had gray hair and eyes that snapped on her like a crocodile before she shut the door and retreated. On his way out he'd smiled at her—a little strangely, she thought. Inside, she found the toilet seat shiny and wet with urine, and she knew what his smile had meant: he had known what she would find.

But what words, what actual words could she have used to tell this to Emile? It all seemed too complex and intimate to tell this stranger, her husband. Probably Emile had a wife and a dozen children already. Simone and Emile's marriage was purely a business transaction; that had been made very clear by the travel agency from which she'd bought the illegal papers and whose name she'd heard through embassy gossip.

Simone weighed the importance of informing Emile that the travel bureau was an embassy joke—a joke that some-day, possibly, the wrong person might not find funny. But all she'd heard was gossip, not news of an official investi-gation, and it was so rare at the embassy that one thing led to the next. If Emile was really a citizen, they wouldn't send him back—but there might be a fine or jail, for which he should be prepared.

She said, "When the U.S. invaded Panama, it was either going to be Panama or they were going into Haiti."

She expected him to ask how she knew, and she could tell him impressively how rumors traveled the embassy grapevine. Then she might mention the rumors about the travel agency. But Emile put his finger to his lips. He said, "Quiet! Are you crazy?"

He said, "Panama or Haiti, nobody here knows the difference. To these whites, all blacks are the same, no matter where we come from. But blacks and Haitian people and Spanish know, we know who to hate and fear. In the Bronx evil priests from Brazil and Puerto Rico are telling their followers that they can be healed with the severed hand of a Haitian, and Haitian boys are turning up dead with their arms hacked off at the wrists."

After this it was awkward to steer the conversation back to the travel bureau. Besides, Simone reasoned, why risk needlessly alarming Emile and further complicating a tricky ride they were trying so hard to keep simple?

Cutting across three lanes of traffic toward the parkway exit, Emile handed Simone a matchbook on which was printed the address of an employment agency where his cousin worked. Emile dropped Simone off in Grand Army Plaza—where, disorientingly, she spotted the Arc de Triomphe. In school the nuns had taught them to recognize the great tourist landmarks of the United States and Europe, but later, in a brochure at the American Center, Simone had seen London Bridge stuck in the Arizona sand.

Emile left her in the center of the plaza amid honking cars she had to dodge in order to reach the sidewalk. But how green and leafy and quiet it seemed, compared to Port-au-Prince!

Miraculously, there was an agency and Emile's *cousine* worked there; miraculously, there was a caregiver job for which, Emile's cousin said, Simone seemed perfectly qualified.

Overqualified, Simone would have said, to care for some rich woman's children. Tears of insult had welled up in her eyes when she realized that "caregiver" meant *au pair*. She said, "In Haiti I was chief assistant to the U.S. Cultural Attaché." But it sounded less important than it had in the airport and failed to work the same magic it had worked on the INS man. Emile's cousins's eyes narrowed—with hatred, it seemed to Simone—and she brushed the air with the back of her hand, sweeping away Simone's past, her education, her embassy job, anything that might have set her apart from any Haitian girl who would be lucky to get a job taking care of some rich woman's children.

Emile's cousin put Simone in a cab to Grand Central Station and repeatedly reminded her to buy a ticket to Hudson Landing. At the last moment she opened the taxi door and kissed Simone good-bye on both cheeks. She said, "You are lucky to have a job and a place. Many Haitian people are freezing to death in camps on the Canadian border."

In the vast granite hive of Grand Central Station everyone was swarming, and Simone lifted her suitcase and ran, though she had plenty of time. She found the right track and the right train and a seat in an empty car, but doubted herself and grew faint with fright when the train pulled out, still empty.

Simone watched the play of light on the wide, flat river, mentally pleading with it not to leave the side of the train. As long as they followed the Hudson, they weren't hurtling out into space. She had seen pictures in magazines of American trees turned orange, but they were brighter and stronger than the whiskery saplings sprouting above the tracks. Some of the hills were barren rubble, like the mountains in Haiti. Every pretty town they passed seemed to be turning its back—on the train, Simone cautioned herself, it had nothing to do with her.

It was a hot September afternoon. Mrs. Porter met Simone at the Hudson Landing station wearing a paint-spattered mouton fur coat, visibly chewed and balding, as if it were made from the pelts of creatures who died gnawing themselves out of traps. The coat was one reason Simone could have believed that Mrs. Porter might practice some strange religion. She was glad when their talk about the paintings in the attic clarified all that.

"Believe it or not," Mrs. Porter said, "I requested some-one from Haiti. The children's wretched public school can hardly manage English. And the dollar being what it is, you can forget the French mademoiselle. Right now, top priority is that I get some work done. When you become a sculptor at forty you've got to hustle to catch up."

Mrs. Porter pursed her lips and blew a thin stream of air up at her frizzy yellow bangs. "Of course when I started sculpting it drove Geoffrey straight up a wall. Three-dimensional *things* that were *me*—he could not endure it. I'll spare you the details of the vicious ways he communi-cated that fact. It's a trial separation, so called. But between us, the verdict's in.

"How tall are you?" Mrs. Porter looked up at Simone. "Wait. Don't bother. Centimeters are useless. In any case, I couldn't have hired *you*. Not with Don Juan in residence. Needless to say, it made it dicey for me to have any female friends. Why do I think I've seen you before? Your face is so familiar . . . Wait. I'm having quite the high-powered *déjà vu*." She flapped one hand in front of her face. "It's *suffocating* up here!"

Mrs. Porter led Simone down the attic stairs and through the second-floor hall, then took the sweeping main staircase and stopped halfway down on a landing.

"The scenic lookout!" she said. Together they surveyed the entrance hall and the huge living room beyond it, with its peeling gilded wallpaper and flaking dandruffy plaster. A patch of blue-green mildew crept toward some crispy hang-ing plants. Purple crayon was scribbled down the white keys of the piano. Everything that could be sat on was thatched with animal hair, although there didn't seem to be any cats or dogs in residence.

"Did I say light housekeeping?" Mrs. Porter asked. "I must have been out of my mind. Look at this place! You'd go insane. When it comes to cleaning you'll just have to find your personal bottom line. You might as well forget the cooking, too. George and Maisie like canned baked beans. They're full of protein and roughage. The beans, that is, not the children. Or else we can actually hire a cook. I was always afraid to, with Geoffrey.

"All you have to do is make sure the kids don't kill each other or you or themselves—and cheer them up! I don't care how. Lift their little spirits somehow! And if you teach them *un petit peu de francais*? Well, that would be *fantastique*."

"Yes, Mrs. Porter," Simone said. "When should I begin?"

"This minute—and that's *Rosemary*! Call me anything else and you're fired!"

SOMETIMES ROSEMARY WORKED on her sculpture through dinner, and Simone ate with the children at the huge yellow-pine kitchen table where, Rosemary explained, twenty indentured child servants once dined on reject potatoes and beer. She said, "Stinginess is a genetic trait, Geoffrey's family has a marker for it. Let us pray that it skips a generation and bypasses Maisie and George."

At first Simone put out regular dinners, place settings and glasses of water, but within days they'd reverted to something more primeval. Huddled at one end of the table, Simone and the children wolfed down their food as if each were standing alone in the kitchen gorging on something forbidden. At first Simone cooked normal meals, but they preferred eating separate dinners. Maisie lived on raw cut-up vegetables, George on breaded fried frozen shrimp. What a great relief it was, the children's desire for repetition, freeing Simone from any guilty allegiance to the adult desire for change.

Simone, too, ate the same meal every night, plates of the rice and red beans she made in a large pot on weekends and reheated in portions with fried plantains that the children liked, too. Rosemary noted approvingly the household's increased plantain consumption. "God's perfect nutritional packages. Potassium city," she said.

Haitian food made Simone feel less homesick, though in Haiti she often ate frozen dinners from the embassy commissary. One night she told George and Maisie, "This is the diet of Haiti. Haitian peasants are lucky when they can get

12

red beans and rice." The children looked sheepish and lectured to, and Simone felt ashamed, because mostly all she had wanted was an excuse to talk about Haiti, just as, after she met Joseph, she took every occasion to mention his name.

Simone was surprised to find plantains for sale at the Hudson Landing supermarket, to which she walked, a mile each way, past the Hudson River estates, along the picturesque low stone walls attractively covered with poison ivy. No blacks or island people ever shopped at the market, but no one seemed to think Simone's being there was unusual or special. In fact, being stared at might have been better than being made to feel transparent, as if everyone could look through her to the more interesting cereal boxes. Simone felt lonelier in the market than she did anywhere else, and it helped only slightly that everyone else seemed lonely, too. No one was selling anything, the shoppers had no one to talk to; recorded music sprinkled down on them like the cold freezer air. How muffled it sounded after the buzz of the markets at home, the cries of the fish and vegetable women, the curses of the porters. Simone longed to hear those sounds, though she knew that she was forgetting how the buzz of the market changed when army or government men came through, and how abruptly it stopped at dusk, replaced by ominous silence and occasional heart-stopping shouts.

Probably the plantains were for vacationers newly returned to Hudson Landing, nostalgic to re-create the food of some happy tropical island. Sometimes Simone lingered— pathetically, she felt—in the vegetable section, as if waiting for a shopper to come along and pick up a bunch of plantains and they could begin a friendship on the basis of starchy fruit. She would have liked to hear herself say out loud what her job was, whom she worked for—naturally to someone who could be trusted not to tell Immigration that she wasn't living in Brooklyn with Emile.

The other place she haunted was the magazine stand—a hundred times more magazines than she'd seen at the em-

bassy, where initially her job had involved skimming *Time*
and *Newsweek* for the names of young dancers and musicians who'd be flattered to travel to Haiti for the U.S. government per diem. Occasionally a ballet troupe came
through, and for days the office was busy with handsome
young Oklahomans who might unexpectedly stretch or do
neck rotations in the middle of a sentence. But after the violence intensified, Simone's duties were mostly confined to
opening Jiffy bags containing videotaped ballets and children's cartoons for Miss McCaffrey to show on the American library VCR.

When Miss McCaffrey hired Simone, after meeting her
at the gallery, she tactfully asked which language Simone
preferred to use in the office and seemed at once disappointed and relieved when Simone chose English. She herself spoke a stilted Creole she'd learned in USIA language
school and read so much about Haiti that she often knew
gossip about pop music and radio stars that was news to
Simone.

So now, like Miss McCaffrey, Simone read fan magazines—as well as magazines about golf, computers, sailing,
gourmet cooking, and martial arts. But she felt she learned
deeper things about people's secret lives from magazines
that counseled American women about their personal fears:
worries about their husbands and children, about over-
weight and cancer, about combining a placid family life
with a profitable career. One alarming article on "Finding
the Perfect Caregiver" suggested that working mothers—
not Rosemary, apparently—investigate their prospective
caregiver's employment record and immigration status.

Many of these magazines advised women not to be too
hard on themselves, to forget the perfect workday *and* the
perfect family dinner, and perhaps this had something to do
with the menus Rosemary occasionally fixed for them all:
underheated canned baked beans, burned hamburgers, pretzels and popcorn they ate directly from the bag. In this, as
in everything, Rosemary gave the impression of a woman
who had just with great effort liberated herself from a

prison of obligation and duty, though it was unclear, exactly, what these duties had been. The quirky, unnutritious diets, the unbrushed hair, the nights they slept in their clothes—all four of them might have been children accidentally left alone. The scale of the house reduced them, its high ceilings and doorways, the sideboards and massive tables hewn for a vanished race of giants.

In a short time Simone and the children discovered each other's secrets; they sensed that they could trust each other not to tell Rosemary. George, who was ten, had a videotape he watched over and over, a *National Geographic* film about life on the Arctic Circle. It showed Eskimos bent over holes in the ice, motionless for hours, then yanking a seal up through a hole that suddenly bubbled with blood. Blood was everywhere, steaming in bowls, smeared on people's mouths, staining patches of scarlet ice where sled dogs fought over the meat. At first George turned off the tape when Simone came into his room, but later he let her watch with him, provided they didn't speak.

Mrs. Porter—Rosemary!—told Simone that George had a problem with grief. He often burst into tears at school, and the other children teased him. Nothing sad had ever happened to him; it was nothing like that. His parents' separation was stressful—but that didn't fully explain it. More likely it was genetic, a character flaw from the start.

Rosemary said, "Poor poor Georgie was born like that: dour, burdened with cares. Even as a baby, he made you think of a depressive CPA reborn in piglet form. I realize that's an awful way to talk about one's child. But we'd all go mad here if we lost our sense of humor. My real worry is that I'm neglecting the children's problems because they're so darn convenient. George and Maisie are too out-to-lunch to fight like normal siblings."

Six-year-old Maisie was a morbid child, too, dreamy and elegiac. She took Simone on her own house tour, a tour of the old and discarded. She said, "This is our piano. It doesn't work. This is our broken swing set. These are George's electric trains that he never plays with." She showed Simone a plot in the yard where their former pets were buried, marked with wooden twig-crosses and rain-streaked Polaroids of the deceased. It seemed an almost suspicious number of newly dead cats and dogs until Maisie explained that the pets had been old, they'd belonged to her parents, some from before they were married. She knew how old each pet was at the hour of its death; she had an actuarial gift for converting dog to human years.

One day Maisie told Simone to watch, and ran to the dining-room doorway. She licked her palms and wet the soles of her feet, then braced her arms and legs against the door frame and climbed up the inside of the doorway and hung beneath the ceiling like one of those suction-animals people here stuck inside car windows. She scrambled down and looked innocent when she heard Rosemary approach. Maisie was black-haired, with skim-milk skin and pink-rimmed rabbity eyes; she wore flowery dresses and frilly panties that showed when she hung upside down.

It startled Simone how quickly she came to love the children. Something about their undemanding melancholy made her want to make them happy, to transform them from two pale will-o'-the-wisps into a flesh-and-blood boy and girl. Soon she found her own moods rising and plummeting dangerously with tiny improvements and declines in the children's spirits.

She had no desire to teach them French, which they had no desire to learn—they spent too much of the day in school to want lessons when they came home. And after that first interview, Rosemary forgot she'd asked.

In the mornings Simone walked George and Maisie down the long, tree-lined driveway and waited with them for the bus to come—and picked them up in the afternoon. She always felt happy, or happier, when at the end of the day she felt the ground tremble and heard the wheezing brakes that signaled the bus's approach. Almost involuntarily, a welcoming smile appeared on her face, and the children saw it and nearly smiled back.

It was safer for the children not to know Simone's secrets: her illegal marriage and the money she'd stolen from Joseph and Inez. But there was one worrisome secret that she couldn't hide, though for a while it almost seemed it might not become an issue.

Rosemary assumed that Simone could drive. The agency must have said so. And when Rosemary tossed her the car keys, Simone caught them in one hand—a reflex that in this context was as good as a lie. Had the agency also lied about Simone's immigration status? Rosemary never asked. Maybe she couldn't imagine a whole category of problems she didn't have. Or perhaps she supposed that Simone, like herself, was simply entitled to be here.

One Saturday Rosemary asked Simone to take the children for haircuts. "The place is called Short Eyes. It's on Route 9. The children know where it is." She gave Simone three twenty-dollar bills and said, "The price is insane, I know it."

Just finding and opening the door of Rosemary's Volvo seemed like an accomplishment and flooded Simone with a warm sense of competence and control. She ordered the children to sit in back and got behind the wheel, and some time later glanced in the mirror and saw them, wide-eyed and pallid.

George said, "Don't you know how to drive?"

"You better tell Mom," said Maisie.

"I can't," Simone answered, and this seemed reasonable to the children.

George rolled into the passenger seat, his face faintly flushed and sweaty. He showed Simone the parts of the car and what to hold down when. She braked and hit the gas and braked. The children tumbled forward.

All day they practiced on back roads, bucking and weaving down the deserted narrow lanes and carefully working their way up to larger, more crowded highways.

"We're like water drops," said Maisie. "Trickling into the river and drowning."

* * *

Happily, the children did know the route to the haircut salon. "It's called Short Eyes?" George told Simone. "That's what they call child molesters in jail in New York City?" When George was anxious, which was most of the time, every sentence was framed as a question.

It took Simone a few seconds to figure out what George meant. Then she said, "How do you know that?"

"Kenny told my mom," George explained. "He tells everyone."

Short Eyes—Kuts for Kids was in a mini-mall designed to suggest a frontier town in a cowboy movie. Inside, the salon had a jungle motif, all zebra skin and rattan. Dozens of long-armed, brown, fake-fur gibbons were suction-cupped to the ceiling. Maisie eyed them competitively, chewing on a knuckle.

A young man in a tight white T-shirt and jeans hovered over a traumatized boy, making predatory mosquitolike swoops around the child's head. Finally he whipped a jungle-print apron off the boy's chest. The child rotated rigidly and grimaced at his mother. He looked as if he'd just had his ears surgically enlarged.

"Fabulous!" His mother pressed some bills in the child's hand. "Give this to Kenny and say thank you very much."

"Thank you very much," repeated the child, and followed his mother out.

"Little geeks," Kenny told Simone. "They're lucky their mommies don't drown them in sacks like kittens. Not these guys." He saluted George and Maisie. "These guys are my buddies. That's because they've seen this . . ."

He reached into a drawer and took out a large, anatomically correct, flesh-colored rubber ear. "They know that this is what happened to the last kid who moved when I was cutting his hair."

The children had seen it and could share with Kenny a conspiratorial smirk, though George kept sneaking looks at the ear till Kenny put it away. Kenny muscled George into the chair, then hooked his arm around Simone's neck and scooted her into a back room.

"So you're working for El Ditzo," he whispered. "Hey, babe, I mean good luck." He pushed Simone away to look at her, then drew her back to his side; it was strangely pleasant, being flopped around like a doll. He said, "Tall women. I love it! You've got a great look, like that actress—what's her name—the one who played that gay junkie hooker Bob Hoskins fell in love with. Jamaican? Trinidadian?"

"Why good luck?" Simone asked.

"Don't tell me," said Kenny. "Haitian! I used to hang out in Brooklyn. Well, for one thing, when you get paid, if you get paid, try to get it in cash. That scumbag could freeze her assets any second now. Have you met the old man? Geoffrey Porter the Fourteenth?"

"No," said Simone. "I mean, not yet." Sometimes the children spent the night with their father; he picked them up at school in the afternoon and took them back there in the morning. He had not come to the house since Simone started work.

"Count yourself lucky," said Kenny. "The guy could freeze anyone's assets. Weirdly straight, very Jack the Ripper, very much in control. It's fabulous to watch the dude, like talking to a schizophrenic, one half of his face looks entitled by birth to tell you what's real and what's not, the other half has to keep checking to make sure the old magic still works. There is nothing you know about that this guy doesn't know better. I always think he's two beats away from telling me how to cut hair. Honestly, you can't blame the babe if her frontal lobe scabs over. The man's screwed everything female and human—well, female, there's that Arabian farm—between here and Albany. Not that there's a whole lot happening in terms of women, present company excepted. It's Rip Van Winkle time up here, seriously asleep. 'Short eyes' is what they call child molesters in the joint, and nobody in this valley knows it. It's my own private joke on the suburban middle, upper-middle, and upper class."

"Why good luck?" Simone repeated. It took Kenny a

moment to work back and find the point at which her attention had quit progressing along with his conversation.

"Well, for one thing, Rosemary jokes about inbreeding, but it's hardly a joke. They naturally select for elegant heads and tiny little brains, the lowest possible cranial capacity without actually being a pinhead. I can tell you, I cut those heads—I need a microscope to fucking find them. The whole family's like a pack of extremely high-fuctioning Afghan hounds. Well, really, the whole neighborhood—it's a longitudinal thing. They're like a bunch of babies, instant erase, no guilt. They wake up in the morning and yesterday's not on the disk. It means they can do anything and not have to worry or pay. Don't trust them is all I'm saying, you can't level with these people. And no matter how weird and sick it gets, don't say Kenny didn't warn you."

The whole conversation was upsetting Simone more than she could say. Emile's cousin at the employment agency had promised that Simone would get room and board and one hundred and twenty dollars a week. But on that first day Rosemary explained that, since she'd listed the job, her own precarious financial status had gone straight down the dumper. Would Simone mind accepting fifty dollars a week until Rosemary stabilized things with her estranged husband? In theory Simone could have taken it up with Emile's cousin in Brooklyn, but she couldn't see going back there or even calling long distance, and if she said she *did* mind and Rosemary fired her—where would she go then?

Even worse, Rosemary paid by check; she was sure Simone would want to start an account at the bank in Hudson Landing. She said, "This is America. A bank account proves you exist." It would also have proved that Simone wasn't living with her husband in Brooklyn and would make it easy to find her if Immigration started looking. Emile had specifically cautioned her never to sign her name or tell anyone—anyone!—one true fact about her past. He said, "You can never tell here what will lead to what." She could be deported or sent to camps up north. He'd told her there was a giant computer that knew everything about you, and once you were in its memory, you would never be free.

Simone took the checks Rosemary proffered on occasional Fridays and filed them in her dresser drawer. Rosemary would never notice that the sums hadn't been drawn. She often described how she'd tried to balance her account two months in a row, then flung her checkbook against the wall and given up forever. Simone supposed she would cash the checks at some time in the future, though right now this future seemed, at best, gelatinous and cloudy. Try as she might, she couldn't see beyond her present existence at Rosemary's which felt at times like house arrest: half prison, half cocoon. But she had come to agree with Emile's cousin—she was lucky to be here.

By now Simone felt very gloomy, but she couldn't show it because she and Kenny had drifted back to the main salon and the children were watching. Kenny said, "The rich are not only richer. They are sleazier than you and me. Again, present company excepted." He stuck his thumb up at George and Maisie. "Okay, George Raft. Let's do it."

George stared into the mirror and sat so still his eyeballs jiggled. He tried not to wince as Kenny assaulted the front of his hair. Finally Kenny stepped back and admired his work and, as an afterthought, fired up his electric clippers and shaved a tiny Batman symbol on the back of George's head. When he finished he held up a hand mirror, and though it took George some time to get the hang of two mirrors, Simone could tell the moment he saw, because his whole face lit up.

"Excellent," George said.

Kenny made Maisie's hair spike up on top and hang down in corkscrew curls—a kind of jellyfish effect. He kissed the children and Simone, and walked them out to the car.

"Speaking of the joint," he said, leaning down into the car, "or should I say the nuthouse, come hang out if you get time off for good behavior. I could use the company. Anyhow, I'll see you around. This is not the largest town when it comes to the young and the hip. It's stronger on the dead and the undead. The overbred and the restless."

Kenny paused and looked around, miming paranoia. In Haiti you learned to be aware of who might be standing nearby—or you learned, as Simone had, to be mindful of what you said. Clearly Emile was right: one must take the same precautions here.

The mini-mall was deserted; a light rain had begun to fall. "Speaking of the undead," Kenny said, "have you met Rosemary's so-called friend and my so-called girlfriend, Shelly?"

"I don't think so," Simone said.

"You don't think so?" Kenny rolled his eyes. "If you don't know, you haven't met her. Shelly's a force of nature. She's the entry under 'Ballbreaker' in the *Guinness Book of World Records*. I just sit back and watch her work. I learn from her, I mean it. I have mothers come in and try to stiff me, bad checks, they left their wallets home, but if I were Shelly they would never *suggest* it. I would be making a profit instead of barely clearing enough to pay some high-school chick to dust those fucking monkeys on the ceiling. Which, let me add, were Shelly's brilliant decorating suggestion."

Mortifyingly, Simone realized that she, too, had forgotten to pay Kenny. She groped in her purse for Rosemary's sixty dollars, but Kenny put his hand on hers and curled her fingers over the bills.

"Forget it," he said. "I know that scene. Believe me. You're going to need it. This is exactly what I mean. Look how I'm running my business. But I may be the last guy left in the valley with a nonbionic human heart. Anyway, I wouldn't want you thinking that all Americans are like that—that we're all like your sleazebag robber baron boss and his artsy batshit wife."

Simone gestured with her head to remind Kenny that the

children were listening. First he did a stagy double take, then winked at Maisie and George.

"They'd be the first to agree," he said. "Tell her, guys. Am I right?"

A FEW NIGHTS later, Rosemary began cooking veal scaloppine with lemon. "Sauté technique from another life," she said, shaking the pan over the flame. She told Simone her friend Shelly was coming for dinner and asked her to set three places. The children were with their father; he'd picked them up at school.

"Shelly's poisonously bitchy," said Rosemary. "But I adore her. Very Southern, very Old South—you have to breed for an edge like that. Her grandfather was a famous Memphis gynecologist who bred prize camellias for a hobby. He would name new species after his favorite patients. When you got down off the table, out of the stirrups, he'd hand you a white flower, a prize specimen of, let's say"—Rosemary held an imaginary flower out to Simone—"*Miss Simone.*" Rosemary laughed. "Very gothic and icky. Definitely one of a kind."

But Shelly wasn't so different from lots of American women Simone had met: pretty, delicate blondes with dewy skin and slicked-back, straight-from-the-shower hair, though with the sharp little teeth and trembly nerves of tiny overbred dogs. She kissed Rosemary as if this were a gesture whose irony she would appreciate, as if they were little girls dressed up, mimicking their mothers.

"Rosemary!" said Shelly. "That coat is a classic! You look like an Eskimo shaman!"

"I live in this coat," said Rosemary. "I wear it in the studio. Actually, it *is* a classic. I found it in the closet I put it in, circa 1967. If the sunlight hits it, it'll shatter like glass.

24

They say the sixties are coming back and I for one am thrilled. I haven't had anything this comfortable for, oh my God, twenty-five years."

"Wear that in Manhattan," Shelly said, "and you get spray-painted as an eco-criminal."

"And they're right," Rosemary said. "I just think there should be allowances for animals that were dead before anyone knew there was a problem. This is Simone. She lives with us and helps takes care of George and Maisie."

As Shelly coolly appraised Simone with an almost consumerlike interest, Rosemary pleaded, "Help me, Shelly. I've been going insane. Whom does Simone look like?"

Shelly said, "I can't believe the scene you've got here. Fabulously *Gone with the Wind*. Well, it's always something. Did I tell you about that client of mine who hired a babysitter named Lolita. A babysitter named Lolita!"

"As far as Geoffrey was concerned," Rosemary said, "they were all named Lolita." She paused and after a deep sigh said, "Simone's from Haiti. Shelly's an interior decorator."

"Haiti," mused Shelly. "Sequined voodoo flags. And of course those great naïve paintings. But that lasted about a month or so, and then you couldn't unload Haitian primitive. Everyone just *fled* back to fabulous fifties or English country chintz." With evident pain, Shelly regarded a monumental oak hutch. "God, Rosemary, I wish you'd let me do *something* with this place. A little white paint and some cheap track lighting—just as a public service."

"My fiancé is a painter in Haiti," said Simone. "He sells to foreign collectors from Europe and the U.S." But Joseph was no longer her fiancé and no longer sold to foreign tourists. Why had she told this lie, unasked, in the midst of a whole other conversation? Why, despite Emile's warnings and her own better judgment, had she volunteered this information that could provoke further questions which might lead from Joseph to Emile and straight to the INS?

It was surprising how little Rosemary had tried to find out about Simone before turning her children over to someone who, for all she knew, might be a former *tonton ma-coute* come over in a rowboat. What kind of mother sent her children out with a caregiver who couldn't drive? Well, Emile had said to keep quiet, and it helped, Simone found, that the level of curiosity here was so dependably low—not from politeness or reserve or reluctance to appear nosy so much as from lack of interest in how others lived. How foolish to let Shelly and Rosemary call this out in her now: the urge to boast and impress them with her artist fiancé.

Perhaps showing off was contagious—people here did it so often. All Simone had to do was walk into the room for someone to start talking, though they rarely spoke directly to her or expected a reply, so that it seemed that any response would be impolite and disruptive. They said to her what they would have said were they all alone in a room, but without the constraint and self-consciousness they might feel, talking to themselves.

Consolingly, this drew Simone closer to the children, whom, she observed, were usually spoken to in exactly the same way. Also, it was helping her absorb the culture more quickly; Miss McCaffrey used to say that to adapt to another country you had to be all eyes and ears, and that the mistake most diplomats made was to be all mouth and larynx. Certainly this was true of Bill Webb, talking constantly to hide his fear of being asked a question he couldn't answer. It had given Simone a chilling sense of what working for him would be like. Miss McCaffrey enjoyed learning new things, but Bill Webb wouldn't like it, and every time it happened, he would take it out on Simone.

Neither Rosemary nor Shelly seemed to have heard Simone mention her fiancé.

"A public service for whom?" Rosemary asked. "For Geoffrey? How long my children and I remain under this roof depends on how puerile and vindictive he chooses to get. This place has been in his family since they stole it from the Indians. The children and I are tenants here or, the way Geoffrey feels, guests—"

"The way Geoffrey *thinks*," corrected Shelly. "It is not an unimportant distinction."

"I forgot," said Rosemary. "Geoffrey doesn't have feelings." She motioned for Shelly and Simone to sit and set out a platter of veal arranged with lemon wedges and parsley. "Ladies, please. Help yourselves. There's salad and risotto."

"*Kenny* has feelings," Shelly said. "Unfortunately, ninety-nine percent of them are about himself and about how, because he is such a nice guy, he is barely earning enough to pay some high-school chick to dust the Velcro monkeys. One half percent is about how I don't love him enough or at all, and the final half percent is about rich and famous movie stars who are, as he eloquently puts it, scumbags, which is why they are rich and famous. I could find this more touching coming from a poor or unsuccessful person than from a man charging thirty dollars a pop to cut rich ugly children's hair." Shelly clapped a hand over her mouth. "Not *all* ugly, of course. George and Maisie are gorgeous."

"Thank you," Rosemary said.

Shelly lifted her fork up in a salute to the food. "This veal is marvelously underdone. No one underdoes veal anymore. Lord, listen to me! First calling the children ugly and then being bitchy about the food. It's so hard for me to switch gears, dealing with other women. With men it's totally different. They insist you be nasty and rotten. It makes them think they can do things with you that they can't do with their wives."

Rosemary said, "Kenny shaved a Batman logo on the back of George's head. George of all people. The funny thing was, George loved it. Maybe there's hope for him yet. And by the way—I don't want to jinx it—George seems to have quit those awful crying jags since Simone has been here. Not that the school would notice any sort of improvement. But he's stopped bringing home those depressing notes about his weeping in class. I suppose George could be throwing them out or just not delivering them, but even that, with Georgie, would be an encouraging sign."

In an effort to conceal how happy Rosemary's saying this made her, Simone pretended to reconsider some rejected veal on her plate. She, too, had noticed that the children seemed less withdrawn than when she had arrived. You still wouldn't call them chatty, but they made efforts at conversation. Maisie told anecdotes from school, mostly about other children's misbehavior. George asked fake-casual questions about upsetting current events. "Is the ozone layer gone yet? That kid in Poughkeepsie who got tortured and killed—did he know the guy who did it?" One evening George had asked Simone to tuck him into bed, but later, when Simone knocked on his door, he'd called out, "No thanks. That's all right."

Shelly said, "George has a problem to overcome. It's called his DNA code."

"I beg your pardon," Rosemary said. "His *father*'s half of the DNA code. The other half is mine."

"Half is a lot," replied Shelly. "It only takes one chromosome."

Rosemary said, "The bluebloods will have a run for their money when the mutants take over. New races that don't require oxygen or ozone."

"You're losin' me, darlin'," Shelly murmured, drifting toward Simone. "What are Haitian men like? Perfect gentlemen, I'm sure."

"My husband is a cabdriver," said Simone. "He gets tired at night. One night he got very angry and threw a beer bottle through a window."

"Charming," said Shelly. "But what do you mean, *husband*? A minute ago he was your *fiancé*."

Simone said, "My husband is in Brooklyn. My fiancé is in Port-au-Prince." Why was she revealing so much—and what was she saying? It was Joseph who had thrown the beer bottle through the window. Earlier that evening he had gone with Simone to an embassy party and been very charming to the USIA couple who were thinking of buying his paintings.

"Simone!" Rosemary cried. "You lucky duck. No wonder you always seem so calm. Maybe I would have been better off if I'd hedged my bets—maybe I could have stuck it out with a husband *and* a fiancé."

"Not if one of them was Geoffrey," said Shelly. "How quickly we forget. Geoffrey wasn't neutral—he was a highly charged negative force."

Rosemary turned from Shelly to Simone with a slow turtlelike swivel that added decades to her age, an impression heightened by the bald spots on her mouton coat. A wizened condor smiled mournfully at Shelly and Simone, and it took a few seconds for Rosemary to come back into its face.

She said, "You two are my reality checks," and toasted them with her wineglass.

That fall it snowed in October and all the leaves dropped at once. For a few hours it was beautiful, white frosting the scarlet maples, but by afternoon the world had turned snail-slime brown and jagged tree limbs littered the ground. Rosemary paced from window to window, monitoring the wreckage.

She said, "Simone, your first snowfall! What a historic event! It never snows in October, you *do* realize that. Freak storms are just the beginning. It's the death rattle of the planet. My personal calculation is that we're about six months from Armageddon."

Simone turned her back and crossed herself. From where she stood Rosemary would see just the appropriate shudder.

Rosemary said, "Those branches will have to be carted away. And those teenage hunks who mow the lawn are surely back in seventh grade. You see I am deteriorating about the housekeeping situation. It's gotten to where I don't give a hoot if a dish ever gets washed. Believe me, I wasn't always this way, but this is my present incarnation.

The decision you have to make is how much disorder you can stand."

Rosemary often mentioned the house's messy state. Was she hinting that she wished the place was cleaner? But why then did she always insist that it was Simone's decision? Simone did her own and the children's laundry and what simple cooking there was. George and Maisie helped with the dishes and with keeping the kitchen and bathroom on the acceptable side of disgusting. How sad—children so heartened by being asked to sponge out the tub! The halls and public rooms of the house seemed dauntingly fragile, like a rusty book that might crumble to powder if you turned its pages.

Simone's own room was bright and spacious, in a sunny wing near the children's. But while the children's rooms were cozy nests layered with dirty clothes and toys, her room had only a single bed, a small dresser, and a battered pine bookcase. The only signs of her presence were a growing stack of women's magazines and, on the wall across from her bed, the painting Joseph had given her.

It was smaller than the canvas that Simone had seen him take down from the gallery wall as a gift for the girlfriend he had before her. Simone used to tell herself that her painting was more precious for being small, and this turned out to be true: she'd been able to bring it with her. The picture he'd given his previous lover was of sexy dancing couples; Simone's was of children lined up outside a country school. Even so, Simone loved her painting and now often found herself staring at it until she felt herself drawn into the scene, becoming one of the children, specifically a tall, thin girl at the end of the line. She could almost hear the bell toll and smell chalk through the classroom windows. But where in Joseph's picture were the white nuns in their brown habits? The teacher he'd painted was pretty and black and wore a short red dress. Staring at Joseph's painting put Simone in a gloomy mood, and in general it seemed wiser to stay out of her room, to be out in the fresh air or elsewhere in the house.

For some reason the debris from the storm was proving hard for Simone to live with; perhaps because the fallen branches represented new, not pre-existing, damage. For a few days Simone studied them through the windows or wandered vaguely around the yard, contemplating the larger branches until, overwhelmed by the size of the job, she'd give up and go back in. Then one foggy morning she went out and dragged all but the heaviest limbs into a series of brushy piles, far from the house at the edge of the lawn where it rolled up against the forest.

Simone hesitated at the tree line, gazing in at the fog and trees: white gauze shot through with black stitches. She filled her lungs and walked in to see how the woods looked from inside. She could hardly see ahead of her and kept checking over her shoulder. Before she began to lose sight of the house, she would give up and go back.

And so she was straining to see the house when she backed into something furry. First she registered its fuzziness, then its revolting, slippery wetness. Her skin and her nerves knew what it was before she turned her head and saw.

A dead sheep, an enormous dead ram, hung upside down from a tree. Its curls were a nicotine yellow except where caked blood had dyed its pelt brown. The sheep's mouth and eyes were wide open and its head flopped off to one side.

A twig raked Simone's forehead as she ran through the woods. She kept scraping her face on the branches, bleating with terror and rage. Her heart raced around in her chest as if it were trying to escape. She felt that someone was watching. She had felt watched when she found the body on the street in Port-au-Prince and looked down, absurdly, to check what she was wearing.

At last she reached the edge of the woods and broke free into open space and ran up the lawn to the mansion. She ran upstairs to Rosemary's studio, where she had never been, but found easily now by following the music from

Rosemary's stereo, the same four notes repeating an insistent, maddening rhythm.

Several small rooms had been broken through and combined to make the studio. Bare patches of plaster where walls were knocked out reminded Simone of Haiti. Rosemary wore goggles, a long-snooted mask, white coveralls, and her fur coat.

"Hit the floor," Rosemary's voice bubbled from inside her mask. "This is a toxic event." She stepped back from a sculpture she had been spraying from a tank and scrutinized it so rapty that Simone had to look, too. It was a female torso with a pendulous belly and a dozen globular breasts that appeared to have been slathered on with a spatula dipped in rubber.

"My Goddess Series," Rosemary explained. "This one's a Demeter figure, very Earth Goddess—Great Mother, with an edge of the Willendorf Venus. The irony is that it's made out of the deadliest space-age fiberglass resin. I think I'll have her holding a broken mirror or some kind of primitive votive object. This Phillip Glass tape can just flip me right into a shamanistic trance state in which for minutes at a time I forget that the whole thing totally misses. Because there is no going back to the time when the art object was pure magic. Primitive people knew things about art that we have forgotten. They knew what images were so powerful you could hardly bear to behold them, what could make your heart stop and congeal on the spot. The Assyrians and the Mayas and the Kwakiutl people—one look at those idols and you just drop straight down to your knees."

Simone's gaze had drifted to the paintings on the walls: prodigiously ugly canvases sharing a feather motif, muddy-colored peacock fans scrubbed into the canvas, as if the main artistic intent was to make a little paint go a long way. But if economy was the point, why was so much paint spilled on the floor?

Joseph's studio was monastically neat, with only an easel, brushes, rags. But there had been disturbing things in Joseph's studio, also.

One night, drunk, Joseph had razored a print of Manet's *Olympia* out of one of his art books.

"Regard," he told Simone. "The smiling silent black mammy and the white bitch colonial whore." Then he dipped a brush in red paint and with sudden violent strokes retouched Manet's painting so that the naked woman looked like a recent victim of a sex-criminal slasher attack. Joseph was a good painter and the result was lifelike and frightening. When he was done he tacked it to his studio wall.

"Two dimensions," Rosemary was saying. "Such obvious limitations. Goodness, Simone! You look like death! Whatever is the matter?"

Simone said, "I saw something in the woods. An animal hung from a tree." She thought of the eyeless family portraits stacked up in the attic and then of all the frightening movies in which the person the heroine runs to is the last one she should trust. Could Rosemary's coat have once been a relative of the creature Simone just saw?

Rosemary put down her brushes. "Oh dear. What was it this time? Not another horse!"

"It was a sheep," Simone replied dully. A sheep seemed like nothing now.

"That's our neighbor up the Hudson. The Count. The man makes Geoffrey's gene pool look like a clear mountain stream. You don't want to know what goes on at the Count's house. I gather that underage children are the least of it. Believe me, we have complained and complained. George and Maisie found the dead horse. But six hundred riverfront acres buys some privacy up here—as it does everywhere, I suppose, the Amazon included. And decadent Bavarian royalty gets cut a certain amount of slack.

"Anyway, you weren't walking in the woods? What a suicidal idea! The story of Little Red Ridinghood is hardly about nothing. Once hunting season starts here, they'll bag you like a quail. Last fall I thought I heard the mail lady; I was walking down the driveway, smiling, still in my nightgown. But it wasn't the mail lady, it was a Buick with

Jersey plates and four guys in Rambo suits eyeballing me through the windshield. At first they looked a little glum, but when they saw me they sucked in their chests. Never have I had such a sense of what kind of morning the deer were having. I dressed and took the first train to the city. I thought: Crackheads may kill me but I'm sure they won't tie me to the roof of their car. Well, *pretty* sure, is what I thought. It's all so neolithic."

Though Simone still made daily trips to the market for groceries and magazines, she no longer liked passing the forests and fields she had lately found so pleasant. When George and Maisie were off at school, she mostly stayed inside. She got better acquainted with the house and knew where the sunlight struck when, so that on the pale chilly autumn days she could track it through the rooms. At two o'clock the sun hit halfway up the servants' staircase, and it was as if Simone had a daily appointment to sit on the steps with her forehead against her knees, sun warming the top of her head.

On the main floor of the mansion was an octagonal library, its leather couches marbled with cracks, its musty books emitting a moldy, botanical smell. Simone passed whole afternoons pulling volumes from the case, reading a page or a chapter, and replacing them somewhere else. Many of the books were ancient, far too fragile to touch; many were birthday or holiday gifts, inscribed from the dead to the dead. There were texts on Latin poetry, gardening, classical art—souvenirs of the interests various Porters had taken up and dropped.

Simone liked the art books best, especially one about the Etruscans. Its photos seemed to know something they were resolved to keep secret. Large stone heads mushroomed out of dwarfish torsos, which in turn grew from the lids of shoebox-sized stone containers. These were funerary vessels to contain the deceased's vital organs, just as the figure's face was meant to hold some trace of the dead person's soul. The figures carried souvenirs of their former occupations. The priestessess held fresh livers from which they used to foretell the future.

Reading about the priestesses prophesying from entrails, Simone felt queasy with dread—as if, like a debt or an unwelcome friend with too much knowledge of her past, something had picked up the scent of her life and followed her here from Haiti. Simone had seen inside a man and a sheep, but who could prophesy from that? At most it said something about the past, but never about the future. And who would want a future visible in a piece of meat that you could buy and toss on a scale and fry with mushrooms and onions?

Near the end of the Etruscan book its author went into a graphic digression on the history of human sacrifice from Abraham to the Aztecs, from the Amazon to the Philippines. An index listed the countries where child sacrifice had been practiced. The long list included Haiti, but not the United States.

One afternoon Simone went into George's room and watched the Eskimo tape. Perhaps with George not present she might understand what he saw. She rewound it to the scene that George most often replayed: a bowl of steaming seal blood being passed around in a circle. The Eskimos seemed lit from within as they took the bowl and drank, and in close-up smiled blissfully and wiped their mouths on their sleeves. It wasn't the blood, Simone thought, but the gratitude, the order—it was what she'd once looked for and found as a girl in church. Wasn't the Mass about flesh and blood? It was entirely different. Sweet grape wine was nothing like the hot blood of a seal.

In the evenings Simone read magazines until she fell into a light sleep, from which she was often woken by the cries of the sleeping children. Frequently the children called out in dreams; once George yelled, "Maisie, stop it!" as if asleep he were having the fight he couldn't risk awake.

Then Simone would get out of bed and go and stand by the children. By then they would have grown quiet but for the pulses fluttering under their skin and the delicate whis-

tles of air escaping their pearly mouths. Simone knew what
Joseph would say: They were spoiled American children.
But she couldn't blame George and Maisie, they hadn't
chosen their lives and asked only the freedom to follow
their sad little preoccupations. Simone's mother was a
piano teacher and had tried to teach Simone; how she'd
felt when her mother gave up on her was how she imagined George felt always. He and Maisie were unhappy
children whose father had just left home, and at moments their faces reminded her of the faces of Haitian
children. They, too, seemed connected to some historic
sorrow, staring out at you from a collective pool of misery and grief.

Simone knew it was foolish of her to so want to make
the children happy. She was asking to have her heart broken, putting such stake in their moods and affections. Any
ties that bound her to them could be severed in a minute,
but the power of their mother and father would last their
entire lives. Sometimes in Haiti embassy people semi-
adopted streetchildren, whom they gently returned to the
street at the end of their tours of duty. For the first time
Simone understood how this love could have been a real
love. How gratifying, how heady it was to hold a child's interest and attention, how confusingly it resembled attention
from a man.

It was frightening to watch breath rattle in the children's
tender throats. In Haiti those sharp intakes of air meant the
loup-garou was near. So many children died there, they
were assumed to be at special risk and people believed in
evil spirits with a special taste for children. The *loup-garou*
was the werewolf crouched under children's windows, silently watching their darkened rooms for a chance to suck
their blood.

Simone had never believed in the *loup-garou*, but nonetheless she felt now as if something was waiting in the
crisp autumn dark for a chance to hurt Maisie and George.
Nor was this simply some voodoo fantasy Simone had im-

ported from Haiti, a stowaway that had hitched a ride like some disease-bearing mosquito. The sheep in the woods seemed like evidence: something thirsty had come near.

FOR SEVERAL EVENINGS Rosemary took the kitchen phone and shut herself in the broom closet, from which she could be heard weeping and screaming and pounding her fist on the door. Finally she emerged one night and cracked the receiver against the wall and lost an entire working day buying a new phone at Sears. In that way it was decided that the children's schedule would change. From now on they would spend weekends in Hudson Landing with their father.

Once these facts were established, Rosemary found them comforting. "It's always better to know," she said. "Things improved considerably when I knew Geoffrey was really leaving. When it finally happens, it's always a great relief. You know what you're up against, it becomes like a wall in your house. You get used to having it there, you even begin to lean on it. If only it weren't for the sadistic pleasure Geoffrey's taking in all this. And the putting of the children at additional risk for spiritual contamination."

It must be so satisfying, Simone thought, to punish the telephone, to whack it against the door frame until the earpiece came flying off. What a lovely, brief distraction from one's own troubles and fears. Simone herself was worried that, with the children gone weekends, her duties would be so diminished that Rosemary might let her go. Not a day went by when Rosemary didn't fret about money and complain about Geoffrey indulging himself while she and the children starved. Though Simone hadn't yet cashed

Rosemary's checks, Rosemary's lips turned white when she wrote them.

She said, "What a ridiculous time to have hired household help! It must be one of those insane things people do in mid-breakup. But the truth is that with this new system we need help more than ever. For some preposterous reason invented to make himself look busy, Geoffrey can no longer pick up the children at school. Simone, if you could drive George and Maisie back and forth between Geoffrey and me, it would spare me the psychic damage of ever having to see him again."

Simone should have been relieved that her job wasn't in danger, but it depressed her to contemplate weekends without the children, the mansion silent but for the tapes Rosemary played while she worked, the ominous repetitious notes that made Simone feel paralyzed and hysterical.

The children were good company. Simone, Maisie, and George could spend hours at Hudson Landing Pizza, ordering Coke and pizza by the slice, watching the other patrons and scratching sesame seeds off breadsticks. Occasionally George asked for a quarter and played a videogame which, as Simone and Maisie watched, he lost within a few seconds. Sometimes the children had school projects the three of them worked on together, maps and cardboard models requiring the use of Rosemary's X-Acto knife, which was so sharp that Simone shivered, rescuing it from George's grasp.

George and Maisie no longer resembled children on the run or in hiding, little refugees prematurely skilled at not attracting attention, aware that any spontaneous noise might mean capture and death. Still, they were appallingly cooperative, rarely argued, and never fought. When they spoke to their father on the phone they mumbled into the receiver. Once, Maisie stretched the phone cord so far that it separated from the new phone; Rosemary gritted her teeth and made little moans while Simone replaced it.

For a week or so the children had been letting Simone tuck them into bed at night. Ironically, these tender moments made Simone dread the children's absence more and feel as if they were leaving for much longer than overnight. George pretended not to need tucking in, yet allowed Simone to do it and chattered out of embarrassment, high-pitched and nonstop.

One night he said, "My dad bought a new Land Rover? For the days when we'll be with him?"

"How nice of him," Simone said, attempting a neutral tone.

Later, when Simone went downstairs, Shelly and Rose-mary were, coincidentally, discussing Geoffrey's sleazy at-tempts to buy the children's love and devotion.

Rosemary said, "Simone, I promise, you will understand tomorrow. The instant you meet the man everything will become clear. The man thinks everything is for sale and available for a price, including those most precious com-modities, his own amusement and pleasure. Luckily he has the wealth to satisfy every infantile male whim, including the million bucks of electronic toys his imaginary advertis-ing business requires. It's an indication, isn't it, of the pas-sionate interest he takes in his children—Simone has been here for what seems like our whole lives and Geoffrey has never met her."

Rosemary poured wine into glasses and brought one to Shelly. "Thank you," said Shelly, and went back to staring out the window. "What are those piles of branches? Burn-ing a friend at the stake? That has always been my secret fear. Joan of Arc made a lasting impression."

Rosemary said, "Simone found a dead sheep in the woods. The Count is up to his old tricks."

"Count Dracula," said Shelly. "It must be hell on prop-erty values. But Simone should be used to it—coming from Haiti and all."

"Ridiculous," said Rosemary. "What do they do in *Haiti*, kill chickens? That's qualitatively different from rites in-volving dead sheep and underage boys."

"Come off it, Rosemary," Shelly said. "They're killing more than chickens in Haiti, aren't they, Simone? I read that the *tonton macoute* employed a stable of insane dwarfs hired exclusively to bite off the testicles of Duvalier's torture victims."

Simone was startled to hear Shelly repeat this old story, which embassy people regularly dusted off to entertain guests and new arrivals. Maybe rumors about the travel bureau had gotten this far as well.

"Shelly!" Rosemary wrung her hands. "Look at poor Simone! Haiti is Simone's country!"

"So what?" Shelly shrugged lightly. "All the more reason to bring it out into the light of day. There are certain truths one has to face, especially about one's own country. I for one wouldn't be a bit surprised to learn those dwarfs were on the CIA payroll."

After a silence Rosemary said, "I wish you were staying for dinner."

"I wish I were, too," said Shelly. "But that dreary photographer in Clintonville is giving a ghastly party."

"Oh, parties." Rosemary sighed dreamily. "I can't do parties anymore. Going to parties with Geoffrey was like party aversion therapy. Always looking around to see who he was flirting with. And when I saw, I'd get a shock—party behavior modification."

"Parties are like everything else," Shelly said. "You have to stay in practice."

"Maybe now," Rosemary said. "If I ever got invited anywhere again . . ."

"What you've got to remember," Shelly said, "is how much Geoffrey stage-managed. It was in his interest to prevent you from trying to have a good time. As with everyone, of course, the roots are all in his childhood. Simone, imagine: the man's anal-sadistic British mother used to give tea parties for his friends, twelve-year-old boys invited in for scones and marmite sandwiches. No wonder he grew up using social occasions to make his loved ones squirm."

"Mothers!" Rosemary threw up her hands. "It's a miracle we survive them. My problem is, I have no memory. I get lonely and forget how it was—and think Geoffrey was bet-

ter than nothing. I need my friends to remind me that in
fact it was worse. I only wish you'd been around, Simone,
though we couldn't have been friends. But after tomorrow
you'll see what I mean. You'll understand what I've suffered."

"Be careful, Simone." Shelly opened her mouth in a
studied, ironic yawn. "Very charming surface. But put
Geoffrey in blackface and inflate him—we're looking at
Baby Doc."

On Saturday morning Simone rose early to wash her hair
and dress with ritual concentration, not—certainly not!—as
she'd dressed for Joseph, but as if for an event. As a girl
she'd worn white to church like the girls in Joseph's paintings, and later she'd had one good dress for important embassy functions. Now she chose a white T-shirt and blue
jeans from the armloads of old clothes that, a few days before, Rosemary had thoughtfully dumped in a pile on the
floor of Simone's room. Simone found a pair of denims that
fit—they were way too long to have been Rosemary's. It
was odd to think she might be wearing the clothes of the
man she was going to meet. Simone put on lipstick and
wiped it off—Rosemary would have noticed.

George appeared in a new sweatshirt and pants he kept
scowling at and tugging. Maisie stood like a Victorian doll
while Simone tied the sash on her dress. Then Rosemary
knelt and squeezed the children as if they were leaving forever.

"Watch out for each other!" she called after them. "You
know what your father is capable of."

Then she caught Simone's sleeve and said, "It's safer to
see Geoffrey as an ever-present threat. Right now he is feeling guilty and, by Porter standards, generous. The unstated
implication is that we can go on living like this indefinitely—me and the kids starving to death in a falling-down
mansion while he spends the cash flow on luxury toys for
his weekend discretional children. And that's the best we
can hope for. At any minute he could decide he wants the

house and full-time children. He has the money and lawyers to do anything he wants."

A few minutes out of the driveway, the children erupted
in conversation. They seemed to have been holding their
breaths while making their getaway. George said, "That kid
who got kicked off the bus for the whole year for tying up
that first-grader with the bus driver's belt?"

"It wasn't the bus driver's belt." Maisie was nearly gag-
ging with contempt. "It belonged to a kid in Special Ed
sixth grade."

George said, "There is no Special Ed sixth grade."

Maisie said, "Yes, there is. Stupid."

The banality, the shrillness, the underlayer of menace—
these were voices Simone recognized, the voices of embassy children in normal American-child conversation. It
was surely, she hoped, another sign of George and Maisie's
improvement. But why did it have to be on the road, where
their happy chatter distracted her and made her driving uncertain? Nor was she sure she liked them being so buoyant
en route to their father's, who might be, as Rosemary
warned, a rival and a threat.

The world was noisier in the rain, quick-tempered and
aggressive, a sudden hail of drops on the roof, the liquid
whisper of passing cars. A cruising police car so frightened
Simone—suppose they asked to see her papers?—that it
seemed a miracle when the police drove on by. When the
road presented a new problem, a left turn across merciless
traffic, Simone froze until George said, "Now. Go ahead.
Turn!"

They drove past the sagging frame houses of greater
Hudson Landing, with their asbestos-shingled porches flat
up against the sidewalk. Simone saw an old woman pushing a child in a grocery cart, the first black faces she had
seen since she'd left Manhattan. Would she be insulted if
Simone waved or said hello? She remembered Emile's
warnings against being friendly to strangers who might be
INS informants.

In the center of the city was the restored business section, old façades of newly sandblasted brick and repainted plaster and siding, like the pristine, just-unwrapped town in George's unused train set.

"There it is!" George and Maisie sang out when they spotted their father's office. Simone pulled into a parking space—well, two parking spaces. George and Maisie ran down the street and vanished into a doorway.

Simone dawdled at a window in which fancy soaps luxuriated in nestlike satiny cushions. Then she followed the children inside. They'd stopped on the landing halfway up the stairs. Their father had met them halfway down and was hugging George and Maisie with a great deal of fuss and commotion. Simone stood at the base of the steps, feeling shy and excluded and stupidly possessive about the children's affection. It was wrong and selfish of her to want them to love her more than their father. Maisie plastered herself against her father's side. George tenderly thumped his back.

Even from below, Geoffrey looked slighter and more boyish than the lumbering monster Simone had been led to expect. He smiled down over the children's heads. "You must be Simone."

When Simone reached the landing he rather formally put out his hand. As they shook hands, he blushed deeply, and despite herself, Simone was flattered. He had shiny brown hair and blue surprised eyes that lit and dimmed like headlights. He seemed drawn to Simone by some interest or force he was actively trying to stifle. She thought of a dieting fat man passing a bakery, so near to what he had loved and renounced and now pretended to ignore. You could step back and watch it in Geoffrey, attraction warring with will, a state of affairs any sentient pastry might take as a personal challenge. All this so appealed to Simone that she slowly backed up until what she read in Geoffrey's eyes was that she was in danger of falling down the stairs.

Geoffrey said, "I got you guys some presents. They're in the office. Go look." Maisie jumped up and kissed his cheek. George consented to pass close enough so his father could ruffle his hair.

Watching the children run past him, Geoffrey seemed at once tense and ardent. Simone saw in him the uneasy boy that Shelly had described, waiting for his friends to discover the lukewarm tea his mum had set out with soggy, crustless sandwiches.

"And I must be Geoffrey," he said. "But I guess you know that. I guess you know my life story and all my personality disorders. You probably know every detail of my classically repressed Anglo-WASP childhood: how my poor homesick mother made icky British snacks and invited my pals for tea."

"Excuse me?" said Simone.

Geoffrey raised his hands, palms outward. "Ah, I can see you do. Rosemary makes quite a thing of it, quite the amateur Freudian. To her, my finding Mum with the marmite jar was the primal scene. But please, come in! Unlike my wife, I know that family therapy is not in your job description."

"Mr. Porter—" said Simone.

"Please. Geoffrey." Geoffrey smiled and Simone forgot whatever she'd planned to say as she tried to reconcile this appealing, slightly gawky person with the devil she'd heard described.

The office consisted of two large white rooms with gray industrial carpet, both smelling strongly of flower perfumes wafting up from the soap store downstairs. One room contained several computers and imposing copy machines. "Star Ship *Enterprise*," Geoffrey said.

"Fire this up," he told George, handing his son a small metal square that—amazingly—George knew how to slip into the right computer slot. The screen lit up and a slew of belching frogs swarmed over the monitor.

"Swamp Thing!" cried George, punching the keyboard until a cartoon zombie lumbered onto the screen, snapping at the frogs.

"Educational and entertaining," Geoffrey told Simone.

"Swamp Thing can't get his froggie dinner till George spells a word."

Simone felt, without turning, Maisie's eyes drill their backs.

"Look at this," said her father, and steered Maisie into the other room—bare but for a drafting table, metal shelves, and art supplies. When Simone took up with Joseph, his girlfriend had just kicked him out of the house and he was living in his studio with only a mattress, his easel, and paints. Simone had confused lack of furniture with the lack of a past to compete with.

Simone thought again of the *Olympia* on the wall of Joseph's studio. How frightened and naked the white girl looked behind all that blood and those wounds! The only item on Geoffrey's wall was a large print of a Madonna surrounded by separate 8 X 10 blowups of her facial features—a lip, a nose, a hooded eye, one beatific eyebrow.

Geoffrey paused in the doorway till Simone caught up and could witness the warming spectacle of him giving his daughter a gift, a picture book wrapped in red tissue and tied with a curly blue bow.

"Read the cover," Geoffrey ordered.

Maisie read, "You are real."

"Bravo," said Geoffrey.

On the next page Maisie read, "Trees are real." She turned another page and a cardboard pine tree popped up from the book. "A house is real," read Maisie, and a Victorian gingerbread house jumped out of the binding.

"You are real," said Geoffrey. "A crucial concept—and one I'm not certain Maisie gets quite enough of with Rosemary for a mother. Of course, the intriguing thing is to say that a house is real and then show the children a cardboard house that *isn't* real at all."

Maisie was engrossed in her pop-up book, George was pounding the computer keyboard. The gifts were precisely on target. Geoffrey knew what his children wanted.

"Look at them!" said Geoffrey. "With Rosemary this wouldn't be fun but simply another example of my uncontrolled sexist aggression, giving the hot technology to George-the-boy, the book to Maisie-the-girl, when in fact George likes the computer and Maisie likes the book."

"I like the computer," said Maisie.

Geoffrey said, "I know you do, honey. But no one gets to do what they like all the time. Do you think Daddy likes designing ad campaigns featuring the body parts of a Piero Madonna to put behind the latest model Japanese family hatchbacks? It cannot be coincidental that this office smells like a bordello. The wonder is that your dad can do it up here and make real New York City money. Everyone does stuff for a living they don't necessarily like, as your friend Simone here will be the first to tell you."

Did Geoffrey mean Simone to say she didn't like caring for George and Maisie? The truth was that she liked her job so much she stayed awake nights fearing she'd lose it. She had come to feel, like Rosemary, that this was the best they could hope for right now, and she longed for it to continue—this interlude of restorative calm after wrenching upheaval and change. Besides, she was so fond of George and Maisie, she would miss them for even a weekend, and she recalled with an unpleasant shock that one such weekend was starting now.

Geoffrey said, "What *I'd* like is serious breakfast."

George and Maisie said, "Yay!"

Simone stepped back, but Geoffrey said, "Please. Come with us, Simone." He tossed George the car keys, and after a few blank moments, George grinned at his father and rushed out, clumping down the stairs. Maisie clung to Geoffrey's hand and chafed her arm against his.

"The Tepee Diner," Geoffrey told Simone. "George and Maisie's favorite. The oldest downscale dining institution in the Hudson Valley. It was my favorite diner when I was George and Maisie's age. Dad and I would sneak off there when Mummy was otherwise engaged."

George and Maisie scrambled into the back seat of the shiny red Land Rover and, unasked, fastened their seat

belts. They all sat for a moment in almost prayerful silence,
inhaling the spicy, optimistic, new-car polymer smell.

The silvery diner caught the sun and flashed it back like
the ocean. Inside, a counter ran the length of one mirrored
wall and across the aisle were two rows of booths uphol-
stered in tangerine vinyl. In the booths sat young couples in
expensive hunt clothes and peevish states of annoyance,
suggesting they'd lost the scent of the fox and settled
grudgingly for this diner. Every party of two or less was
reading *The New York Times*.

The waitress wore black leggings and a tight flowered
mini-skirt. Protruding from the pocket of her oversize
man's shirt was an antique pack of cigarettes.

"Thirty-year-old Luckys?" Geoffrey said. "That's pushing the envelope, healthwise."

"Purely decorative," said the waitress. "Your lungs
would vaporize if you smoked one."

Geoffrey consulting with the children about what they
wanted to eat was such a touching sight that even the tough
little waitress registered and approved.

"French toast all around," Geoffrey said. "Fresh-
squeezed orange juice. Coffee." To Simone he said, "I
know it's not called French toast in French. Do they have
French toast in Haiti?"

"In Haiti," said George, "they eat rice and beans and the
children are lucky to get it."

The waitress turned and walked away. "That's my boy!"
said Geoffrey.

The French toast was made from crusty baguettes, diag-
onally sliced, encircled by banana and strawberry slices
suggesting flower sexual parts. Simone lowered her head
and ate, grateful for the taste of the food and for its power
to distract and free her from the steamy curtain of intensity
that seemed to encircle their table. She wondered where it
had come from, this pressure and isolation, as if the four of
them were taking a shower instead of just eating breakfast.

Only slowly did the fog clear enough for Simone to notice an obese couple, two beach balls with heads and legs, in a nearby booth. The man was involved in complicated negotiation with the waitress, who finally removed their plates—untouched stacks of pancakes. Soon she returned with new plates, new pancakes, new negotiations, these apparently about syrups and pour-jars of fruit toppings. The couple moped in silence, then took a few resentful bites.

"It's a diet," Geoffrey whispered. "I've seen them do this before. A good fight with the waitress not only delays gratification but cuts down on their calorie intake and gives them an adrenaline rush so they metabolize faster. Listen to me. I sound so cruel. It's all those years with Rosemary. She wore off on me, I suppose. I keep trying to locate some vein of sympathy for all of us poor souls in hell, fat people included.

"But finally I can't do it, it's basically so disgusting. I can just imagine how that little scene must look to someone from Haiti, someone from the country with the world's lowest per capita income." Geoffrey paused for credit for knowing this fact about Haiti, then looked to see if George or Maisie needed help cutting their French toast. Maisie didn't and George did. Wisely, Geoffrey left them both alone.

"What I *can* sympathize with," he said, "is how every second of a fat man's life can turn into a test, a major battle between self-control and the power of desire. Every minor temptation is a crossroads with a traffic cop holding up his hand. Every chance to be bad seems like a decision: give up or break on through. And eventually you see the cop's a skull and bones, he's wearing your own death—death's scaring you and at the same time mocking you for being scared. Well, there's no longer any choice. It's your *duty* to get into trouble."

Geoffrey's tone made it clear that what he meant by trouble was not what the fat couple meant. Simone hadn't known many men very well, but a high percentage, it seemed, talked as if women were a disease from which they had or hadn't recovered. Geoffrey was the only one who talked about running roadblocks when what he meant, or what she thought he meant, was going to bed with women. Several times, in Inez's car, they had run into roadblocks. Simone remembered peering into the dark to see how many men were around, and if they looked as if they would torch your car, just because they could. Not even these painful memories could dampen Simone's pleasure in Geoffrey's having chosen to confide in her his very private and personal thoughts. Not every man would talk this way to his children's caregiver.

Geoffrey said, "That skull and bones always seemed to me to be saying: Last chance. In a blink of an eye you'll be dead or old, with all the leisure in the world to regret what you didn't do, getting up twenty times a night just to take a piss, and every time you wake up you see the face of a different woman you didn't sleep with. The pressure got unbearable. It's a wonder I didn't snap. For six months now I've been celibate, totally sworn off women. It's a kind of trial period—a dry-out time, so to speak."

This was welcome news to Simone; it would keep things between them simpler. But how exactly did it fit in with his flirting with the waitress? "The point of the experiment," Geoffrey said, "is to stop thinking with my dick."

Simone glanced at the children, sawing obliviously at their toast. Simone took a gummy bite that required some time to chew.

After another few mouthfuls she asked, "When should I come for the children tomorrow?" though Rosemary had specifically instructed her that George and Maisie were to be home no later than three. What would she do now if Geoffrey said six-thirty?

Geoffrey said, "I'm sure that Rosemary has an opinion on this." Gratefully, Simone told him what Rosemary's opinion was.

"Three is early," Geoffrey said, "but I'll do anything to keep the peace."

"Should I pick them up at your house?" Simone held her breath, awaiting his answer. Tomorrow, Sunday afternoon—it was unlikely he'd be at his office. If he wanted her to go to his house, Simone would have to agree, though it made her nervous to find a new place without the children along for guidance.

A funny spark passed between them—Simone caught it right away. Geoffrey said, "No no no! The office would be fine."

He didn't want her to come to his house. He didn't want any discussion. A pinpoint chill scratched up Simone's spine and she hunched her shoulders and shivered.

On the beach near the village where Simone's grandmother lived, there was a ruined stone castle in which a pirate was said to have stacked the corpses of nine wives. People said this was why the water temperature dropped in that part of the cove. When Simone was a little girl she'd been afraid to swim near there, and now, as she looked at Geoffrey, she remembered why: the castle watching you from the shore, the icy shock of the water.

IN SEVERAL OF her magazines Simone had read warnings: Women driving alone should always check the front and back seats before entering a vehicle. But where could an intruder have found room to hide in Rosemary's Volvo? Simone's anxiety filled the whole car—and ambushed her when she got in.

Leaving Geoffrey's office, she missed the children intensely and felt barely capable of making her way home alone. She reminded herself of how long and how well she had functioned before she knew them, traveled from Port-au-Prince to New York without George and Maisie's support. But rage and pain were great navigators, and besides, she hadn't been driving.

Simone's heart began to thrum like a moth in a jar. Luckily she had to stay on the road and couldn't afford to panic, and after a moment the fluttering stopped, leaving her giddy and weak. She squinted against the flickering sun that jumped out from behind the black trees in the huge locker full of dead sheep pretending to be a forest.

Simone told herself, This is peaceful. In Haiti there was war, bursts of automatic fire and bodies in the street. On the night of the last election she'd lain in bed, waiting for Joseph. Everyone expected violence, she'd heard shots from every direction, but she wasn't worried that Joseph might be hurt—she was afraid he was with someone else. Probably he was with Inez; probably she knew that. What a small, selfish person she'd been in that vast sea of trouble and pain. So it followed that her motives for leaving Haiti seemed, from this distance, small and pathetic. She would have felt better about her life if she had left for political reasons; the victims of history were heroic in ways that the victims of heartbreak were not. But perhaps it had all worked out for the best; for the moment she was safe, and after the turmoil she'd left behind, a moment of safety was fine.

Here people got in line and took turns. Cars crawled through drive-in banks. No one stumbled by the road beneath impossible burdens, the bent real-life versions of the happy laundresses Joseph painted. No wonder Americans loved the sight of people with laundry on their heads! They all had washing machines and a car to carry their clothes. This was life like clockwork. This was peace, not war. And yet it didn't seem peaceful, though Simone could not have said why.

Simone got back to Rosemary's with no idea how she'd got there. She stood in the foyer, listening for music or for the squeal of Rosemary's air compressor. The house was eerily quiet. Was Rosemary asleep upstairs? Simone had the Volvo. Rosemary never walked. Had Shelly taken her somewhere? How much time would Simone have to pass until she could go get the children?

Then Simone heard a rustling like the dry scratch of a mouse and tracked the noise to the living room, where she found Rosemary on the couch, extending one limp hand to Simone from her shroud of a navy blanket.

"Oh, Simone, you're here," she gasped. "Oh thank God. Thank God you've come." Rosemary pushed the covers down a few inches. Her forehead glistened with sweat.

"I can't breathe," she whispered. "I'm having some kind of attack." Simone could tell it was not a habitual thing Rosemary knew how to handle. In Port-au-Prince she had seen a woman have a seizure on the street. The woman was alone when she fell and no one came to help; people watched, keeping their distance, until the woman stopped twitching.

"We'll have to try the Instacare Clinic," Rosemary managed to pant. "Shapiro will be out running some dismal marathon and his answering service is so deaf you just call and scream and hang up."

A look of concentration—of listening—came over Rosemary's face. "Shit," she said, "here it comes again," and her chest swelled and collapsed with a harsh rhythmic croak. An unwilled thought came to Simone—the frogs on George's computer—and its giddy inappropriateness made her realize how scared she was. What if Rosemary died and Simone was left here alone, an illegal alien with a dead employer? What did it mean that, on the drive here, her own heart had acted up, too? Was it weather, air pressure, some contagious disease? Wasn't it human to take on the feelings of those with whom you lived closely? Simone had come to share Miss McCaffrey's pleasure when a dance performance went well, and Joseph's political angers and Inez's twitchy boredom.

On the way to the clinic Rosemary said, "Turn right. No, I meant left." Emergency seemed to have oiled the wheels so Simone could make tricky U-turns.

At last they found the red brick building. "Fast-food medical care," Rosemary said. "The last wrinkle they have yet to iron out is the drive-in appendectomy."

A woman behind a window took Rosemary's credit card. Simone was relieved that Rosemary seemed able to manage without her help. Rosemary said, "This is going to sound hypochondriacal, but I'm in acute respiratory failure."

"Don't worry, dear." The receptionist smiled. "Leave the diagnosis to Doctor."

"Come this way," she said, and Rosemary shot a wild look at Simone. Both of them followed the woman into a curtained-off cubicle.

"Hop on the table," said the woman. "You'll want to take off that fur coat. Doctor won't hear a heartbeat, and then where will we be?"

On her way out the woman drew the curtain. They could hear her and the doctor yelling back and forth.

"How was I supposed to know he's her nephew?" the

doctor said. "The worst kind of teenage shithead, the absolute scum of the earth. I don't ask, I don't want to ask how he broke the arm. Okay, I'm not as gentle as I might be, seeing if I can set it. He keeps screaming, 'Aunt Suzie! Aunt Suzie!' How am I supposed to know Aunt Suzie is Susan, my goddamn nurse?"

A white-haired man yanked open the curtain and told Rosemary and Simone, "What we have around here is what they call organized chaos. Know anyone who wants a job?"

Simone looked at Rosemary. Were they expected to answer?

"I'm Dr. Worms," he told them. "Believe me, I've heard every possible joke about my name. What's the problem, young lady?"

Rosemary burst into tears and in a strangled voice managed to convey the fact that she couldn't breathe.

"There, there." The doctor patted her shoulder. "I know how it is. You're the one who can't get sick. The hubby can get sick and the kids can get sick but you can't let up for a minute."

He felt the glands under Rosemary's neck and put a stethoscope to her heart. He said, "You know, there *is* one thing women do better . . ." and waited till Rosemary asked, "What?"

"Everything!" The doctor grinned. "I think you'll be fine. Short of hooking you up to a million bucks' worth of electronics better suited to an auto shop than a human, I have to go with my hunch, which is that physically you're shipshape. Something's just getting to you. How many kids do you have?"

"Two," said Rosemary.

"Three," the doctor corrected her.

"Three?" Rosemary looked bewildered. Was there one she'd forgotten?

"Three counting your husband," he said.

Rosemary said, "I guess you know my husband."

The doctor said, "I'm just like him."

* * *

A few days later Rosemary saw her regular doctor for a checkup. This was after much discussion with Simone and then on the phone with Shelly, asking Shelly the same questions she had just asked Simone: Was something really wrong with her? Should she bother with the doctor? Wasn't it normal that Rosemary should feel a tiny bit fried the first weekend her children spent with their psycho father?

But it hadn't just been in her head. She had had physical symptoms. Who knew what fatal condition Dr. Worms—Dr. Worms!—might have overlooked. What kind of physician hears you can't breathe and makes dumb jokes about your husband? What had he done in another state to wind up working at that clinic?

Simone's father had died suddenly of an aneurysm of the brain and her mother, some years later, succumbed in a matter of days to meningitis. That both of them had been fully alive and then, dizzyingly, dead made Simone feel unqualified to give medical advice.

Rosemary came home from Dr. Shapiro's office with an armload of pamphlets that she dumped on the kitchen table and read, a paragraph from each one. "I've been kidding myself," she said. "Talking bananas and potassium and eating potato chips and toxic fumes. You can only fool the body so long. Our whole lives will have to change."

The first change was a treadmill Rosemary bought at a sports shop. "Nordic skiers are indestructible," she said. "Excepting, I guess, the Finns, who all have coronaries at fifty. Don't the Finns go cross-country skiing? I guess not enough to counteract all that reindeer butter."

From then on Rosemary could often be found skipping on the conveyor belt—even this she chose to do in her mouton coat. She said, "I must look like a grocery item trying to escape. What I *feel* like is a guinea pig in an abusive lab experiment." She put the treadmill near the telephone so she could work out while chatting with Shelly. Rosemary told Simone it was easier to talk to Geoffrey now that she knew she was secretly fitting him into her exercise routine.

Every so often Rosemary tried to get George to try the

treadmill. She said the exercise would do him good, but George shook his head firmly no.

"Can you imagine!" Rosemary said. "I would have loved it when I was his age!"

Maisie stood at a distance watching with what Simone alone recognized as the superiority of a child who can climb straight up the walls.

Rosemary changed her diet: no more burned-burger-and-pretzel dinners. Now she lived on moderate portions of Simone's rice and beans and plantains. Everything came up for review, what was healthy and what wasn't. Some things were psychologically good and physically bad, and the relative merits had to be carefully weighed. Luckily, the spiritual benefits of Rosemary's sculpture canceled the risk of liver damage from the fiberglass and resins.

Part of Rosemary's program for mental health was to get out of the house more. Simone heard her ask Shelly on the phone, "Who's doing the Halloween party?" Rosemary was silent a moment, then said, "Oh, I see. No, I don't think I know them."

After that Rosemary paid new attention to the telephone and the mail, and once Simone heard her say, to a pile of junk flyers, "Come on, *someone* must celebrate Halloween. I'd settle for a charity bash, the Cerebral Palsy Harvest Moon Ball."

Simone coughed to make her presence known and to stop Rosemary from humbling herself before the mail. Without missing a beat Rosemary said, "Despite what one hears about charities, they're grotesquely efficient. The day Geoffrey moved out, all the envelopes with envelopes inside got redirected elsewhere."

A few days before Halloween, Rosemary appeared in the kitchen. Maisie swallowed her corn flakes and pointed as if at an apparition. George said, "I can't believe it. Mom's got up for breakfast!"

"Shut up, George." Rosemary smiled. "I don't appreciate the implications. Listen, I've got a brilliant idea. Halloween at the mall! I heard about it on the radio—it's supposed to be terrific. Costumes! Prizes! Trick or treat! Free candy for the kiddies! Bob-bob-bobbing for apples!"

George and Maisie and Simone looked at each other, and George rolled his eyes. Several times the children had asked if they could go to the mall for Halloween, but Rosemary had brushed the question off into some indefinite future.

After the children left for school Rosemary considered costumes. "Let's be creative," she urged Simone. "This is a chance to expand their nonexistent art education, or at least work around the rigidity of those minimum-security prisons known as public schools. What do you think George should be? Perhaps something therapeutic, a lion or a tiger. It might do him good to go around roaring like the king of the jungle."

Simone had a dismaying vision of George in a humiliating kitty-cat suit, and when it seemed that Rosemary might have fixed on this idea, Simone cast about frantically for an alternative that would spare him.

She said, "Maybe George could be an Eskimo," and regretted it at once. The Eskimos were George's secret—and she had given it away. Would he understand how anxious she'd been to save him from Halloween as a kitty?

"An Eskimo?" Rosemary said. "An Eskimo? There may be such a thing as *too* creative. George, let me point out, is a white person. But wait. This could be genius. Recycle some old furs from the attic, creepy shaman stuff. I'm sure he'd like some kind of harpoon, very weaponesque and phallic, always appropriate for the shaky pre-adolescent ego. And Maisie? We could do Maisie as the Death of Little Nell. Come on, I'm joking, Little Nell is precisely what we want to avoid. We want something healthy, organic, American. What about Pocahontas? The only Native American Hudson Landing is going to see."

Rosemary and Simone foraged in the attic and found a smelly fur parka for George and a feathered Indian bonnet for Maisie.

"Perfect!" Rosemary said. "Let's surprise them. No peeking till Halloween!"

On Halloween the children came home from school and took one look at their costumes, and their faces crumpled.

"What's the matter?" Rosemary asked through clenched teeth. "What seems to be the trouble?"

George gave Simone an accusing look. Clearly he thought she'd told his mother about the Eskimo videotape. There was no way to invoke the kitty-cat she'd rescued him from being.

"These feathers are from a bird," Maisie said.

"A dead bird," Rosemary pointed out. "By that point plumage was the least of its problems. But I like this evidence in you, Maisie, of correct ecological thinking. The feather bonnet was unconscious of me, a mistake I won't repeat. Meanwhile, put it on for now and let me paint your face. You will be sadder being the only kid without a costume than worrying about some chicken that died ages before you were born. Besides, it's nature red in tooth and claw. Do you think Pocahontas worried about dead birds?"

The night was dark and sheeted with rain. Rosemary's nose inched toward the windshield.

"Every car in the opposite lane," she said, "is full of guys dressed as Diana Ross and the Supremes."

The children had grumpily donned their costumes and now were taking it out on each other. "Quit it!" Maisie shrieked. "George is poking me with his harpoon!"

"They're really very much improved," Rosemary told Simone. "A few months ago even sibling conflict was beyond their energy level. I really have to say, Simone, that your friendship has made a difference."

This was almost enough to reconcile Simone to the humiliations of her own costume: high heels and a little black shirt and a gold lamé mini-skirt. Simone and Rosemary were dressed respectively, as Tina and Ike Turner.

Finding the gold skirt for Simone had inspired Rosemary, who seemed relieved, even overjoyed, that Simone knew who Tina Turner was. In fact, her music video had been the

most popular request on the American Center TV. That had
pleased Miss McCaffrey, who liked Tina Turner as much as
ballet, the difference being they couldn't afford to bring
Tina Turner to Haiti. Rosemary had teased Simone's hair
till it looked like an agitated turkey, then darkened her own
face with makeup, spray-dyed her own hair black, and now
looked rather natty in a boy's white tuxedo. For the first
time in months Rosemary had shed her mouton coat.

"It's our Carnival," she said. "Or our *excuse* for Carnival
or Mardi Gras or whatever. The one night out of the whole
year we get to dress up and act out."

Simone felt as if objecting to her costume would be a sin
against the culture. That had been Miss McCaffrey's phrase,
"sinning against the culture"; several times she'd told
Simone that the greatest statesmen were the ones who
would sit on the floor of the tent and eat the eye of the
sheep. Still, the reference to Mardi Gras filled Simone with
misgivings; she had always had a terrible time at Carnival
in Port-au-Prince. Last year Joseph contrived to get lost in
the crowd and disappeared for days, which at least excused
Simone from having to fake the Carnival spirit. Even—
especially—as a child the ecstatic mobs alarmed her.
Though she longed to be the sort of person who enjoyed
that sort of surrender and could briefly forget herself and
lean on the arms of the crowd, she hated it when crowds
picked up and moved without anyone seeming to will it.

Rosemary had definitely caught the spirit. Tonight as
they'd left the house, she'd taken a long swig from a vodka
bottle in the freezer. She'd said, "All I need is the silver
coke spoon to make my costume complete. Georgie,
where's that cheap electric guitar we bought and you never
played?"

Now from the back seat George said, "There was this
drunk driver on TV? He wiped out this mom and kids, they
were on bikes? And they took away his license and he went
to jail for life?"

"Relax, George," said Rosemary. "One swig of vodka

does not a DWI make. What gives me the willies," she told Simone, "is that in six years *they'll* be driving."

"Six years for me," said George. "Ten years for her."

Rosemary was looping wide circles around the mall parking lot. She said, "Geoffrey had that male fetish about parking right by the entrance. I myself never had any desire to compete in that arena." They parked a mile from any other cars and hiked out into the rain.

Simone tottered behind the others on her ice-pick heels. George waited for her to catch up and then said, "Did you tell my mom about the Eskimo tape?"

"No," replied Simone. "I did not. But I had to do something. Your mother was planning to dress you as a lion or a tiger." Once more telling the truth had involved going too far. It was wrong to make these children feel any more misunderstood by their parents—wrong of Simone to incriminate Rosemary in order to clear herself. But the force of the truth seemed to work on George, who believed and appeared to forgive her. The brisk walk through the cold drizzly lot made their talk heartfelt and intense.

George said, "Simone, if you tell anyone I'll never speak to you again."

Simone knew that George meant it. She said, "Don't worry. I won't." There was no point asking him why he needed this secret kept. The tape was not about hunting or blood but about George's secret religion. The igloo was a refuge to him, a haven where things were simple, uncomplicated by sarcasm or ambiguous adult nuance. Well, why shouldn't people have ceremonies that gave them some courage or hope, just so long as it didn't involve killing something for the occasion? Sometimes Simone envied believers their spirits and loas, whose tricks and whims and grudges so neatly explained the world. If your lover left you it might be consoling to think that someone had prayed to Erzulie and turned the goddess of love against you. Joseph said that voodoo was an instrument of ignorance and repression which should be rooted out of the people even if nothing took root in its place. Yet he was surprisingly tol-

erant of Inez's flirtation with voodoo and amused by her
stories about the jewelry and perfumes her rich friends put
on Erzulie's altar to secure her help with an affair, a seduction, or a revenge. It had taken Simone this long to hear
how it must have sounded to Joseph—Inez prattling on
about women who would do *anything* for love.

The white atomic light of the mall made Simone's eyeballs ache. It took all her bravery and resolve to put one
foot in front of the other, and she couldn't have done it had
she let herself think how they looked—an Indian, an Eskimo, and two black rock-and-rollers. Her mini-skirt rode
up on her thighs as she swayed on the needle heels.

Rosemary said, "I love it! Look at us! I love going as the
Third World contingent! *Isn't* it like Carnival in Haiti?"

But except for the fact that people wore costumes, it was
the opposite of Carnival. Glaring and white instead of dark
and hot, indoors instead of out, everyone in discreet little
groups instead of jammed tight in one mass, and instead of
a throbbing drone of music, drums, and voices, a watery
stillness broken by bursts of mothers and children yelling.
Though the mall was overheated its white glare suggested
a freezer, with gangs of costumed little mites swarming
over the shelves.

Many women were dressed like cats, young mothers in
black tights and pointy ears with curled tails and drawn-on
whiskers, often with several toddlers dressed like a litter of
kittens. These women seemed not to know each other or to
be surprised by each other's presence, or even to find it interesting that they'd all had the same idea. Each time they
passed one of these cats Simone looked at George as if to
say: Behold what you might have been, a fate far crueler
than Eskimo furs in the steamy mall. George understood
what Simone's look signified, and their wordless communication made Simone feel connected with him and chosen.

"Mom?" George ventured, without hope. "Carry my harpoon?"

"I will not," said Rosemary. "I've already got the guitar.

Besides, it's part of your costume. You could have left it home."

"It's the only part of my costume I liked," said George.

"What did I tell you?" Rosemary asked Simone. "Boys! If the Eskimos had hand grenades, he would have liked that better."

In the doorway of every shop costumed teenage employees doled out candy. The children darted from store to store in an acquisitive frenzy while their toddler siblings stumbled after them, drooling and confused. The craving for foul-tasting sugar treats was irresistible and contagious. George and Maisie were soon drawn in, filling orange plastic bags. Rosemary dipped into Maisie's bag, fishing for Tootsie Rolls. She tossed a candy to Simone; it was medicinal and delicious.

"Admit it, Simone," Rosemary said. *"Black Orpheus,* USA." She was pointing to a tall figure carrying a sickle and wearing a long gray robe with a peaked hood over his domelike forehead. His lantern face was chalky white; his bloodshot, charcoal-encircled eyes were caked with the dust of the grave.

They passed a child disguised as a computer desk, half hidden by a huge cardboard box topped with cardboard office equipment. A family of dinosaurs followed with backs and tails of foam packing material spray-painted like reptile skin. A woman in an eyepatch and a cocked hat pushed an old-fashioned baby carriage rigged with masts and flags, a rolling pirate ship in which an infant pirate lay sleeping. An elderly Indian woman in a white sari sat outside an import store, dispensing bright green coconut treats and having her photo taken with children. In Port-au-Prince there was a roti shop where Simone and Joseph sometimes ate. Once Simone took Miss McCaffrey there and watched with admiration as she mopped the curry with the roti and never spilled a drop.

Rosemary cried, "This is the avant-garde cutting edge of American creativity! All the wasted talent, the buried gifts,

the juice with nowhere to flow. One holiday a year for all
this talent to come pouring forth!"

Behind the window of the novelty store a teenage boy in
black leather and spiked hair was flipping through greeting
cards. George and Maisie watched, fascinated, as he
searched for the right birthday or anniversary message.

"Wouldn't you know it?" Rosemary cried. "All this color
and creativity and my children gravitate to the garden-
variety low-rent teen heavy-metal fascist. God, I hate sugar
and how it affects them. Look at all those poor kids zapped
on Red Dye #2. All right, George and Maisie, that's it. The
minute those bags of poison are full, we're out of here, I
mean it."

On the drive home George said, "Did you see that guy
dressed as Death?"

"The Grim Reaper," Rosemary corrected. "That's what
the sickle is for. The idea is that he goes around harvesting
lives like alfalfa. Totally primitive, obviously. I don't know
where it comes from. Do *you* know, Simone? I know Mr.
Bones is big in Mexico. What about in Haiti?"

Simone said, "In voodoo there is Baron Samedi, the god
of mischief and death. He wears a top hat and tails and
plays evil tricks and comes out at night in the graveyard."

Maisie said, "In school they told us that if our generation
doesn't drink or smoke we'll live to be a hundred and ten."

"Good luck," Rosemary said. "But you're interrupting. I
asked Simone a question."

George said, "The science teacher brought a horse's heart
into class and we all held it and passed it around."

"How interesting," pronounced Rosemary. "I didn't
know you had a science teacher. Considering the education
budget up here, it's probably a moonlighting dietitian."

"There's this thing they've been saying in school?"
George said. "About Bloody Mary? The Queen of England? The one who chopped people's heads off? They say
that if you go into the bathroom and don't turn on the light
and say Bloody Mary fifty-five times, you'll see her face in
the mirror."

"That's absurd!" For some reason Rosemary was yelling. "You kids must like scaring yourselves into a state of abject terror. I guess that's what Halloween's about, the grisly pleasure children take in tormenting themselves with everything we try to protect them from all the rest of the year."

The next morning Simone heard Rosemary repeat this on the phone to Shelly, though in a calmer tone. She presented it as a theory that had occurred to her the night before, along with her searing vision of buried homegrown American creativity—two bursts of insight for which she could thank her fascinating Halloween at the mall. Then Rosemary said, "Oh really? Where was it? Who was there?"

Even Shelly must have been moved by the longing in Rosemary's tone. For the next pause ended with Rosemary saying, "Definitely! We'd love to!"

"SHELLY ADORES YOU," Rosemary said. "She insists you come along."

Adores, thought Simone, was a little strong. But it did seem that Rosemary and Shelly wanted Simone around. You couldn't say they liked her, exactly—whom exactly did they like? Not once had Simone revealed one true fact about her past, and no one ever asked her, not even from politeness or when conversation faltered. In any case, it was extremely rare that Rosemary and Shelly stopped talking; and Simone, like the children, served as the still point they yammered around. Everyone here spoke so freely and confessed so much about their lives, as if they were strangers meeting just this once on a plane or a train. But where was everyone going, and how would they know when they got there?

Simone sensed that the women valued her presence the way a lawyer might value an item of evidence—a convincing courtroom exhibit in their ongoing case against men. Simone was younger than they were, taller, beautiful, and black. The fact that she wasn't living happily with a man proved that it wasn't their fault. It could happen to anyone, it was simply how things were.

At other times they saw her differently, which let them see themselves differently, too. Then Simone wasn't a woman without a man but a woman with *two* men, a husband *and* a fiancé whom she had left to make a life for herself in Hudson Landing. In this version they were three independent women who had followed their own lights:

66

Shelly had her decorating business, Rosemary her art, Simone her blossoming career as George and Maisie's caregiver.

Rosemary's and Shelly's need for Simone gave her a certain power that she tried to deserve and maintain by acting confident, even superior, though she felt that she was unluckier in love than Rosemary and Shelly combined. At least Shelly had Kenny, and Rosemary had two children as proof of twice having been found attractive. All Simone had was an illegal marriage certificate, a ninety-minute cab ride with Emile, one small painting, and a stub from a plane ticket Joseph unintentionally bought her.

Before they left for Shelly's house, Rosemary smoked a joint. "The difference between a drunk driver and a stoned driver," she informed Simone, "is that a drunk driver runs a lot of red lights and a stoned driver stops at a lot of green ones. And given the road conditions—Saturday night in Budweiserville—it's better to stop on the green, don't you think? So what if it's paranoia?"

Rosemary drove so slowly that Simone found her own foot bearing down on an imaginary gas pedal. Braking several times for every stop, Rosemary jounced them toward Shelly's house. Simone blamed the marijuana. Rosemary wasn't the most confidence-inspiring driver, but this was something special. Anyway, Simone asked herself, who was she to criticize?

Rosemary said, "I've noticed a funny thing. I'm a better driver when the children are around. I'm more confident in general that I won't fall off the edge of the world."

Simone was amazed that Rosemary should have experienced this, too. She herself took it for granted, how much safer she felt with the children. But she so rarely knew if Rosemary was even registering the children's presence.

"One good thing about dope," Rosemary said, "is that it makes me more aware of the children even when they *aren't* around. Thank God for Shelly inviting us over to-night, anything to take my mind off the idea of those poor little funny bunnies in their father's so-called care. It's so sick, I feel as if they were a *man* out with another *woman*. Actually, it's worse. I never felt like this when Geoffrey was off having his adventures. You know, Simone, I never asked: What did you think of Geoffrey?"

Simone searched for a single word that could function as either compliment or insult. "Interesting," she said.

"Interesting!" Rosemary cried. "Certainly you don't mean interesting to *talk* to! You can't even gossip with Geoffrey because it's not about himself. His intense self-involvement is such a perverted—and successful—way of ensuring your devotion. You're so honored just to show up as a blip on his radar screen!"

They turned a corner and Shelly's house popped out of a field like the Victorian cottage in Maisie's book, which indeed it resembled. The house was lit so that every scrolly detail stood out against the dark sky.

Dressed in black pants, a red silk shirt, and high heels, Shelly greeted them at the door and gave them each a dry, perfumy peck on the cheek. She seemed impatient for them to begin admiring the house, to notice how crossing the doorstep had rocketed them from gingerbread to ultra-modern. The entrance hall was a windowless black tunnel with pink-and-violet neon tubing defining the edge of the walls.

"It's marvelous in the daytime," Rosemary explained to Simone. "You creep through this dark little hall and then the sunlight in the living room slams you in the head. It's got a funhouse-entrance feeling: butterflies in your stomach."

"I worship you, Rosemary," Shelly said. "Not only is that exactly what I was trying to do in this hall, that is exactly what I *told* you I was trying to do in this hall."

Beyond the hall the living room soared; one whole wall was glass. Lighting from some invisible source bounced its high beams off Kenny, reclining like an odalisque on a black leather chaise lounge. The rest of the furniture was kidney-shaped, in shades of turquoise, gray, and pink plastic, except for a large rectangular glass-and-black-wrought-iron table.

Kenny jumped up and kissed Rosemary, who in turn kissed the air through which she regarded the table, obviously disappointed to see only four places set. She had been counting on Shelly to introduce her to new people who in the future might have parties and save her from another Halloween at the mall with its thrilling social insights.

Shelly said, "I gather you all know each other. I thought it would make things more comfy to keep it family and small."

Kenny leaned close to kiss Simone. "We are in hell," he whispered. "Dinner party hell."

Shelly led Simone over to an immense wooden sculpture, not unlike the ruined children's swing set on Rosemary's lawn, only more deteriorated and overgrown with creeping ivy.

"My jungle gym," said Shelly. "My solitary bit of wildness. I'd go mad without it. You don't think I would *choose* to live with Formica and all this tacky fifties detritus I made my mama throw out thirty years ago! The only thing that gave me the heart to go on was the visual joke, all this cartoony-colored plastic constipated fifties junk against the soaring late-sixties space. Twice, a writer from *Architectural Digest* almost came; both times he got sick and canceled. Meanwhile, I've got about two more years and it's time to do it all over. In my old age I plan to have a house that is not also a place of business.

"Meanwhile"—Shelly picked up a bottle—"join me in an experiment. Ginseng-flavored wine. Genghis Khan brand. Look at this red-and-black Last-Emperor-death-of-the-Dowager-Empress label. This paramecium in the wine store guaranteed a special sort of high."

Kenny toasted the wine with his beer bottle. "This paramecium in the wine store," he mimicked. "The woman's totally fucking bananas."

Shelly didn't smile. She said, "I don't suppose this is the time to discuss who here might or might not benefit most from ginseng's supposed aphrodisiac qualities."

Simone took a sip of greenish liquid that tasted like fermented mothballs.

"Okay, okay," said Shelly. "I can see from your stricken faces." She whisked away their glasses and replaced them with new glasses of ambery cold white wine.

"An unpretentious little California Chardonnay," she said. "The ginseng was just a test."

"A test of what?" Rosemary said. "Did we pass or fail?"

"As they said in grade school," Shelly said, "you know who you are. And it goes on your permanent record."

"What permanent record?" said Kenny.

"I love this guy," said Shelly. "He believes there's a permanent record."

Shelly shooed her guests toward a grouping of black couches so aeronautic Simone felt compelled to sit quickly before the furniture took off. The couches were set at oblique angles: any attempt at conversation ensured an instant stiff neck. Rosemary and Simone sat at opposite ends of one couch, Shelly and Kenny in the center of another. Kenny massaged Shelly's shoulder with absentminded pincering grabs.

Rosemary sighed piteously. "The children are with Geoffrey."

Shelly said, "Are we talking about the children or are we talking about Geoffrey? I mean, we *can* talk about the children—for a limited amount of time—but not one minute on Geoffrey. There must be another topic. What about the proposed county dump? Can't we get something going on that?"

"We can try," said Kenny. "But Geoffrey probably fucking supports it. Geoffrey's family probably owns the land that the dump's slated to be built on. Probably through some Wall Street WASP lawyers, Smith, Peabody, Smith and Asshole."

"Don't be silly, Kenny," said Rosemary. "Geoffrey and his family can afford to be ecological."

"They can feed the world population," said Kenny. "It's just not in their business interests."

"Dinner's served!" Shelly tip-tapped into the kitchen and returned with four elegant salad plates. She set the plates on the table. "Y'all come and eat," she said. Simone sat next to Rosemary, across from Shelly and Kenny.

The plates were painted with landscapes of a tropical beach at sunset, and each held baby asparagus stalks bent to look like swaying palms. "In honor of Simone," Shelly said. "Our new friend from the islands."

The asparagus demanded much covert but focused ripping and shredding. Over the noise Kenny asked Rosemary, "Did Shelly tell you we saw Geoffrey?"

"I was sparing her," Shelly explained. "The very definition of friendship and tact."

"Saw him where?" With studied casualness, Rosemary popped an asparagus tip in her mouth.

"At a horrid party," said Shelly. "Actually it was the party I told you about, at that creepy photographer's house."

"Was he with anyone?" asked Rosemary.

Shelly said, "I believe the photographer was *with* some unfortunate twelve-year-old nymphet."

"I mean Geoffrey," Rosemary said.

"Geoffrey?" said Shelly. "Who could tell? We were all too busy being forced to watch botanical pornography."

"Slides," said Kenny. "Art shots of flowers. Can you believe that shit?"

"Apparently," said Shelly, "our host is a famous flower photographer. You know: glossy calendars and upscale seed catalogues. It turned out we'd been invited for a show of his new work. As if my being a decorator had nothing to do with it. His new work! Flower genitalia projected six feet tall, every poppy or iris like peeking up somebody's

skirt. We sat there meekly, helpless prisoners of giant hol-
lyhock organs. My grandfather all over again, the
gynecologist-slash-camellia breeder. The grotesque thing is
that women are still falling for it. After the slide show our
host was *mobbed*. Women were sticking to him like pollen
to a bee."

"It was fascist," Kenny said. "Any party that makes you
stop what you're doing and do what everyone else is doing
is fascist. Even singing 'Happy Birthday.' "

Rosemary said, "Was Geoffrey with someone? Tell me,
Kenny. I can take it."

"I can't take it," Shelly said. "In fact, it makes me feel
a sudden overwhelming need for lobster and Japanese soba
noodles." She stood and cleared the asparagus plates and
reappeared with a large glass bowl through which one
could glimpse a tangle of mossy-colored pasta.

"These lobsters did not want to die," Shelly said, waving
a chunk of pinkish meat on her fork, triumphant proof that
in the end the lobsters' wishes had counted for nothing. "I
had a hard time accepting my role in the deaths of two recently living creatures."

Kenny said, "You're better off sticking to supermarket
chicken. Then you get underpaid black women down South
doing the killing for you—hacking up poultry and their
own hands under disgusting conditions."

"Yankees compulsively pick on the South," Shelly told
Simone.

"Yankees?" said Kenny. "Fuck that."

A decorous silence fell over their struggles with their
pasta. Finally Shelly stood and said, "Kenny, help me with
the choucroute." She and Kenny shared a private laugh.
Simone looked away.

After they left Rosemary said, "Southern women. They
simply cannot get beyond these primitive dominance
games. Like female penguins fighting over the biggest rock.
They keep having to make it obnoxiously clear whom the
male belongs to. Or if the male happens to belong to *you*—
well then, who can steal him if she wants to. They're still

back one evolutionary stage: monkeys competing for mates. They wouldn't want to delude you into trusting your female friends, and they feel compelled to remind you of this. It's their way of being honest."

Who knew how long Rosemary might have continued this analysis of her friend if Kenny hadn't entered with a platter of sausage, potatoes, and sauerkraut? Shelly followed close behind with spoons and a two-tined fork.

"Peasant food," Shelly announced.

"Cold-weather food," Rosemary said. "Oh marvelous, marvelous, thank you!"

The food was so delicious Simone had to work at not bolting it down. She was used to eating with Maisie and George in private, puppylike frenzies of hunger. She tried not to think of the children dining with their father, surely not on fried plantains, raw vegetables, and frozen shrimp. Most likely they were at the Tepee Diner, eating the normal American diet of normal American children. For a moment Simone couldn't think what such a diet might consist of. At the embassy on the Fourth of July they'd served hot dogs, corn, and fried chicken, but Simone had never seen anyone here eat anything like that.

"Knowing Geoffrey," Rosemary said, "right at this minute he's got the children smothered in animal fat, stuffing their faces with ten-pound sirloin steaks in one of those Mafioso beef-and-lasagna joints he always secretly liked."

"Villa Carnivora," said Kenny.

Shelly pushed her plate away, then reluctantly retrieved it, carved one last piece of sausage and popped it into her mouth. "I honestly don't know how men do it." She waved her knife at the remaining sausage. "Detach themselves that way. I mean, actually slice and chew these things and not let themselves make the obvious natural phallic association. Well, I suppose detachment and denial are testosterone breakdown products—"

"Shelly," cried Rosemary. "Please! Some of us are still eating!"

Kenny took his time chewing, deliberately swallowed,

and said, "It doesn't bother me. The way I can get past eating this is I pretend it's a piece of dogshit."

"Come on, now," Rosemary said. "Please."

"Savage!" said Shelly. "I'm mortally wounded by that
dagger aimed at the heart of my culinary pretensions. Perhaps it's time for some music to soothe the savage whatever."

Shelly set down the phonograph needle and loud applause rasped from the speakers, long enough for Shelly to
pull Kenny to his feet. Simone heard a choked-up vibrato
guitar, then two men crooning a love song. Simone felt that
each of the men had in mind some real woman and believed this was his only chance to say what was in his
heart: *Tonight we'll meet, at the dark end of the street . . .*

At first Kenny was playacting, whirling and tilting
Shelly. Only a practiced dancer could have overplayed it
like that, and Simone knew from how Shelly moved in his
arms that they were used to dancing together. Shelly was
performing, too, tossing her head and shrieking when
Kenny dipped her too close to the ground.

"My mother always said," Kenny announced to the
room, "that everything interesting begins with a slow
dance."

At first he and Shelly were entertaining themselves and
in theory Rosemary and Simone, but soon the showing off
stopped and Simone could feel herself drop off the edge of
their visual field. She wondered which was worse, the aggressive sexual display or the moment when real desire
kicked in and they were aware only of each other. Simone
closed her eyes and listened to the two men pouring themselves into the song. She thought of the night she'd come
home after seeing Joseph and Inez in the café: how she'd
lain awake, hating the heat, the dark, the rub of the sheets
on her skin.

The voices paused for a tremulous, overwrought guitar
break, and as if the singers had left the room, Shelly and
Kenny danced closer. Simone remembered a quiet Sunday
afternoon she and Joseph and Inez went for coffee. On the

way they'd passed musicians singing on a corner, a melancholy slow rumba they hardly appeared to be playing but that seemed to ooze out of them while their minds were somewhere else. A couple danced in the center of a circle, a gray-haired sinewy old man and a beautiful straight-backed young woman, a haughty, disdainful half-smile on her face, her skirt bunched up in her hand.

Simone didn't, wouldn't dance. Joseph had teased her about it, but kindly, as lovers make fun of one another's quirks. But *Inez* danced, that was clear; you could tell from how she rolled her shoulders and shifted her feet to the beat. Only now did Simone see Joseph's sideways glance. In Joseph's paintings dancing couples melted and flowed into each other. But Simone had remained convinced—dancing didn't make you happy. The best thing that could be said for it was that no song lasted forever.

Laughing, slightly breathless, Kenny and Shelly sank down onto a couch. Kenny twisted around and burrowed his face into Shelly's neck. He seemed unaware of the others, genuinely aroused. Simone was alarmed and fascinated. How far was he planning to take this?

Shelly scooted forward. "Time for dessert!" she said.

Kenny blinked and for a moment looked petulant and injured—like George and Maisie, thought Simone, when she woke them early for school. Then Kenny's face formed a skin, like an egg on a plate, and he again became Mr. Short Eyes, the young man who swiped so confidently at the children's hair and dragged you around by the shoulders. All evening that part of Kenny had been curiously submerged, replaced by the quieter, fuzzy-bear Kenny deferentially cursing at Shelly.

"Anyway," Kenny said now, "that's not my kind of music. Black people imitating white people imitating hillbilly trash. I like forties swing, old standards, Cole Porter, old jazz, Chet Baker, Bud Powell, Bird, all those beautiful cats: live-fast, die-young, leave a good-looking corpse. What's Haitian music like, Simone?"

Simone had often been asked this by the American arts groups and dancers who visited Port-au-Prince, and each time she answered, her answer had grown shorter. They had not wanted to hear about the African roots of Caribbean rhythm—and neither, Simone knew, did Kenny.

"Very good to dance to," replied Simone, smiling stiffly, hearing herself sound like a cheery islander promoting the Caribbean on TV. She had never smiled so often and so falsely as since she'd come to Hudson Landing. Miss McCaffrey had smiled a lot but never required it of Simone.

Shelly said, "Kenny, we should get married—that is, to other people. Then we could have an adulterous love affair and maybe get something going."

"Fuck you," said Kenny good-humoredly.

"Say what you will," said Shelly. "But one mustn't underestimate the greatness of adultery—the song we've just been hearing is a kind of hymn. Let's face it, life is hotter at the dark end of the street. Courtly love was about that, it's the basis of modern civilization. Rosemary, you were married and you never cheated once. I can't believe you blew your one chance for a grand *amour*."

Rosemary's fingers worked distractedly, tweezing fur from her coat. She said, "Geoffrey got enough chances for both of us. That was the whole point of our separation."

Shelly said, "That is never the 'whole point.' Am I right, Simone?"

"Leave Simone alone," Rosemary said. "How is she supposed to know? Listen to what I was thinking while you two were dancing. When Geoffrey and I first got married—this was centuries ago, when we were supposedly happy—I had a peculiar dream that turned out to be prophetic. I dreamed Geoffrey was ordering me around, barking out all sorts of commands and hurtful little suggestions: 'Wash the dishes. Exercise more. Spring for a decent haircut. Try to speak, or at least pretend to speak, so someone can understand.' I woke up very upset, not having yet seen in my waking life what I would later recognize as Geoffrey's

standard m.o. I woke Geoffrey and told him the dream,
wanting comfort, I guess. And Geoffrey opened one eye
and said, 'Don't have dreams like that!' "

Shelly went over to a chaise lounge and settled herself as
languidly as molded plastic permitted.

"The thing I hate about wine," she told Kenny, "is it's
so punishingly fairy-godmother. For hours I'll be skimming along in Cinderella's magic coach and then suddenly I'm scraping the ground, and it's back to mice and
a pumpkin!"

Half a block from Geoffrey's office Simone heard Latin
music. Involuntarily, her step quickened and fell in with the
beat until she was doing a sneaky merengue down the
empty sidewalk. It wasn't that she was immune to rhythm,
but surrendering to it felt private, not something you would
choose to do when other people were doing it, too. In Haiti
she had a radio and sometimes danced around her room,
but to move that way in public seemed exhibitionistic, as
Shelly and Kenny had so convincingly demonstrated last
night. On the other hand, losing Joseph to Inez had made
it debatable where, exactly, and how far Simone's sort of
modest self-restraint got you.

No one heard Simone knock. She opened the door to
find Geoffrey and the children dancing around his office.
Maisie was doing a creditable samba, with both elbows
pumping and her tiny clawlike fists shaking phantom mara-
cas over her head. George made do with a shuffling transfer
from foot to foot, twitching his shoulders and smiling when
he felt obliged.

The children's faces shone unrecognizably. Simone could
watch light come up in their eyes as their father danced between them, dancing with each in turn, falling into each
one's style, not mimicking but giving them his total re-
spectful attention.

A man's voice shouted in Spanish, intermittent staccato
cries, ragged, shattered, and undeceived by the saxophones'
offers of consolation. Effervescing to the rhythm, sending

bubbles through tubes of light was a magnificent jukebox that hadn't been there yesterday when Simone brought the children.

Eventually Geoffrey noticed Simone and danced across the room and dragged her into the center of the floor and into a kind of tango. There wasn't time to explain that she didn't dance, or maybe she missed the moment, concentrating on not tripping as he spun her around and the sticky carpet fibers grabbed mischievously at her feet.

Soon Simone was dancing, or at least she wasn't *not* dancing. By then it would have seemed clumsy and rude to balk and back away. Anyhow, they weren't dancing so much as clowning around; Geoffrey's exaggerated tango and tight, silly grin were the equivalent of Kenny's playacting last night. Here, it seemed, couples started dancing by making fun of dancing. In Haiti they just locked in tight and started grinding away.

Even so, Geoffrey's closeness left Simone quite out of breath. If she'd tried to speak, her voice might have shook and distracted her from her effort not to seem like a mannequin Geoffrey was pushing. Simone recalled an exercise Rosemary did on her treadmill, mentally traveling from cell to cell, persuading each to relax. But in this context the thought of Rosemary put Simone's cells on full alert.

Geoffrey was the same height as Simone, which made the dance, however excruciating, smoother and less problematic than dancing with Joseph would have been. Joseph was shorter than Simone, she could admit that now. One night she and Joseph and Inez had gone to a bar where there was dancing. Joseph asked Simone to dance; she smiled and shook her head no. Simone had to admit it had crossed her mind, the fact that Joseph was shorter. How would she look on the dance floor with a man who was shoulder-height? Now this seemed conclusive proof that she hadn't loved him enough, so that his leaving her was inevitable, she'd brought it on herself. After Simone refused him, Joseph had asked Inez. There was a funny moment before Inez said no. The world shut down like a stopped clock and then started up again.

Geoffrey steered Simone nearer the music and paused there, admiring the elaborate chrome-and-neon jukebox until Simone caught on and shouted in his ear, "Oh, how beautiful!"

"*C'est très belle*, no?" said Geoffrey. "The kids and I picked it out." Simone saw him wink over her shoulder—at the children, she guessed.

The music stopped, but before she could escape, Geoffrey punched a button. A violin played an introduction and another song began.

"*This ma-a-gic moment*," Geoffrey sang along, and gathered Simone in another dance. "The best thing about having your own jukebox is you can program it yourself. This one is stocked exclusively with songs about ecstasy, desperation, and heartbreak."

Ecstasy, desperation, and heartbreak? Simone found Geoffrey's chattiness reassuring, regardless of its content. At embassy parties she'd often seen dancing couples jabbering away, presumably to signal that all this had nothing to do with sex but was just conversation to music. She couldn't remember ever seeing Haitians talk while they were dancing, and last night Shelly and Kenny had stopped talking soon after the dancing began.

Geoffrey said, "This song comes as close as anything to describing falling in love." Simone tensed and it seemed to her that Geoffrey felt it and tightened his hold. Men so rarely said "falling in love." Just uttering those three words changed the terms between you.

"The pity," Geoffrey went on, "is that for twenty years these guys have been playing roadhouses on the strip, being rediscovered and doing nostalgia tours, and then going back to roadhouses. Is this how we treat our poets?"

At once relieved and let down that Geoffrey had dropped the subject of love, Simone decided that he reminded her endearingly of George chattering to mask his desire for

Simone to tuck him in at night. For a moment she could see something of George in Geoffrey, or something of Geoffrey in George: Geoffrey with the edges rubbed off or as yet undeveloped. How rarely she noticed any trace of Rosemary and Geoffrey in their children. Often she forgot and was shocked to recall that they were George and Maisie's parents.

Simone's limbs loosened slightly, but not to a point that anyone might confuse with grace or compliance. Then she saw George and Maisie watching her dance with Geoffrey, their mouths and eyes forming little round o's of betrayal and confusion. It was plain to her: this wasn't neutral to them. No matter what Simone thought she was doing, she was dancing with their father.

The children were living witnesses to the history of their parents' marriage: what their father did, what their mother said, how their father answered. Who knew what attention George and Maisie had seen their father pay other women? Who knew if, as a survival technique, they'd attuned themselves to the distant early-warning signals of adult lassitude and enchantment? Perhaps as they watched Simone and Geoffrey, they were detecting traces of pleasure, attraction, even desire—emotions too risky and volatile for Simone to consider right now.

She remembered the rainy parking lot on Halloween night, George asking if she'd told Rosemary about his Eskimo tape. The children's confidence could still be lost—that is, if she'd ever had it. Suddenly it struck Simone with the force of a revelation that the secrets the children entrusted her with were only decoy secrets. George's Eskimo tape, Maisie's climbing the walls—they were the bait they threw Simone to lure her off the track.

The important, inviolate secrets were those they kept on the grownups' behalf. Those secrets were caustic and had the power to burn them and disfigure their lives. Simone might have been annoyed at the children, who, she now believed, had withheld the truth and tricked her into feeling trusted and valued—if it hadn't seemed so childish to be angry at children for knowing things so dangerous they couldn't risk telling her.

Simone's body took over and extricated her from the dance. Every muscle locked at once. Geoffrey couldn't budge her. "What's wrong?" he said, as his gaze followed Simone's to the children. "Uh-oh," he said. "Bingo!"

He bowed and told Simone, "Thank you," and glided over to the jukebox. He pushed a button and the music gagged to a stop.

"Oops! I meant to do that!" Geoffrey grinned. He hunkered down by the children and gathered them in his arms.

"Huddle time," he whispered. "Urgent bulletin from central command. Do not, I repeat, do not under any circumstances tell your mother that Simone and I were dancing. Obviously you could see for yourselves that it was perfectly innocent and no different in any way from me dancing with you. But you know your mother and her history of insanity and paranoia."

"We know Mom, all right," George agreed, rapidly cheering up.

"The idea is not to slander your poor tormented mother. Even if the torment originates in demonic fantasies from her own brain. The idea is to save all of us additional trials and tribulations."

Poor Rosemary, indeed! thought Simone. What defense did she have against this onslaught of articulate, conspiratorial, fatherly charm?

"Get it?" Geoffrey said.

"Got it!" George saluted.

"I get it." Maisie drew the words out, projecting extreme irritation and boredom.

Geoffrey looked up at Simone. "Maisie wants the world to know how tiresome she thinks this has gotten—all the times these martyred children have had to keep their father's non-secrets."

He put his face up close to the children's. "All right,

men. Back to the trenches. Fortitude. Be brave. In case of enemy capture, what and how much do you disclose?"

"Name, rank, and serial number?" said George.

"Report for action!" Geoffrey said.

MAISIE AND GEORGE introduced Simone to the addictive pleasure of hickory nuts, small wild nuts with a vein of sweet meat you had to dig out with a pin. Partly it was the labor itself, the minuscule reward, the disproportionate joy of prying loose a slightly larger crumb—it kept you hungry and desirous in ways a bag of shelled walnuts could never. How wasteful that the difficult should seem so much more precious, so that the practically unattainable was valued most of all. In that way shelling hickory nuts was like being in love, Simone thought. Rosemary had called it a triumph to show up as a blip on Geoffrey's radar screen, and Simone had never loved Joseph so much as when she knew she had lost him.

Simone and the children spent evenings at the kitchen table picking at the hickory nuts with catatonic concentration. Their lives took on a squirrel motif that persisted to bedtime, when Maisie insisted Simone read aloud from a book in which talking squirrels discoursed tediously about the acorn supply. Simone and the children were hoarding, too, stockpiling nuts for the winter whose approach they felt in the wet chill wind already slapping at them from the Hudson. They had grocery bags full of nuts stored up—but suppose they ran out, and snow fell, and they couldn't find more? This seemed, as the autumn wound down, an unendurable prospect.

Often Simone thought of how Joseph imagined America: a land of white people with black servants bringing them cellular phones by the pool. Where in Joseph's vision was the celestial peace of being with the children in the drafty kitchen, digging out nut-meats with safety pins? Joseph had imagined California, where it was always warm and never damp and icy, as it was now in Hudson Landing.

One afternoon the children came home from school and the sky was so blue and bright that it tricked Simone into forgetting how short the days had grown. She and the children decided to hunt for hickory nuts in the woods, and as they crossed the lawn Simone said, "Look up. What do you see?"

"Clouds," George said.

"What do you see in the clouds?" Simone asked.

Maisie was wearing large heart-shaped sunglasses she'd got as a present from Shelly, and now she tilted them forward to better see the sky.

"Seafood," George said finally. "An octopus and a lobster."

"A horse's head," said Maisie.

They walked on in silence until they reached the trees. Maisie said, "I can make clouds move by concentrating on them."

"Sure you can," said George.

"Let's talk about our fears," Maisie said.

"Let's not," said George. "She always wants to talk about her fears."

Ordinarily Simone might be curious about what Maisie was afraid of, but it was the last thing she wished to discuss walking through the woods with the children. She had been frightened of the forest since she found the dead sheep.

"My worst fear is horses," Maisie said.

"We found a dead horse," George said.

Before Simone could decide whether or not to pursue this subject, Maisie said, "I mean live horses. The most beautiful thing in the world. I wish Mom would let me take riding lessons. I would be scared that I'd get trampled. But that would be a good way to die. Not like the guinea pig baby at school where the guinea pig mother ate it."

"Hamster," said George. "Don't you know *any*thing?"

"Guinea pig," said Maisie.

"Hush," said Simone. Absurdly she was seized with fear that Maisie's talking about horses would somehow cause them to find another dead one dangling from a tree. She looked around for the shaggy bark that would mean nuts had fallen nearby.

"A lot of times I'm afraid of old people," said George. "Sometimes you don't know what they're going to say and—"

Just then something whistled past and smacked Simone on the side of the head. In fact, it had not hit her, just hit the air near her face, hit the air with the violent crack of a diver cannonballing into water. It felt like someone blowing into her ear through a long thin metal pipe. Pressure galloped in her skull and swelled inside her throat. Then something struck a birch tree, and splinters exploded off the bark.

The last yellow leaves showered down like a hail of coins. Afterward the tree kept shaking for a very long time.

"Was that a gun?" asked George.

The answer was a crackle of gunfire, the delicate pop of a shot. Simone threw the children to the ground and covered them with her body.

"What's going to happen?" said George.

"Nothing's going to happen," snapped Simone. Another bullet streaked overhead. Maisie buried her head in Simone's shoulder and began to cry.

A minute passed, then another. There were no more shots. "Stay down," said Simone. "Stay down until I tell you to get up."

"What's going to happen?" repeated George.

"Nothing. Nothing," answered Simone, and this time nothing did. In a while they lifted their heads and looked at each other. They squirmed around till they lay with their heads together, their legs like the spokes of a wheel. All three of them could have been children playing in the dead leaves.

"Are we allowed to talk?" George whispered.

Simone said, "I guess. Don't move."

"There's this kid?" said George. "In our school? His dad grew up around here? And one year when his dad was in high school there was this squirrel population explosion and kids got paid fifteen cents for every dead squirrel they brought in?"

"Cheap," said Maisie.

"So this kid's dad took his gun and popped fifty squirrels and took them home in a bag? But his dad, I mean, the dad's dad got mad and made the mom skin the squirrels and put them in the freezer? The mom—the dad's mom—had to figure out all different ways to cook them? The kid's dad still eats squirrel. He takes the squirrel legs to work and cooks them in the microwave."

"Gross," pronounced Maisie. Then she said, "Maybe hickory nuts have feelings. Maybe God was punishing us for eating them."

"Yeah, sure," said George.

Maisie whispered, "The shooting stopped."

"Who *was* that, anyway?" asked George. "Who was shooting at us?"

"I don't know," said Simone. Why did the children think she had answers? "Not *at* us. Just *near* us. Maybe it was a hunter."

Maisie said, "Hunting season starts Monday. It's all Mom's talked about for weeks."

"Or a serial killer?" suggested George.

"What's that?" Maisie asked, and then said quickly, "I don't want to hear."

"They go around killing people?" said George. "It's what they do on vacation? They'll stab somebody in Florida and then take a car ride up the coast and strangle somebody in Maine?"

"Kids, too?" Maisie asked.

"Some specialize in kids," said George. "I think they're called something else. Did you hear about that kid whose dad set him on fire with a can of gasoline?"

Simone tried to listen through their talk to the sounds of the forest. She felt somehow that they were alone, that the danger had passed, though before the shooting started she hadn't felt anything special, either. How strange, she thought, that she'd grown up in a country where killings were a daily occurrence, and she'd had to come to this peaceful American forest to nearly get herself shot.

"Be quiet for five minutes," she said. "Then we will very quietly and slowly get up and go home."

Maisie said, "I don't think we should go home. I don't think we should tell Mom."

Some instinct signaled Simone and the children: Rosemary must not be told. If she found out she might forbid them to leave the house ever again, or she might even fire Simone for having put George and Maisie at risk. Alternatively, perhaps more likely, Rosemary might not react at all. Then Simone and the children would feel cheated of their experience, with no excuse for the tremors that still shook their legs and shocked them into functioning as one creature with three heads and a single brain that knew they needed to get away—go somewhere and tell someone.

"Let's go see Kenny," Maisie said, and they piled into the car. Simone had never driven at dusk; the prospect was unnerving. But whatever spared them this afternoon would just have to save them again.

Everything about driving to Short Eyes tested the limits of Simone's courage. She could never have managed if she hadn't so recently been so afraid. The only route she knew was the one she took that first day, small roads into larger roads and finally onto Route 9. She wondered if she would always have to recapitulate the beginning; in Port-au-Prince there was a crazy woman who used to get stalled on the street and had to go all the way back to her house to get herself going again.

Kenny seemed genuinely happy to see them, which in itself moved Simone. She always felt so indebted when a man registered her presence.

A little boy sat in Kenny's chair—a tiny, dark-haired prince. "*Modified* spike," his mother was saying. "Modified is the operative word."

Kenny abandoned his victim when Simone and the children walked in, a reprieve for which the little boy dazzled them with a smile.

"You know that kid?" George asked Maisie.

"No," whispered Maisie. "Do you?"

"*Ola!*" said Kenny. "*Bonjour!* Yo!"

George said, "Yo!"

Maisie said, "Kenny! *Bonjour!*" The children seemed more cheerful already.

Kenny came closer and said to Simone, "Jesus Christ. I'm sorry about the other night. Shelly's dinner party—Nightmare Alley, right? I don't know what comes over me whenever I'm with Shelly. I cannot believe the evil shit I hear come out of my mouth. My whole vocabulary changes. Fucking this, fucking that. This is shit, that is shit, it's all a fucking motherfucker."

Kenny became aware of the children and the boy's mother, staring. To the children he said, "You guys have heard shit like this before. Christ, I mean bad language.

"Women secretly love it," he said. "The more outrageous the better. They never tell their husbands." Was Kenny still talking about language? Was that what women loved? Did he mean the little boy's mother? She shot a hostile glance at Simone.

"Isn't Shelly a killer?" Kenny asked. "And I use that word advisedly. Whenever she comes to the salon—which, thank God, isn't often—I'm always super aware of where the scissors are." Simone noticed on the counter large apothecary jars full of pointy scissors, like torture implements, stewing in blue disinfectant. How unreassuring they must be to the timid child!

Kenny said, "It's not that there aren't women around. Some really beautiful women. But I'm terrified of Shelly.

She would definitely rip your balls off and serve them—hush puppies, am I right?—to a close family member. I'd love to spend some time with you, Simone. We could drive to Connecticut. I would have to cross state lines before I felt safe from Shelly."

Simone said, "My boyfriend gets jealous, too." Why was she lying like this? Joseph never once asked what she did when she wasn't with him. He thought she died when he wasn't around and came back to life when he was. Sexual jealousy was not in the range of things you would logically feel for a zombie, nor was it a problem if you believed you were the only man in the world. But it seemed important to establish the fact that there was a boyfriend who would ride along like a ghost chaperon if she took a trip with Kenny.

Kenny said, "If he's in Haiti, he's got no business being jealous. If *Shelly* was in Haiti, I'd be cutting a fairly wide swath through the local female population. But speaking of doing damage—you guys look like a total wipeout. You look like somebody dragged you here from Rosemary's house on your faces. You want a Valium, Simone? How about you, kids? A baby Tylenol? A Pepsi?"

"A baby Tylenol and Pepsi," replied Maisie.

"Someone shot at us?" said George. "We were walking in the woods near our house and someone shot at us. I think it was a .357 magnum? You should have seen what it did to our tree."

"A .357? I doubt it," said Kenny. He looked at Simone for corroboration.

"Someone shot at us," said Simone.

Kenny laughed. "The Count, I'll bet. Your neighbor to the south."

"Really?" said George. Kenny's salutary effect on the children evaporated in a flash.

"Joke," said Kenny. "The Count is a criminal and a freak but not a murderer. Or anyway, not of humans. Listen to Uncle Kenny. This is hunting season. You are considered a nine-point buck until you are proven human. Only the desperate or deeply impaired venture off the blacktop. After two six-packs you guys look like Bambi's mom and two Bambis. Simone, didn't Rosemary warn you? Some years she can't talk about anything else."

Simone was trying to remember the story Rosemary told about seeing a carful of hunters and fleeing to the city. Where were George and Maisie then? That had not been clear. It was often hard to tell from Rosemary's stories when they happened or whom they happened to, or what exactly they meant.

Abruptly the little boy's mother said, "I saw the most adorable item. Two doors down they're selling these darling Red Ridinghood capes, cute and warm and made for kids who have to go anywhere near the forest during the annual bloodbath the locals call deer season. The capes made me wish all over again that I'd had a girl. But I'm not having another child, not even to get a daughter. She *did* have these terrific red baseball caps. I got one for Max."

"Two doors down from *here*?" said Kenny.

"Good Witch of the East," said the woman. "Where did you think I meant?"

"Oh, Glenda's place," said Kenny. "Glenda's my buddy. Far out. Another total fuzzball with a blue-chip business sense."

He finished cutting the little boy's hair. The boy and his mother left.

"Button up," Kenny told George and Maisie. "Let's hit it. We're out of here. Uncle Kenny is going to treat you guys to one red cape and one red hat."

Shooing Simone and the children out, Kenny said, "Hey, dig it. Over there's the jingling cash register, and I'm leaving the joint unlocked."

He led them several doors down to a store with a crowded, dusty window and a sign that said, in swirling letters, GOOD WITCH OF THE EAST. Zither music played on a stereo, crystalline and frantic. The air smelled of potpourri, like the soap shop under Geoffrey's office, but with a faint insecticide edge.

Guarding the door, large sinister wooden frogs affected debonair poses. On a table were drinks trays made from butterfly wings. A large stone cherub pouted, unappreciative for having been rescued from somebody's tombstone and set down among the painted hatboxes full of rolls of watered-silk ribbons, soft-sculpture bedroom slippers representing Nancy and Ronald Reagan in bed, brightly colored, overdesigned toys that failed to catch the children's attention except for one tiny expensive set of doll's woodworking tools. Simone wondered what principle of selection had gathered these items together.

"Good taste and magic." A trilling voice rang out as if in answer to Simone's unspoken question. A stout, sweet-looking woman swayed in from the back of the shop in a two-piece outfit ingeniously knotted from many flowered silk scarves. "I'm Glenda," she said. "Simple introductions are not Kenny's strong suit."

"Eat shit," said Kenny genially. "Simone, Maisie, and Big George. Glenda, what it *is*, babe?"

"Same old," said Glenda, and a lovely smile glorified her doughy face. It was always instructive to see what women turned into around Kenny. "The usual shnorrers and kleptos. Did I tell you about that old Native American guy the Sweat Lodge Church flew in from Utah and dumped. He came in trying to sell me some kind of animal pelt. He put it down on the counter and it was crawling with maggots! Little white blind grubby things wriggling down the display case. I started screaming, I made him take it away. Then I went next door and bought a six-pack of Black Flag. Very unorganic. Can you smell it?"

"Yuck," Maisie agreed.

Glenda turned to Maisie. "Whooo are yooou?"

"The caterpillar!" said Maisie. "In *Alice in Wonderland*."

"Exactly," Glenda told her. "I love your look. I could *sell* you in here."

"Yeah," said George. "Give her away!" This aspect of

George troubled Simone even more than his sadness: how quickly he allied himself with whoever was on the offensive, especially when it was at the expense of his sister or his mother. When Geoffrey made fun of Rosemary, it was George who chimed in, though at home he showed her a puppylike, unrequited devotion.

"How's Shelly?" Glenda said.

Kenny turned over a cobalt-blue vase, as if examining it for listening devices. "Russia will be a democracy," he said. "But we'll still have Shelly."

Glenda said, "What about *you*, Simone?"

Simone replied, "I take care of the children."

"Simone takes care of the children," said Kenny, "while she reconnoiters and marshals her forces to take New York City by storm. She could be a model or an actress like Cicely Tyson's niece. Look at her, Glenda? Don't you think Simone could be a movie star?"

"Absolutely," Glenda answered.

The children were appraising Simone with new interest and concern. They had never considered that they might be a way station on her road to success. That this disturbed them pleased Simone, though she knew it was wrong of her to want the children to worry more or feel less secure than they already did.

Maisie prompted Kenny: "Are we getting the cape?"

"How old are you, dear?" said Glenda. Simone, without thinking, put her arm around George.

"Six," Maisie replied.

"Six going on thirty-six," Glenda said. "The perfect Victorian mini-adult. Kenny, did I tell you this ugly story? A woman came into the shop this week, you know that survivalist couple, Vietnam vet, they live in that camouflage station wagon? He waits for her out in the car—"

"Check," said Kenny. "The one with the bowie knife in her belt. Half a dozen ratty children."

"Exactly. And one of the children glommed onto an egg"—Glenda pointed to a straw basket full of marbleized stone eggs—"and simply would not let go. The mother's prying its fingers loose, and by now the baby's howling and the poor woman asks if I take food stamps."

"Do you?" said Kenny. "I get asked all the time."

"The hell you do," said Glenda. "The question was: Did I want to give the child a malachite egg from Oaxaca? The answer was: No, I did not. So I make all sorts of lame little jokes. No, I'm sorry, I can't. But when the mother finally drags the kid out, I am totaled by guilt, thinking about how this woman can't buy anything pretty for her kids, and next week some rich witch will MasterCard a two-hundred-dollar doll-carpentry set for a grandchild whose name she can't remember. I could have given the kid that egg. It cost me four bucks wholesale."

Kenny said, "You thought this after she left the store or you thought this after her car left the parking lot?"

"All right," Glenda said. "Anyway, I decided I wanted to do something for kids in general. And I remembered that poor little girl last year who was blown away by hunters on her back-yard swing set. It was inspiration—Little Red Ridinghood! I *saw* these little capes in which kids would be visible and safe. Then I came up with red baseball caps, not to gender-discriminate."

"Fuckin-A not to," said Kenny.

Simone stared at Glenda. She wished there was some way of asking about the little girl shot in her yard without alarming George and Maisie.

"How much?" Kenny asked.

"Seventeen ninety-five for the capes," said Glenda. "Eight ninety-five for the caps. Reasonable, no?"

"Outrageous," Kenny said. "I'll take one of each. Actually they *are* reasonable when what we're buying is protection."

"Protective magic," said Glenda. She handed Kenny a cape and a hat, and he passed them along to the children, saying, "Wear them in good health, kids. Don't get killed." Glenda led the children to look at themselves in a mirror in the back of the shop.

"I left my wallet at the salon!" Kenny yelled to Glenda.

Glenda called back, "I trust you."

"She shouldn't," Kenny told Simone. "Others have made that mistake."

Maisie wore her cape home and George kept on his baseball cap. Rosemary said, "What is this? I thought we *did* Halloween. Or have the children joined some kind of cult or team?"

"It's a present from Kenny," Maisie said. "So hunters won't think we're deer and shoot us."

"I'm amazed Kenny knows what month it is," Rosemary said. "Let alone that a slip of paper allows our neighbors to use helpless children for target practice when they run out of mailboxes."

Simone and George and Maisie eyed each other and said nothing. Rosemary was in an excellent humor they didn't want to spoil with the news that someone might have tried to kill them in the forest. Her good mood dated from several days ago when an invitation had come, asking them to a wedding to be held Thanksgiving Day.

"The nerve!" Rosemary told Shelly, whom she had called right away. "Don't they think people have families? Do they think the world has nothing to do on a national family holiday, that they're so important we'll drop everything, stiff the relatives, cancel our own Thanksgivings, and answer the DeWitts' summons to join them in celebrating the marriage of their daughter Batsy?"

Realizing that the children were listening, Rosemary covered the receiver. "I mean your cousin Betsy. Don't you *ever* call her Batsy."

"Are we going to have Thanksgiving?" George asked.

Rosemary put a finger to her lips and got quiet, listening to Shelly, and looked briefly distraught before she managed to sound suitably delighted. "Oh, you're invited, too? Great! We'll see each other there!"

Now Rosemary could join Shelly in slandering their future hosts with the brio and clear consciences available only to the invited. Discussions of the wedding were so frequent and all-involving that Rosemary gave up the ski track while talking on the phone, and her entire exercise and diet program soon fell by the wayside. It was as if she had been in training for something that was finally about to happen, or had done active penance to *make* it happen, like a pilgrim crawling on her knees to pray at a holy shrine. Shelly kept warning Rosemary not to expect too much from this wedding: the catapult that would rocket her back into social life. And indeed Rosemary did seem to be steeling herself for disappointment, taking care to let it be known that she didn't even want to go.

"The DeWitts are cousins," she told Shelly on the phone. "In other words, I have no choice. All right, *Geoffrey's* cousins. But like it or not, they are related to my children by the thin tea that in the Porter family passes for blood. Which means Geoffrey will be at the wedding. I really *shouldn't* go. It's criminal to hand him the power that my seeing him there will give him. But I so want to *observe* it. I wouldn't miss this fabulous scene, the double-barreled phenomenon of Old Money *and* New Age vulgar self-display. The groom's a Sufi homeopath veterinarian. The family is just dying.

"Of course they have to allow it—there's only Rick DeWitt left. His second wife, the bride's stepmother, is a Manhattan gynecologist! How did Rick meet a gynecologist is what *I* want to know. The consulting gynecologist at the dry-out clinic! I *know* your grandfather was a gynecologist, Shelly. This is different; that was Memphis. In any case, Rick DeWitt's the reason one has to go. And of course the house and the setting. The food will be vile, as always . . ."

After a silence Rosemary said, "Squid? You must be joking! How did you find out? Okay. Answer it. Talk to you later."

"Call waiting." Rosemary made a face at Simone as she hung up the phone. "They're serving squid at a Thanksgiving wedding! Extraordinary, no? I swear this country is getting more Third World every minute! Apparently Shelly has done some decorating for the groom.

I wish she'd stop talking about room furnishing as if it were high art."

Rosemary refused to consider the possibility that Simone was not invited. "You are going," she said. "For the purposes of the invitation you are my holiday-weekend houseguest. To leave a guest home to fend for herself on Thanksgiving would go against our culture. I don't know what the etiquette is for bringing one's caregiver; there might be some barbaric seating mistake, like putting you with the children. So let's just say you are our guest, everything will be much smoother."

Meanwhile, there was the crisis of what Simone and Rosemary would wear. Simone had the one good linen dress she'd worn to embassy parties, white but not so white that a diplomat might hand her his empty glass and half-eaten hors d'oeuvre wadded up in a napkin. Rosemary squinted at Simone and finally offered her opinion that a good jacket might almost—almost!—pull things out of the fire. She left open the question of where this jacket would come from.

Rosemary emptied her closet, a heroic achievement. The closet was so large she could stand inside it and fight her way into various outfits, some of which, the most promising, she wore as far as the closet door and said, "Hideous, right?" No response was expected from Simone, who sat on Rosemary's bed. In between consultations Rosemary chatted to keep Simone entertained.

"Don't imagine I'm unaware," Rosemary called from the closet, "that twenty years of outgrown clothes are occupying a space large enough to house a small family. But what am I supposed to do? Invite a homeless family to come and live in my closet?"

Rosemary struggled with some tangled hangers, then shoved the whole mess back in. "The trouble with so-called stability is that nothing gets thrown out. You can see the purpose of an occasional war or plague from a housecleaning point of view. As the memory goes, we cling to the artifact. Hence this house: the Porters' memories have been gone for about three centuries. I've come to think that memory loss is a contagious condition transmitted through sexual contact."

Working from the front of her closet back, Rosemary tried on outfits in reverse chronological order, or, as she told Simone, back through her previous incarnations. The black clothes of the eighties gave way to seventies bell-bottoms and the fitted shirts that gave everyone round shoulders and knobby wrists. Rosemary held up a vintage cowboy shirt, stained an improbable fuchsia at the armpits and neck. She said, "This garment has had a toxic reaction to human bodily fluids."

Watching Rosemary try on clothes was like watching a movie backward; with every reel the actors get younger and the dead reappear. Rosemary in a daisy-printed blouse or a housedress with cabbage roses offered brief sad glimpses of the Rosemary of the past, very much at the start of things, trusting and still hopeful enough to walk around in flowers. Every outfit Rosemary experimented with intensified her "look"—the look of a cartoon creature with its paw in an electric socket.

"Maternity stuff!" Rosemary cried, and was silent awhile.

"It's hopeless," she said at last. "I'll just have to wait for inspiration to strike and then throw something together. The pittance we get from Geoffrey prohibits buying anything good. Perhaps I should go as Ike Turner again. Relax, I'm joking, Simone. Let's make sure the children look fabulous. Then you and I can slip by unnoticed. Let's work on getting George to consider some other look besides Child Revivalist Preacher."

The children were excited by the prospect of a wedding with its vague titillating connection to adult sexual secrets. And like their mother, they welcomed an invitation—the first since Simone had been here—to participate in a social event at somewhere homier than the mall.

Didn't George and Maisie have friends and didn't their friends have birthdays? Their accounts of school life were

eerily unpeopled, a moonscape of empty classrooms in
which only teachers had names, but not, apparently, the
ability to see the invisible George and Maisie, who floated
through their days from which they returned every afternoon with bags stuffed full of half-completed mimeoed
pages of math problems or spelling words. These they hid
from their mother, not just because they did badly, but to
avoid Rosemary's rants on the theme of public education
and how many trees were sacrificed daily to bore her children to death.

Maisie asked what the bride was going to wear. George
asked about the food, less from anticipation than from fear
he might not like it. Simone referred them to Rosemary,
who told them the wedding was at the home of a rich
branch of their father's family whose blond, bovine daughter was marrying some gold-digging New Age witch doctor
and would most likely dress appropriately. The food was
squid, not exactly the children's favorite, and anyway, there
wouldn't be enough, so probably they should eat first.

"What's a witch doctor?" asked Maisie.

"A witch doctor," explained Rosemary, "is what ignorant
people call shamans in tribal cultures. Shamans practice
magic, can cure the sick or make the healthy fall ill, and in
their spare time stir up natural phenomena, volcanoes,
earthquakes, and such. They are especially good on hysterical paralysis and demon possession. Ask Simone about it.
Haiti's the witch-doctor Mayo Clinic."

Maisie said, "I can move clouds by looking at them."

George asked, "How could they make you sick? What
kind of sickness would it be?"

"Hold it!" ordered Rosemary. "Your cousin Betsy's
fiancé is not a bona fide witch doctor. That was a figure of
speech. I should have said: a bogus medical practitioner
who gives people sugar pills for their pets and charges
them—though not, I gather, very much. Apparently he ac-
cepts barter, which on principle we like, though we're also
grateful to capitalism for providing us with this house.
Grateful, I mean, for *Geoffrey's* house and however long he

allows us to stay here. Shelly decorated the groom's living room and the groom doctored Shelly's cat."

"What happened to the cat?" asked George.

"It died, actually," Rosemary said.

THANKSGIVING CAME, UNSEASONABLY warm, a bright November morning. On their own the children took baths and emerged wrapped in towels, their smooth skins rosy and fragrant and ever so lightly steaming. Simone watched George comb his wet hair in the hall mirror, in such a deep meditative state that he didn't see her. Maisie appeared, looking gift-wrapped in red velvet, black ribbon, white lace. George put on a sweatshirt and sweatpants, a sober businesslike gray.

Only Rosemary's outfit came as something of a shock. A ruglike rectangular poncho hung almost to her ankles, a rough tan-and-brown-striped wool blanket that smelled as if it had just been yanked off some llama. Underneath she wore a black mini-dress, black heels, black fishnet stockings.

She must have caught the expressions on Simone's and the children's faces. She said, "One advantage of having money and talent is that one can get away with looking as if one slept in one's clothes. What you three fashion plates don't realize is that it's going to be freezing. The ceremony will probably be on a knoll in the middle of a windswept tundra. Why do upper-middle and upper-class youth always want to get married at Stonehenge?"

Under one arm Rosemary carried what looked like a groundhog but turned out to be a mink jacket for Simone. She said, "A genuine fifties bolero. *Très très chic.* This is not Port-au-Prince, girl. You'll freeze in that little *shmatte.*"

The jacket was dry and prickly and several sizes too

100

small, a hair shirt that chafed Simone's underarms, rucking up her dress. Discomfort intensified Simone's annoyance at herself for acceding once again to Rosemary's fashion advice.

"You look sensational!" Rosemary said. "Like a high-class Haitian hooker."

Rosemary drove cautiously, not wanting to miss the gate. Maisie said, "People tie balloons outside when they're having a party."

"How would you know?" asked George. "You've never been to a party."

"I have," Maisie said.

Rosemary said, "There will not be balloons in this case. Balloons are not these people's style."

They turned into a driveway flanked by cobblestone gateposts. On each post bobbled a cluster of pink and silver balloons.

"I told you there'd be balloons!" Maisie cried.

"With Arabic writing!" Rosemary crowed. "The DeWitts must be expiring!"

The driveway seemed several times longer than the road from home. Finally they reached the house: a white segmented Palladian dinosaur creeping down toward the Hudson. Small groups chatted on the rolling lawn, while braver guests advanced warily to admire the view of river, as if the river were a sleeping child or dog they were afraid of waking. Most of the men wore dark suits, a few had on raincoats and Irish tweed caps. The older women wore expensive, slightly baggy wool coats. The younger ones had on elegant suits in shades of olive and putty. Their eyes followed Rosemary, Simone, and the children, but their heads stayed neatly in place.

"The bar is on the verandah," Rosemary whispered to Simone, "and that is where we are heading. Slowly—this ridiculous grass is like a Cuisinart on these heels. God, these women all look like generals in the Milanese fashion army."

Tending the bar was a friendly young man with an earring. "Don't tell me. You're an actor," Rosemary said. "Bartenders are always actors."

"No, ma'am," said the bartender. "I'm a high-school senior."

"Well, you should be an actor," Rosemary said. "I know it's one in the afternoon, but I'll have a martini. And Coca-Cola for the kids. George and Maisie! Three glasses of Coke all wedding. That's the limit! Understand?" Rosemary smiled at the bartender so he would mark and enforce this limit, and he grinned back from the infinite wisdom of the few years he had on George.

If this were a Haitian wedding, Simone might have asked for rum. But now to be inconspicuous she said, "I'll have the same."

"The same Coke or the same martini?" asked the bartender.

"Martini," said Simone.

She and Rosemary stood at the top of the steps facing the lawn, cautiously sipping their oily, chemical-tasting drinks. Finally one of the big-shouldered suits turned out to have Shelly inside it, and Rosemary raced across the grass, trailed by Simone and the children. Rosemary's heels sank into the lawn and obliged her to walk on her toes.

Rosemary pursed her lips in a kiss that, to Simone's surprise, landed on the grizzled cheek of the man to whom Shelly was speaking: a rumpled, handsome, elderly fellow with a shock of pure white hair.

"Rick!" cried Rosemary. "Good to see you! Congratulations! George and Maisie, do you remember Daddy's cousin Richard?"

"Yes," said George. "I mean, I'm not sure."

"Good to see you." Rick DeWitt shook the children's hands. To George he said, "I see you have already found the bar, young man." George nodded, beaming with pleasure.

Rick, too, had already found the bar—several days ago, it seemed. Being anywhere near him made you gulp your drink to catch up. Simone took a swallow of gin and felt it slither down her spine. Before the others arrived, Rick had been giving Shelly his undivided attention, but now he seemed perfectly happy to share it with Rosemary and Simone.

"This is Simone, our houseguest." Rosemary's diction sounded inexplicably drawling and Shellylike.

"Pleased to meet you. Welcome." Rick grasped Simone's hand in his warm bony palm.

"Permanent houseguest-in-residence," said Shelly, and Simone got instantly tense. All this could lead so easily to someone asking the wrong questions, to curiosity, embarrassment, more curiosity, and worse. Luckily it looked as if Simone's immigration problems would be the least of her host's concerns; and luckily Shelly wasn't really talking about Simone, but only using words as noise to reclaim Rick's attention. Rick's eyes swam toward Shelly, missed, and drifted out toward the wedding.

"Ah, yes." He sighed dramatically. "Congratulations."

"A Sufi homeopath veterinarian," Shelly said. "Isn't that unique? Well, it must be nice to have another doctor in the family."

"Shelly!" Rosemary said.

Rick DeWitt said, "Want to know the worst part? I console myself with the thought that Ronald Reagan went through worse. His daughter married a yoga teacher, as I'm sure you remember. They missed the presidential inauguration—the yoga teacher had to work! But why should I think a yoga teacher is worse than a homeopath? We've got Sufi blessings on the balloons and the paper napkins. The neighbors think we're hosting a PLO convention."

"Where's Betsy?" said Rosemary. "Where's the blushing bride?"

"My daughter?" said Rick. "I'm about to go find her."

A companionable silence fell on the group as they watched Rick weave across the lawn. "Totally hammered," said Shelly.

"Wouldn't *you* be?" said Rosemary. "I'm getting there

myself. Have you seen Geoffrey? This will be the first time I've seen him in, I don't know, months."

"Rosemary, your outfit's terrific," said Shelly. "You look like a whore *and* her gaucho pimp put together in one fashion statement."

Rosemary said, "What I like about this outfit is the ambivalence it projects."

"That's awfully private," Shelly said. "Schizophrenia has never really caught on as a design principle, though there have been a few tasteless attempts at the bag-lady look."

"Are you saying I look like a bag lady?" asked Rosemary.

Just then Kenny came up. "Did someone say schizophrenia? I thought I heard my middle name. Shelly, the wild mushroom and puff pastry triangles are *primo*. Find the waiter, go on."

"Men!" Shelly said. "First they stuff you with little butter pastries, and then they make comments about your thighs."

"Your thighs are great," murmured Kenny distantly, gazing around the group. "Simone, you look beautiful! Unbelievably hot! Like an incredibly classy high-priced Caribbean hooker. Don't get offended, okay? You know me well enough by now to know I mean it as a compliment."

"She won't get offended," Rosemary assured Kenny. "That's exactly what I told her."

But in fact it had sounded quite different coming this time from Kenny. Simone was annoyed at herself for feeling pleased and flattered because a man thought she could pass for a credible whore and not get laughed off the streets.

A waiter in a tuxedo appeared on the porch and clapped his hands until silence spread from group to group. "We're starting the ceremony," he said. "I'm Barry, your Pied Piper."

"It was my impression," Rosemary said, "that the Pied Piper appealed exclusively to rats and little children."

"You're being too literal," Shelly said. "It's a problem you have."

The guests formed a tractable mass that spread around the side of the house and down a gravel path. "Are they going into the stable?" asked Rosemary. "Simone, can you see up ahead?"

Shelly said, "Not exactly a stable. An architecturally significant landmark Dutch-colonial barn."

Rosemary asked, "Is this where the *wedding* is?"

"Jesus was born in one," Kenny said.

"That was a Jewish-carpenter social occasion," said Shelly. "The same rules hardly apply."

"Though perhaps for a Sufi homeopath . . ." said Rosemary.

"I love mixed marriages," said Shelly. "They're so much sexier." She and Rosemary wobbled ahead. Kenny held Simone back.

"The first nice day this week," he said, "you and I are going for a drive to Connecticut. I'll take you across state boundaries. It's probably a federal crime. Meet me at the salon—I'll cancel the afternoon. I'll tell the answering service I'm having a triple bypass."

Simone and Kenny had to hurry to catch up with Shelly and Rosemary, who were squeezing through the stable door, just behind George and Maisie. The barn smelled of rotted hay and manure with a *soupçon* of gardenias. Craning their necks, the guests pressed deeper inside.

Rosemary said, "These heels were not designed for straw-and-cowshit wear."

A man standing behind Simone and Kenny told his companion, "They wanted a kind of cathedral effect, like the stalls were little chapels. Combined with a Bethlehem manger thing, a really holy place. Not some Episcopal church that the robber barons built on land they stole from the Native Americans. And the truly beautiful thing, the part that really makes it, is that all the food that's left over from the wedding is being trucked down to the city and distributed to the homeless."

"Friends of the groom," Kenny whispered to Simone.

If the horse barn was a cathedral, the horses must have been priests, patiently waiting in their wooden boxes for sinners to come for confession, occasionally snorting and lifting their heads, which caused the crowd to ripple and make room, except for a few women who made a point of standing near the horses, aggressively stroking their noses and cooing in their ears.

The minister, a round-faced young woman with a helmet of yellow hair, grabbed the bridal couple and opened the gate to an empty paddock. She pushed the couple inside the stall and shoved them around to face her. Purple lipstick and kohl around her eyes gave the hefty blond bride a bruised, Oriental look that went nicely with her ankle-length black skirt and long-sleeved shiny black blouse.

"My God," breathed Rosemary. "Batsy's dressed to marry the Ayatollah."

"Actually the guy looks like Wyatt Earp," said Shelly. "She'll be fine if he spends half the time on her that he must lavish on that mustache."

"Hey, I know that guy," said Kenny. "He is a total scum." Simone checked nervously for eavesdroppers, but everyone stared straight ahead.

"Is Geoffrey missing this?" Rosemary said. "Do you think there could be somewhere else he had to be on Thanksgiving?"

The minister's syrupy, moneyed voice flowed out over the stable. "I'm Charlotte Hunt," she said. "I'm the ninety-fifth woman to be ordained by the Congregational Church of New York." There was a smattering of applause. "I'm honored to have been asked here today to help marry Betsy and Ethan, not only because it's always great to see a couple really in love, but also because of the spirit of compromise that my being here symbolizes—and the wonderfully positive feelings that this gives me about the marriage.

"I know that I was not Ethan's first choice to perform the marriage ceremony. He would have preferred someone of his own faith, a Sufi, or at least a Muslim. But Ethan compromised, just as Betsy compromised and agreed to hold the service in this humble manger instead of what Ethan calls my European church. Some of us wish it *were* European. Paris or Rome would be nifty."

A few laughs gave the minister time to catch a quick breath and say, "Like gaggles of you present today, Betsy and I are cousins. I knew her as a baby."

"I can't see," Maisie wailed, and Kenny lifted her up. George, Simone realized, couldn't see either, but preferred being wedged between two walls of adults to being picked up and risking unwanted attention from a stableful of strangers.

"Betsy and Ethan came to talk to me in my office," the minister was saying. "And the minute I saw them together I knew this marriage would succeed. It may not be a popular thing to say nowadays. But what made me so certain was that I could sense immediately a powerful current of sexual attraction."

In front of Simone the sea of bobbing heads froze: icebergs rocking on an Arctic bay that had suddenly turned solid.

"First they spoke with me together," said the minister, "and then individually, and when Betsy was in my office she said the most marvelous thing. She said that Ethan was a homeopath everywhere but in bed. She said that bed was one place where he definitely does not think that less is more."

Kenny covered Maisie's ears. With a squawk of protest, Maisie pried off Kenny's hands. The mood of the crowd was such that no one turned to investigate Maisie's squawking.

"So it struck me," said the minister, "that this stable was the perfect place to join these two together, a place to remind us of that stronger, more urgent river flowing beneath what we, perhaps foolishly, call civilization. Ethan has asked that I read aloud from the poems of Rumi, a Persian poet whose erotic verse shows us even today how sexual,

genital love is a mirror for the love of God and our fellow
man."

The minister unfolded a sheet of paper and read, " 'My
soul is beyond desire, my ears are drunk, in one hand is a
wine goblet, in the other my lover's hair, my desire, my
only desire . . .' "

Everyone in the stable inhaled and seemed to get stuck
there, as if another breath might provoke still more intimate
revelations. Simone could feel the collective swell of relief
when the minister said, "And now by the powers vested in
me by the State of New York . . ." How grateful they were
for the familiarity of the civil ceremony with its safe
categoric abstract promises to love, honor, and obey.

"Obey!" hissed Rosemary. "Can you believe that—love,
honor, and *obey*! The last couple in the twentieth century to
include that in the service! Is female obedience making a
comeback?"

"It's a Muslim thing," said Shelly. "Limited application."

"You may now kiss," said the reverend, and the couple
kissed passionately, perhaps feeling some obligation to
make good their sexual boasts. While the guests cleared the
stable the newlyweds remained in the stall, licking each
other's faces.

Tables had been set up under a huge striped tent, heated
by mammoth blowers from which gusted a hot desert wind,
disastrously for the wilting ferns strewn about on the tables.
Perhaps it was the ferns that added a stale-icebox vegetable
aroma to the more pleasant party smells of perfume, liquor,
and cigarettes.

The children had their own tent, to which Simone and
Rosemary delivered them.

"I'll go with you," Rosemary told Simone, "so you
won't look like their caregiver."

In the smaller tent fifty overdressed children milled uneasily among the tables, eyeing each other hostilely, as if in
a game of musical chairs.

"Upper-class children!" said Rosemary. "Where else in

the world do the poor little robots wait to do what they're told?"

Not in Haiti, Simone could have said, but thought better of it. Packs of children roamed Port-au-Prince, seemingly without families. You imagined them sleeping in a lump, huddled together like puppies.

"All right, children," Rosemary cried. "Everyone take a seat. Soon someone—not me—will come along and bring you little people some food. Goodness, where are your parents? There are tiny babies here! Maisie, you can get carrot sticks from the grownup tent. I don't know what they plan to feed you. Hamburgers or something equally imaginative. George and Maisie, keep an eye on this zoo. Come get me and Simone if you need us."

In the other tent, the adult tent, Shelly and Kenny had saved them places at a round table at which five guests—a man and four women—were already seated.

"Count!" said Rosemary. "Good to see you!" A faint smile of greeting twitched the lips of a ruddy-faced man with a ginger mustache and closely cropped reddish hair. Was this the famous pervert who strung dead animals up in the forest? Was this the killer Simone had imagined shooting at them in the woods? The Count she'd pictured was tall and cruel, puckered with dueling scars. But the actual Count was plump and shiny, like a packaged pastry, iced with loads of unhealthy but not necessarily toxic chemicals.

Surrounding the Count were two lovely storklike women with thin arms and pointy elbows that defied the laws of physics supporting their large drooping heads. Occasionally they lifted their chins, like telephones off a cradle, and leaned over and whispered in the Count's ear, messages that made the Count go silly with delight or as close to silliness as his pained tic of a smile permitted. It was impossible to picture him participating gravely and without irony in rituals involving sheep.

But didn't people want that, their hands plunged in animal blood—or at least the thrill of watching someone do the plunging for them? What about those voodoo services

included in package tours of Port-au-Prince, busloads of
tourists nervously patting their wallets in time to the fren-
zied drums while sinewy dancers leaped about and a poor
chicken lost its life. Simone had gone to several of these
with the ballet dancers from Oklahoma, though she told
them she was a Catholic, voodoo was not her religion. She
explained that voodoo was the faith of the villages and the
poor, and the dancers tried to look sympathetic instead of
how they really felt: happy, flushed from the heat, admiring
the drumming and the writhing, handsome Haitian versions
of themselves.

Simone wondered what the Count thought of the wedding service among the animals. And why were these
women talking to him like those other women spoke to the
horses?

On Simone's left, two ladies had just discovered that one
of them lived in the country while the other came up from
the city for weekends.

"I don't think I could stand it," the country woman said.
"All that dirt and pollution and noise and crime, the sen-
sory and moral compromises just to get through the average
day. You have to develop a shell to survive—it's a city of
hard-boiled eggs."

"Maybe," reflected the city woman. "But if I lived in the
country I'd lose my shell completely. I'd become a mushy
cauliflower from lack of stimulation."

"I suppose in the city one could have great dinner parties," the country woman admitted. "That is, until war
broke out in the streets and made it dicey to get to them.
The dinner-party scene in Beirut must be in terrible shape."

"And where do *you* live?" the city woman asked
Simone, as if to enlist her on the side of either country or
city, perhaps figuring that, Simone being black, smart
money was on the city.

"I am from Haiti," Simone replied. She straightened her
shoulders defensively, as if to ward off further questions.

"Haiti," said the city woman. "My husband and I spent
two weeks there. What a beautiful country, but economical-

ly—my God. The people live in poverty, deep deep poverty. They're also incredibly spiritual people. For weeks after I got home I felt like a better person for having known them. We bought this beautiful sequined flag of Boussou, the god of agriculture."

"At least here," the country woman told Simone, "you can wear that cute mink jacket. If this were the city, you'd be taking your life in your hands."

Meanwhile, across the table, the Count was introducing his female companions. "This is Morgan," he said. "And on my right is Silver. Why do wealthy American families name their offspring after horses?"

"Or dogs," said Rosemary. "Half of Geoffrey's family were named after thoroughbred hounds. Uncle Rex and Cousin Springer to name just two. Half the first names that sound like old-money last names were actually borrowed from old-money dogs."

Kenny said, "If they did that in my family, I'd have a Cousin Rin Tin Tin." There was a silence. People looked at Kenny and looked away. Kenny refilled his champagne glass.

"Rex," the Count said finally, "is a German name, no?"

"It's fashion," said Shelly wearily, "just like everything else. All the little girls are named Melissa, all the boys are named Max. Back home the blacks give their kids fabulous names: Farouk and Valvoline. But up here . . . I have a client who named her son Luigi after some Italian designer's kid she saw in a photo spread in *Vogue*. Luigi!"

"It's a great responsibility," said Rosemary. "It comes back on you if you screw up. How utterly cynical of us to name our baby son after the last dead king of England. I soon realized that 'George' was as close to 'Geoffrey' as we could get without having a Geoffrey Porter the Fifteenth. That was the extent of Geoffrey's rebellion against family tradition. I wasn't going to let that happen again when it was time to name Maisie. We knew there was a Henry James novel about a little girl named Maisie. We both thought we'd read the novel—mistakenly, as it turned out. How were we supposed to know that *that* Maisie was an unfortunate waiflike victim of ugly, selfish adult divorce? Which is precisely what I mean about names coming back to haunt you. Imagine your child's name exposing not only your marital problems but the fact that you've been lying about something you've always pretended to have read."

"I met a Jewish fellow once," the Count said, "who claimed he could tell from a Jewish man's name his age within five years."

"I'm sure," said Shelly. "Ten years ago they were all Scott and Heather. Five years ago every Jewish child was Joshua or Rachel."

"And five years from now?" Rosemary asked.

"Mary and Jesus," said Kenny.

Rosemary said, "The hardest thing about sculpture is naming a piece when it's done. Sometimes I'll just let a piece sit and rot until it surrenders and *tells* me its name."

This failed to generate any of the questions Rosemary might have liked about her work. Happily a waiter appeared with a tray of clattery dishes. This young man was clearly not an actor but a high-school student at a painful stage; every shameful sexual thought had broken out on his face.

"How many want squid salad?" he asked.

When he left, Shelly said, "How clever to match the food with the help. Like different wines for different courses. After the squid, hardbodies take our orders for roast beef."

"Shelly!" said Rosemary. "That is genuinely cruel." Then, more quietly, Rosemary said, "Wait a minute. I can feel it. All my danger sensors are blinking at once. Geoffrey must be here."

"What ESP," said Shelly. "I saw him about ten minutes ago but kept quiet for your sake. I thought if I didn't say anything he might just disappear."

Rosemary said, "I wish I'd worn my mouton coat. I feel very exposed in this poncho."

"Fasten your seat belts," said Shelly. "We're in for a bumpy ride."

"Am I just paranoid," Rosemary asked, "or is he headed this way?" Simone noticed that Kenny's hand had clenched around the knife with which he'd been alternately chasing and cutting a rubbery circle of squid.

"What's this?" inquired the Count, literally sniffing the air, on which he'd caught a piquant whiff of emotional turmoil.

"I cannot handle it," Rosemary said. "Coming here was a big mistake. I cannot deal with seeing Geoffrey in this public venue."

"No problem," said Shelly, leaping up. "I'll head him off at the pass."

The whole table watched Shelly run over and interpose her tense little body between them and Geoffrey. Too far away to overhear, they watched Shelly and Geoffrey talking. They seemed to Simone to sway like snakes, or like a snake and a mongoose, but more taut and alert, more like tunneling rodents fighting over a burrow. Geoffrey kept leaning backward and moving closer and backing off in a way that made Simone think: He's frightened of Shelly, too.

Returning to the table, Shelly stuck her thumb in the air. "Very graceful," she said. "Very clean. I explained that having to talk to him now would blow all Rosemary's circuits. Rosemary, don't ever say I never went to the mat for you."

"Great," muttered Rosemary. "Thus confirming his view of me as a borderline schizo."

"I was doing you a favor," said Shelly. "What gratitude!" She turned to the others. "The moral is, don't interfere in a marriage. It's like getting trampled by a herd of elephants."

Rosemary chewed on a piece of squid. Her circuits looked blown, regardless. She said, "Simone, finish your salad. In between courses let's go check on the children."

At first it seemed like a good idea—being anywhere else but this table, but as Simone followed Rosemary out of the tent and toward the children's tent, they saw Geoffrey walking in front of them, generating a kind of force field they dropped farther back to avoid.

Though Geoffrey seemed unaware of their presence, perhaps he knew they were there. Because by the time they reached the children's tent he had moved far away from the entrance, where the three of them might have been obliged to stand side by side as they watched the magic show in progress. In the few seconds it took to locate George and Maisie, Simone felt unreasonably anxious, as if they might somehow have disappeared.

"I don't know if I can get through this," Rosemary whispered to Simone.

The magician, a suave sadistic Viking in a top hat and tails, was making a boy from the audience pick playing cards from a deck. Each time he guessed the boy's card, he said, "Can't you do better than that?" The boy was on the edge of tears. Twenty children and a half dozen adults watched, stunned and utterly silent. At last the magician thanked the boy and sent him back to his seat and the whole group applauded with insane relief.

The magician took off his top hat and ran his hand through his plastered-down hair and asked for volunteers to come inspect his hat. No one in the audience spoke. A toddler started crying.

"Chickens!" said the magician. "I'll show you." And he tilted the shiny black topper he'd just worn on his head. "Empty, no?" No one said a word.

"Empty!" said the magician. "Like your little noggins. How quiet we are today. Well, maybe now we get a response." He yanked a white rabbit out of the hat and held it by its ears. The bunny looked pink and defenseless, swimming in the air like a newborn.

"Ooooh," chorused the children, more from shock than pleasure.

"He's hurting it!" one girl cried out.

"Not at all," said the magician. "This is my friend Bobo. Say hello to Bobo, children."

"Hi, Bobo," said a few voices.

Rosemary said, "Child abuse and rabbit abuse. Fabulous combination. Believe me, a geek show is not standard fare for our weddings and children's birthdays. But why am I apologizing to you? In Haiti, plenty of social occasions must feature animal sacrifice. I just cannot fathom who the adult in charge here is—who is protecting these children from this obvious sexual freak."

Simone looked across the tent and her eyes met Geoffrey's. She nodded, and Geoffrey gave her a quick military salute.

"Now I need a lady volunteer from my audience." The magician stared over the children's heads at Rosemary and Simone. Simone was afraid he'd call on her and she'd be too timid to refuse. Then she'd have to lie in a coffin and let him saw her in half. She thought of Baron Samedi, the voodoo god of death, dressed like the magician in a top hat and tails. In Haiti children were frequently warned to avoid dark spirits, but American parents invited them in to entertain their young.

The magician considered her and then passed her over for Rosemary. Simone wasn't sure if she should be relieved or insulted. Without taking his eyes off Rosemary, the magician switched on a record player. A wheezy, ghoulish violin waltz crackled through the static.

"May I have the honor of this dance?" the magician asked.

"I don't think so," Rosemary said.

"I will be very insulted," the magician said, and sashayed toward her across the tent. The audience twisted around to see whom he'd chosen. Simone caught the moment when George and Maisie realized it was their mother. She watched them watch the magician reach for Rosemary's hand.

Rosemary resisted, then crumpled, undermined by politeness and by the fear of being a bad sport. She reluctantly took the magician's hand and followed him into the center.

George and Maisie looked around. Then they got up and went to their father, cutting across the magician's path, annoying the magician and alarming Rosemary, who murmured "George and Maisie?" as if calling out in a dream.

Geoffrey put one arm around each of the children and they stood poised for attack or defense. But what was there to fight about? No one was in danger. A magician performing for children had asked for a volunteer.

Neither the magician nor Rosemary appeared to know how to waltz, and he dragged her around with only the most casual relation to the music. The magician's back was straight, his elbows locked, his face turned stiffly away. His evening clothes and her poncho made for an interesting pairing. It was upsetting to watch how Rosemary detached herself and complied.

Simone thought of how in Haiti *tonton macoute* asked women to dance, and if the women refused, the *tonton macoute* would chase them and beat them with their sticks. You learned to keep away from dancing crowds or stand far from the music. But this blond magician was nothing like the *tonton macoute*, all he could do was embarrass you. He couldn't take your house or kill you or imprison someone you loved.

Half twirling, half pushing Rosemary till her back was to the audience, the magician shouted, "Children, I would like your help now—counting from one to three . . .

"One!" His eyes drilled the crowd till it echoed, "One!"

"Two!" said the magician.

"Two!" said the crowd.

"Three!" said the magician.

"Three!"

The magician snapped his wrist and clawed and fumbled at Rosemary's back as if he meant to produce from it yet another rabbit. At first it looked as if he had come up with something pink and embryonic. Then he snapped it in the air and it unfolded—a very large pink satin brassiere he was pretending to have just extracted by magic from under Rosemary's poncho. Even the children could tell it was several times Rosemary's size, but it looked so naked, so exposed and organic, you felt it had come fresh from contact with a woman's breasts—had recently cradled in the dark something tender and fleshy and warm. It looked like a body part itself, more like skin than cloth. A few older children laughed harshly.

"Look!" a chorus of children warned Rosemary, who had to twist around in a magician's arms to see the pink brassiere. It took her awhile to process what she was seeing, and then she smiled a terrible grin of complicity and shame, a smile meant to diminish the significance of the occasion but which instead excited tragic pity and terror. The children folded under the pressure of that smile. All their mothers were humiliated, threatened, in sexual danger, faking acceptance and pleasure to save them from being afraid. A howl of laughter and misery went up from the children, which the magician chose to interpret as a positive response, and modestly bowed his head in acknowledgment.

George and Maisie pressed against their father. His arms were around them tightly. Then a woman's voice cried, "They're cutting the cake!" And the children streamed from the tent.

On the way to the main tent Simone and Rosemary met a woman walking briskly in the other direction. The woman wore a monk's robe made from a grimy red blanket. Simone recognized Glenda from the shop in which they'd got Maisie's Red Ridinghood cape.

"I love this wedding, don't you?" Glenda wrinkled her face. "Betsy and Ethan are such good people."

Everyone had gathered for the cutting of the cake, a frosted monster that loomed so hugely over the bride and groom that both their trembling hands were needed to pick up the knife and attack it. The cake reminded Simone of the Aztec pyramids in the human sacrifice book, and she imagined the priests pitching human hearts down from the highest point.

As the couple cut into the bottom lawyer, the groom no-

ticed for the first time the decoration on top of the cake: a
little boy and girl Pilgrim couple under a bridal canopy.
Still holding the knife, the groom stopped and glowered at
his bride, who smiled apologetically at the crowd and took
the knife from his hand. Her smile implied that he was ec-
centric, maybe, but not dangerous or homicidal.

"Lord," Shelly whispered. "She *is* marrying the Ayatollah."

The groom addressed the wedding guests: "The whole
purpose of this ceremony was to create a new Thanksgiving. To turn around the holiday by giving it new meaning,
a day of real Thanksgiving, a celebration of caring and love
not based on exploitation, on stealing land from native people and eating endangered species."

"Of course not," Rosemary whispered.

"The whole point," said the groom, "was a kind of
atonement for what Betsy's family has done here, ripping
off the land and the people and ignoring the will of Allah."

It was very impressive, how smoothly the crowd absorbed this, perhaps because they'd had so much recent
practice in transcending their situation, in just going blank
and ignoring what was transpiring around them. Simone
thought of the Manet *Olympia* on Joseph's studio wall and
of how sometimes tourists and embassy people came to
look at his paintings and saw the bloody nude woman and
nodded and went on to something else.

"And now," the groom was saying, "the icing on the
cake, so to speak, is these tacky little Pilgrims." He plucked
the decorations off the cake and showed them to the crowd,
two black-clothed angels with tiny feet mired in clouds of
white sugar. "After everything we tried to do, after all our
efforts—we wind up with this gross symbol of all the evil
that Betsy's ancestors helped to bring about. This reminder
of who really owned the land and of what happened to the
native people who so freely shared the knowledge of how
to survive on the planet."

The bride must have known her people; she knew how
much they could handle. She took the knife and closed the

groom's hand over hers and carved a wedge of cake. Flash-bulbs popped and the crowd erupted in a modulated ripple of applause—the perfect volume, the perfect length, the perfect pitch of excitement.

AFTER THE WEDDING the children went off with their father for the Thanksgiving weekend, and Simone didn't see them again until Monday after school. The minute they stepped down from the bus she knew that something was wrong.

George and Maisie stood nearly immobile except for their anxious little faces, looking around till they found Simone and, when they found her, looking away. Simone longed to run and embrace them, but they seemed too fragile: two eggshells with their centers blown out, bundled in winter coats. Surely it was an optical trick of the foggy November light—the children floated in clouds of breath, faraway, dazzling, and insubstantial.

George said, "Hi," and that was the extent of their conversation. They turned and trudged up the driveway, Maisie ahead of George, who had paused politely to wait for Simone, who for a moment couldn't move.

All three of them dragged their feet through the slimy pebbles at a far more leisurely pace than the drizzly weather might have suggested. There was nowhere they wanted to go, nowhere they wanted to be. The drafty house held no more appeal than the slushy driveway.

They had almost reached the front door when George announced, "I have a note from school."

Simone said, "Let me see it," and George dolorously complied, producing from his pack a crumpled envelope, dusted with crumbs. Though Rosemary's name was typed on the unsealed note, it never occurred to Simone not to open and read it.

The letter was from George's teacher, informing Mrs. Porter that George had burst into tears for no reason during quiet reading time. Rosemary was encouraged to feel free to call the school and set up an appointment with the staff psychologist, in whose opinion George might be showing signs of subclinical depression. Would Rosemary please sign the note and send it back with her child?

"Could you forge Mom's signature?" George asked.

Simone said, "Your mother will find out. You had better tell her." In fact, it wasn't clear at all that forgery wouldn't work. But Simone wanted Rosemary to see the note, she wanted adult help with this.

Adult help from Rosemary? What had Simone been thinking? When Rosemary read the note, the adult bat was what she resembled, flapping and swooping around the room while emitting high sonic shrieks. "What's *this* about?" she demanded of George. "I thought we were *through* with this."

George said, "It's about a lot of things." He waited a few beats, studying his mother. "I hated that magician—"

"Look what I drew!" Maisie unfolded a thick sheet of yellow paper on which she'd drawn leopards and tigers in advanced states of rigor mortis. "It's called *Jungle Grave-yard*." She grinned expectantly at Rosemary. Simone wondered: Was she protecting George or competing with him for attention?

Rosemary said, "I'm sure that drawing is the most creative *objet* to see the light of day in that school. Psychologists! Imagine if they'd turned their dirty little minds loose on Hieronymus Bosch! They'd have loved to treat Van Gogh right out of artistic existence. It's amazing how much better medical care Van Gogh's gotten after his death. Every week some doctor comes up with a new diagnosis."

Only then did Rosemary turn to George and say, "Are

we still on *that*? That absurd magician? I thought we settled that at the wedding after you kids finished sulking.
George, you are becoming a genuine obsessive. How
many years do you plan to spend bent out of shape over
nothing? You are not going to try and convince a sentient
adult, your mother, that you cried at school because your
mom was drafted as a magic show volunteer and you, a
grownup boy of ten, are still fried about it.

"Anyway, we should be thankful that your teacher noticed. Eight bomb scares a week in the senior high, cocaine
at junior-high lunch, two dozen major safety violations in
the first-grade classroom—and with all that, they have
nothing to do but pay attention to minor fluctuations in my
children's moods."

But gradually, Simone began to realize that "minor fluctuations" hardly described the children's steady decline.
Helplessly Simone watched them slide back into the
troughs of distraction and grief she liked to think she'd rescued them from during the three months she'd been with
them.

The children were hiding something; their eyes no longer
met hers. They'd stopped arguing and chattering and mostly
stayed in their rooms. George switched off the Eskimo tape
when anyone came near and, instead of asking Simone to
tuck him into bed, turned on his radio and listened to the
comforting, inexorable countdown of the top ten hits.
Maisie seemed much too enervated to even think about
climbing a doorway.

One night Simone heard mumbling from the children's
bathroom and tiptoed near and heard George, whispering in
the dark, "Bloody Mary. Bloody Mary. Bloody Mary."

Could all this have been the magician's fault, as
George halfheartedly claimed? Or had something disturbing occurred during their weekend with their father? Either explanation seemed preferable to the more personal
one Simone imagined: she had worked some small magic
on the children, and the spell had worn off. That was
what had happened with Joseph—for the first few weeks

Simone lived with him he'd quit drinking and chasing women. How flattering to imagine that you could bring about permanent change when, in fact, if your influence worked at all, it was only for a second, a brief float in the buoying sea of warm self-satisfaction before the person's true nature rolled in again and slammed you back into the beach.

It was insane for Simone to suppose she could make the children happy. All this was George and Maisie's drama, Simone was only watching. This was the children's entire lives and only a part of hers, though it was dizzying to contemplate what the rest of her life might be, exactly.

Simone wanted to say to someone: I am worried about George and Maisie. But there was no one she could tell. No one would understand. Rosemary was too volatile, the subject was too explosive. Nor could she consult Geoffrey in case it was somehow his fault; if not, it would only make him blame Rosemary more.

Several times it occurred to her: Kenny knew George and Maisie. After the shooting in the woods, he was the first person Maisie thought to go see. Kenny had a neutral view of their lives, comparatively speaking.

At the wedding Kenny had invited Simone to go for a drive to Connecticut. If she took him up on it, quickly, before he forgot, she could use a long ride to another state to ask his advice about George and Maisie. Or perhaps he would only confirm what Simone secretly feared: There was nothing she could do. They were not her children.

Was Simone just seeking a reason to go visit Kenny? She had to be very clear about this—then maybe Kenny would be, too. It was impossible to tell with a man how something might be taken. She would hate her visit to be misunderstood as a sexual invitation or as an acceptance of the invitation implicit in every move Kenny made. Men made it so hard to remember who you ordinarily were. Just by asking her to meet him at a café Joseph had transformed her into a smiling, agreeable person who answered every question yes; and it was this changed, acquiescent Simone who woke up the next day in Joseph's bed.

One afternoon a light bulb in the kitchen went out with an alarming pop. When Simone replaced it, Maisie asked if she could have the burnt-out bulb.

Simone said, "No, it's dangerous." Maisie fixed her with a look. She needed it for something—for some game or ritual, Simone sensed, that was not to be interfered with. For the first time it struck Simone that these were the children who had cut the eyes out of the family portraits upstairs. She had never thought of that as a story about George and Maisie but only as a story about what their mother had let them do.

That evening as Simone was walking past the sun porch, she found George watching Maisie bury the light bulb in a flower pot full of pebbles and dirt. Maisie said to Simone, "It was our pet. I don't know if you can watch this."

Simone said, "Fine, I am busy," and hurried past the door.

The next day Simone got in the car and drove to Kenny's salon. When Simone walked in, it took Kenny a second to cover his surprise beneath a foxlike, carnivorous interest in this tasty turn of events.

No customers were in the shop. Kenny grabbed his jacket, flipped the CLOSED sign over, and locked the door. "Let's head for the border," he said.

Soon Simone was scrunched in the passenger seat of Kenny's tiny red car, practically scraping the blacktop as they rocketed over the roads. The engine whined like a bratty child, prohibiting grownup conversation. Kenny called out impressive facts about torsion and pickup speed while oversteering wildly and, it seemed, independently of what the car was doing.

"Look how she holds the pavement," Kenny yelled, skidding toward the shoulder. Gravel sprayed the undercarriage. Simone shut her eyes.

"We are now approaching Connecticut," Kenny said. "Run away with the rich and famous!"

How pretty it was, this winding lane through stubbled fields and towns smelling of woodsmoke rather than, as in Haiti, of smoldering rubber tires. You didn't expect, as you might there, some terrifying event, roadblocks and men with machetes screaming into your car. There, memos circulated through the embassy discouraging travel to the provinces, but here you could take any route, any turn, stop at any antique store. The white siding on the old houses bordered the optimistic blue sky with a clean, geometric edge that filled you with pride in human achievement. How honestly this world winked back at you in the bright autumn sun. Simone almost felt safe to surrender herself to the landscape whipping by.

Even Kenny, intent on the road, registered Simone's enjoyment. "Riding around in fast cars," he said, "is every American's birthright."

Simone was relieved that crossing the New York border did not involve uniformed guards scrutinizing her papers. There was no way to make Kenny understand the luxury of a road without roadblocks, to explain without lecturing him and spoiling his good time. Simone felt a pang of missing Miss McCaffrey, with her insatiable appetite for trivial details of Haitian life. Here it was almost impossible for Simone to mention Haiti without feeling that she was rambling on, being boring and self-involved. Emile had said this would be the case; he'd said it would make it easier not to reveal too much. It upset her to think about Emile now, it made her feel awkward and clumsy, as if Emile had meant more to her, hurt her more than he did, or as if he were really her husband and might disapprove of her being with Kenny.

Immediately, as if she'd summoned it with improper thinking, a yellow New York City cab nearly ran them off the road. Kenny said, "Fucking weekenders," though it was a Wednesday. "I see more and more city fucking cabs up here in the country. Rich scumbags miss their train at

Grand Central and can't wait two hours for the next train
and go hail a fucking cab. Well, okay, here we are. Welcome to Connecticut! Free at last, free at last! Great God
A'mighty, free at last! Though God only knows where I get
the idea Shelly's radar stops at the border. Besides, what am
I worried about—what have we got to hide?"

"Nothing," said Simone.

Nothing changed from state to state, but Kenny behaved
as if they had crossed into a new country whose exotic cus-
toms needed explaining. He plucked his radar detector off
the dashboard and, leaning across Simone, stuffed it into
the glove compartment.

"Connecticut and Virginia," he said. "The most fascist
states in the nation. What I hate is how suddenly the side
of the road gets so *coiffed*."

Kenny made a screeching turn into the parking lot of a
rambling, mustard-colored frame barn.

"THE WALDORF HOTEL." Kenny read the sign. "That's what
I love about this place. Woodchuck delusions of grandeur.
Relax—it's not really a hotel, just a redneck bar. Though I
guess they do have some rooms upstairs for guys too
sluiced to drive home. I've always wanted to register at one
of those cornpone inns, sign in under a phony name, and
disappear forever. Especially if I had company—what do
you say, Simone? Shelly wouldn't eat here if an atom bomb
hit and it was the last greasy spoon on the face of the
planet."

Inside the vast low-ceilinged bar the air was cool and
dark and beery. The wood paneling was covered with license plates and animal heads. Simone studied a giant
moose, its glassy eyes fixed on some distant point between
melancholy and rage.

"I see you're digging the taxidermy," said Kenny. "This
place is closer to a voodoo temple than the regulars would
like to admit."

Simone followed Kenny to a table, off by itself. On the
table was a shiny checked cloth and a ruby glass oil lamp,
which, when Kenny picked it up, began to flicker and sput-

ter. "This place could blow sky-high," he said. "Incinerated in a second. Kenny, cool out, man. You can relax. You are not with Shelly."

Simone nodded confirmingly and found herself envying Shelly. Kenny talked about her so much—it hardly mattered what he said. There had never been a man who mentioned Simone so often.

"The down side of Connecticut is what saves it," said Kenny. "We're right in the middle of that manicured shit and actual humans still live here."

The nearest other customers—a woman with a puff of downy white hair and a pastel-blue pantsuit, a grizzled old cowboy in a grommeted shirt and a bola tie—leaned over their table, holding hands and gazing into each other's eyes.

"An all-purpose cheaters' bar," Kenny said. "Nighttime it's guys from Torrington cruising for rural nookie. Afternoons, your geriatric lovers cheating on social security. I know that's what I'm looking at as I approach my golden years. I'll be lucky to get *that* much when I'm that old fart's age."

Simone's smile, meant to suggest that Kenny was being too modest, accidentally signaled the waitress, who drifted over to their table and hovered there without speaking, projecting the same disconsolate rage as the moose on the wall. Kenny ordered a New England fried seafood plate and a Miller draft.

"Five minutes over the border," he told Simone, "and they hit you with freaking New England. But deep fry is the only thing these places can halfway do."

Simone said, "I'll have the same."

Kenny turned to watch the waitress walk back to the kitchen. "Bermuda shorts in November." He shook his head. "This place is authentic."

Kenny flipped through the panels in their private jukebox, then plugged in a quarter and sang along, "*Today I passed you on the street. And my heart fell at your feet.* Hank Williams! The guy makes me want to howl like a dog. Want to know something strange? When I'm with

Shelly, there's all this music I can't admit I like. And when *she* plays certain stuff—like that song she had me grinding to when we were all at her house that night—I feel compelled to give her shit for saying she likes *that*. Christ, I sound like some boring chick analyzing her relationship. How about it, Simone? Want to dance?"

Simone shook her head. "No one's dancing."

"Of course not," Kenny agreed. "It would be totally out of line to dance here." But they gazed at the empty dance floor as if someone were. Kenny said, "I'll bet they've got places like this in Haiti."

Simone thought: Yes on the beery smell, no on everything else. This did not feel dangerous, like the Carrefour bar to which Inez took her and Joseph, and where Joseph had asked first Simone and then Inez to dance.

A few nights later they went back to the bar. It was as if they expected something to be continued or concluded, and every small act felt significant and as heavy as moving through water. Just riding around in Inez's car required enormous effort. A bottle of rum went around and the three of them kept drinking and finished it as they got to the bar and went in and ordered more.

At one point Simone awoke from an abstracted moment and saw Inez out on the dance floor dancing with a Dominican whore. Both women had slight, boyish bodies, though the whore was much darker; both were concentrating hard, rubbing their bellies together to the music but otherwise hardly moving. Finally Inez sat down and leaned over and whispered to Joseph. Her mouth kept moving against his ear until Joseph laughed and got up and danced the same way with the same whore—just as close, just as absorbed, just a little bit taller.

That night as Inez drove Simone and Joseph home in her convertible sports car, Simone half hoped for a roadblock—for someone to line the three of them up and shoot them in the head. It seemed so much less painful and tedious than what she sensed coming next. Why was she even surprised when a few days later she saw Inez and Joseph together in the café? Simone thought of Shelly and Kenny dancing at Shelly's house. She thought: This is how I am spending my life—watching other people dance.

While they waited for their food, Kenny said, "We had a high-school science teacher, a real genetics nut. He was breeding six-toed bunnies. He started out with one normal and one freak rabbit and allowed the six-toes to live and eighty-sixed the rest, and by spring every student got to take home a six-toed Easter bunny. The whole school knew what was going on—no one said a word. Amazing, the outrageous shit you could pull in those days.

"Not that it's so different now. It's all a big breeding experiment organized by the rich. All those bitches at the wedding checking out the horses, doing quick little chromosome counts, calculating the market price to console themselves as they watched Betsy court major bloodline pollution. Those people didn't come over on the *Mayflower* to marry Sufi homeopaths. It makes you understand how slavery could exist, pricing your fellow humans by the state of their dental health."

Kenny shook his head. "I can't believe myself. Jesus. Simone, forgive me. I am heartily sorry for comparing WASP wedding etiquette with the historical tragedy of your race . . . Hey. You know what these tiny jukeboxes always make me think of?"

Before Kenny could tell her, the waitress brought their meals: platters of mysterious, crusty items garnished with apple rings bleeding onto the lettuce. Simone took a bite of what appeared to be a potato and a thin film of fishy oil evenly coated her mouth.

"Salty," said Kenny. "I don't need my blood pressure taken to know this is sending it through the roof."

Simone ate a shrimp shell by mistake and raggedly cleared her throat. She realized it was her turn to continue the conversation, an obligation she had rarely felt since coming to this country. Finding herself so rusty at simple adult chat made her clutch at anything relevant to blood pressure or salt.

She said, "Salt is very important to the Haitian people. In Haiti many people believe that salt will bring a zombie back to life. That is why sorcerers who are said to have private armies of zombies are extremely careful about what their zombies eat."

Kenny said, "Simone, you are the most interesting woman I have ever met. Not every chick you take out has the scoop on zombie diet. I'm so used to these boring, predictable women. When I'm with them I don't have to listen—we could be doing a movie I wrote the script for myself."

Predictable would not have been Simone's word for American women, though maybe if this were her country their train of thought might seem more on track. Simone had given up trying to follow Rosemary and Shelly as they switchbacked and careened from one topic to the next. Still, she liked it that Kenny had made a distinction between her and boring women.

"Many people believe in spirits," she said. "Some Haitian people believe in devils who prey only on children. The *loup-garou* is our werewolf; it has red eyes and red hair. When a child gets sick, they say a *loup-garou* is drinking its blood."

"God," said Kenny. "Don't little kids have enough problems without their own designer vampires?"

"George and Maisie do," Simone said.

Kenny said, "Worry not. George and Maisie will grow up and marry Mom and Dad. Respectively. Or maybe they'll both grow up and marry Dad. They'll fight about the estate and the inheritance and reconcile and clone themselves and repeat it the next generation. I'm sure there's a zillion Haitian kids who would trade lives with George and Maisie, get that good food and the rich guilty dad and the mansion up on the river."

"I like George and Maisie," said Simone. She couldn't have said this to Joseph. All he would see was their money and the color of their skin. But at least he talked about color—it was a permissible topic. No one here ever talked about race unless they were mindlessly rattling on, and if they caught themselves, it was a social mistake and they quickly changed the subject.

"That's a problem," said Kenny. "George and Maisie are screwed. The mom's a cross between Tinker Bell and the Bride of Frankenstein, the dad's the son Peter Pan would have if he'd had a baby with Jack the Ripper. Wait. What's your damage, Simone? You *do* know who Jack the Ripper is? Or do you not know how I can say such nasty things about handsome young Geoffrey Porter? I mean, is that bewildered look cultural or specific?"

Simone realized it was useless to ask Kenny more about the children. They were obviously not a subject he could keep his mind on for very long.

"Don't explain," Kenny said. "I understand the confusion. You haven't seen Geoffrey's sadistic side, just the boyish charm. This is a common temporary blindness affecting only females."

In fact, it did confuse Simone, the discrepancy between her vision of Geoffrey and the monster others painted. Ever since they had danced in his office, she had thought about him often. She liked to think about him before she fell asleep. She looked forward to seeing him; he was nice to her and flirtatious enough to make her feel briefly more cheerful. Sometimes she imagined scenes in which she confessed to being an illegal alien; instinct told her that Geoffrey was the one to ask for help. Here, just as in Haiti, money and family counted. Clearly she had stopped seeing Geoffrey as the threat Rosemary described, the evil destroyer who could on a whim dismantle their entire lives. Even now, the thought of him seemed like a secret charm that made Simone feel less nervous about saying the right thing to Kenny.

Still, there remained the mystery of why Geoffrey didn't want Simone at his house. He always picked up the children at his office and returned them there on Sunday. Simone had offered to come to his house, but he said finding it was tricky, it would take forever just to give her directions. Once, he'd told her that Rosemary was capable of having his house watched; it was better if women, even Simone, weren't observed dropping by. Simone knew this was unlikely—how could Rosemary afford a detective? Maybe the place was a mess, or maybe women stayed overnight and left embarrassing evidence.

"Look at them," Kenny was saying; he meant the elderly couple. "You can never tell about people's secret sexual lives. Behind closed doors Mr. Joe Average may be into all manner of weirdness. Take the Count. On the surface he's your basic Eurotrash queen. But give the guy a mask, a whip, a couple of pretty boys, sheep—well, it's a heady combination, anything could go down."

Simone was eager to pursue this, to learn more about the Count. But just then the waitress brought their coffee and lingered at their table until the moment passed for asking about sex with ritually slaughtered animals.

Kenny watched Simone stir sugar into her coffee. He said, "I've never seen anyone use so much sweet stuff in my life. It confirms what I've come to think about you, Simone—you're a liberated person. No one here is free enough to use that much white sugar. You know, Simone, if some time you and I were to make it, it would be the first time I ever slept with a woman my own height."

How was Simone supposed to respond to this? Was Kenny serious or joking? She stared down at the table, not even knowing, herself, exactly what Kenny might read on her face—encouragement or dismissal.

Kenny put three spoons of sugar in his coffee and stirred it meditatively. He said, "I have the little house and the little car. Now I need the little wife and the little kids to go with it. I'd really be there for my kids, not like my own dad, that type-B lump of protoplasm we saw only at dinner and Sunday lunch, not like that scumbag Geoffrey wrecking every good thing he had. I still have the instincts for being with kids that most guys today have lost—it's a de-evolutionary thing, it went out with the mating instinct. Tell me that George doesn't walk out of my shop feeling better than when he walked in! I'd be the Dad of the Century. Am I right or what?

"The problem is, I keep getting involved with killer Amazons from hell like Shelly. Not what any sane person would exactly call mother material. You'd have to be a lunatic to do that to a kid. The world is full of nice women, genuinely good-hearted humans, but the ones I'm attracted to are bigger slimeballs than me. And it isn't only white chicks. I used to see this black girl in Brooklyn. You remember that movie where Pam Grier played the psycho whore who gave guys blowjobs with a razor blade in her mouth? This chick had razor blades in her soul, it was just slower-acting . . ."

Kenny winked at Simone over his coffee cup. "Speaking of Shelly . . . We'll take a Godfather oath of silence about this afternoon. *Cosa nostra*, right? We don't even have to repeat how much sugar we put in our coffee. I'll go nuts if I hear Shelly call sugar 'white death' one more time."

On the way home Kenny drove past his house, a white vinyl-sided bungalow next to a satellite dish so large the house looked like its maintenance shack. It was neither the city apartment nor the gritty cave in which Simone had pictured Kenny dwelling.

Kenny said, "When I was in high school I had a crush on my Spanish teacher. She lived in an apartment on a corner by a dry cleaner's. I worked weekends at the A & P so I could afford to get my jeans dry-cleaned. I could get a hard-on just hanging out in front of her house. Once, I actually ran into her in the street outside her door. I said hello in this strangled voice—total humiliation. But now when I drive past my *own* house I get that same weird hard-on. It's almost as if I'm thinking I'll come out of the house and see *me*. And I know it's crazy—I mean, this time I know no one's home."

GEORGE AND MAISIE were deeply alarmed that Rosemary might forget Christmas. Of all the worries plaguing them, this was one they would admit, perhaps because it seemed relatively safe or especially urgent. They must have heard the lack of conviction in Simone's reassurances, because one evening Maisie was driven to ask, "Are we having a tree?"

"A tree?" Rosemary glanced up from her plate of hot dogs and Cheez Doodles. Her eager, uncomprehending smile confirmed the children's worst fears.

"A Christmas tree," said Maisie.

"Christmas?" Rosemary repeated. "When exactly is it?" George burst into tears.

"Oh, George, loosen up," Rosemary had said. "Of course we're having Christmas." But as yet she had given no sign of holiday awareness.

By contrast, the neighborhood around Geoffrey's office was gift-wrapped with bows and holly berries and clumps of bulbous Styrofoam bells. When the children saw this, the weekend after Thanksgiving weekend, they flung themselves on their father as if he had decorated the storefronts himself.

"Cool Christmas stuff," George said.

"Thank you," Geoffrey said. "Now you guys go into the office. I have top-secret matters to discuss with Simone."

Maisie asked, "Is this about our presents?"

George said, "Shut up, stupid."

135

Geoffrey said, "Your sister is not stupid and don't tell her to shut up."

The children were happy to leave Simone conferring with their father, for this was the only season when adult conspiracy was encouraged, even required. When they were out of earshot, Geoffrey said, "Simone, I need your help."

She knew that Maisie was probably right: he meant consumer advice. But his asking for her help was confusing and seductive. If only he didn't look at her as if he were *interested* in who she was, as if there were a chance that what she said might amuse or delight him.

"Christmas is less than three weeks away and I have no idea what to get them." Geoffrey's wry smile was at once superior and sheepish, the grimace of a young boy compromised into good behavior. "I can't believe how every year I fall in the same trap. Everyone knows the holiday's lost whatever meaning it had. It's a manifestation of our acquisitive materialist values. I know this must sound disingenuous coming from the guy who just blew three grand on a Wurlitzer so his kids could see it bubble. But buying things is enjoyable, at least in this culture, and it's the culture we live in, I can't fight it alone. And if I held my ground and said no, who would suffer? George and Maisie—that's who!

"Meanwhile, I go through Purgatory like clockwork each December. I feel I'm being tested on how well I know my kids. Have I noticed how they've changed since last Christmas? Have I registered their desires, their passions and hungers and fears? And no matter what, I fail the test; I buy too much or too little—some stupid toy that's too old or too young, too complex or too simple."

Yet just weeks before, Simone recalled, Geoffrey had bought George the computer game and Maisie the book—gifts they both enjoyed. He had gotten the jukebox, too, and the children had loved it. Buying things for George and Maisie was what Geoffrey did best. Had he forgotten or lost the skill? Had something happened in between? Or was it the fact of Christmas that made him lose confidence in what he knew?

Geoffrey said, "Tell me honestly, which do you think is worse: not having the money to buy your kids Christmas presents or being so out of touch that you don't know what to get them?"

Simone could have told him. It would have been so satisfying to ventilate Geoffrey's cocoon with a few selected razory scenes from the lives of Haitian children. She could describe babies living in cardboard boxes, children scrapping over garbage behind the Holiday Inn. How tempting to watch Geoffrey's handsome face go slack with dismay as he comprehended that this was not the dizzy non sequitur Rosemary had accustomed him to expect. Haitian children knew that not having food was worse than too many choices. The reproof of their situation would resurface throughout Geoffrey's evening, a mild headache of conscience that would fade and disappear by morning.

Geoffrey said, "Have you noticed that the children seem a little down in the dumps? Of course, under normal circumstances they're hardly the happiest kids in the world. But it seems to me they took a major dive sometime around Thanksgiving. And the fact is, I love those kids, bizarre little warts and all."

It was strangely exhilarating to hear Geoffrey remark on this change in the children, which Simone had observed but thought she might have imagined; it was reassuring just to know she could still tell what was real, and moving to hear someone, anyone, claim to love George and Maisie. Of course Rosemary loved them, but with a passion that tracked erratically between hysteria and neglect, a love that could send them out in a car with someone who couldn't drive and then turn around and forbid them to ever ride in a car again. Geoffrey was always the person who paid the closest and most consistent attention. Why hadn't Simone consulted him first, instead of trying Kenny? Because it would have seemed disloyal to Rosemary to ask Geoffrey's help. But it was very different when Geoffrey brought it up.

She could hardly refuse to talk to the man about his own son and daughter.

But before she had even begun to decide how to approach his question, Geoffrey asked, very quietly, "Have the children mentioned anything?"

A chill tickled the back of Simone's neck and rippled along her spine. Geoffrey didn't sound like an anxious parent casting about for answers that might explain why his children seemed anxious and depressed. He sounded as if he knew exactly what the children might have mentioned and was trying to find out if they'd mentioned it to Simone.

"For example?" Simone asked.

"I have no idea," Geoffrey said.

Then, though she'd been trying not to, Simone thought of her magazines and their chilling statistics on how many American fathers sexually interfered with their children. In one article a panel of doctors agreed that these days when a child was sad you had to consider that first. Hadn't Kenny said you could never tell about people's secret lives? Nothing about the Count made you think right away of sheep. Simone remembered Joseph saying something similar—you could never be sure what anyone did in bed in the dark. Was this something all men knew and felt compelled to tell you? Perhaps Joseph had been warning her not to trust him with Inez. Simone had liked what she and Joseph did in bed in the dark. But after he left she worried that she'd done it all wrong.

From inside Geoffrey's office came the raised voices of the children arguing volubly over the computer controls. George and Maisie sounded more normal, more vital than they had all week. Their giddy, shrill, contentious voices persuaded Simone that whatever their problems might be, incest wasn't among them. They would not sound so light-hearted to be remanded into their father's care. But what went on in Geoffrey's house that he didn't want Simone seeing?

"What engages them?" Geoffrey implored. "Who *are* George and Maisie?"

The landing trapped the building heat in a suffocating pocket, and sickeningly, the staircase seemed to accordion in and out. Simone filled her lungs with radiator air. Then she heard herself say, "George likes Eskimos. And Maisie collects old light bulbs and buries them in pots."

"Whatever for?" said Geoffrey.

"I don't know," Simone answered. "Like a funeral, I suppose."

Why had she told Geoffrey this? Suppose the children found out? She wanted to make Geoffrey promise to keep it secret, though how could she impress on him how crucial secrecy was? How dangerously easy it was to betray even those you loved when the impulse to tell the truth got mixed up with the desire to please. The children had trusted her not to tell. They had meant for her to tell no one.

Outside, a light snow had begun to fall. The wind flicked ice against the glass, demanding Simone's attention. She was very uneasy about driving home in bad weather. When had it gotten so dark out? How far from an oncoming car did you dim your lights?

"Eskimos?" Geoffrey was saying. "Light-bulb funerals? My children have these great interests and I'm the last to know it!"

The snow kept up through the night and all Saturday morning. Among the things it muffled was any sense of time, so that it hardly seemed unusual when on Saturday, around noon, Rosemary called Simone to the kitchen to help her finish a bottle of bourbon.

"I'm done for the day," Rosemary said. "*Venus Number V* has to dry overnight. Besides, I've come to think it's healthy for me to take weekends off, observe the normal five-day grind like a regular working stiff. And with this white garbage falling from the sky, it's difficult to scare up the minimal inspiration needed to convince oneself that art is worth doing, that it's not all the product of vanity, boredom, and duty."

Rosemary filled two glasses with whiskey and handed

one to Simone. "I would appreciate not being informed that
it's too early to start drinking."

Drinking at noon had not been, until now, one of Rosemary's vices, but Simone could see where Rosemary might
be in need of extra cheer. She seemed unusually perturbed,
even by normal standards. She poured a cup of black coffee
and drank it to chase the bourbon. Even in the mouton coat
she looked shivery and cold.

"Ugh," she said. "I hate bourbon. It always reminds me
of Shelly. How ironic that the demographic group most
worried about racial pollution should gravitate to the liquor
with the most toxic impurities and potential teratogens."
She paused to scowl out the window. "God, I despise the
snow."

The snow had tossed its white sheet over the world and
turned it into furniture in a house where a death has occurred and now stands empty, awaiting the movers. Simone
had never felt so isolated. She was a lifetime from civilization, an eternity from the children. The ten miles or so to
Geoffrey's house had become an uncrossable wasteland.
She would never get out, never again. She was stuck here
forever and ever.

Rosemary said, "You know how I found out about
Geoffrey's last femme fatale? I was returning a videotape
he borrowed for the kids, some simpering cotton-candy
piece of animated fluff. And there wasn't a receipt for it, or
the girls at the video store couldn't find it. When I said my
husband had rented the tape and I repeated Geoffrey's
name, everyone got silent and shot guilty glances at this
one girl—the usual blond subliterate trollop, very PG-13.

"And you know what I wondered? This is the priceless
part. I wondered was this better or worse than when the
pizza girl used to give Geoffrey free pizzas? For that's what
my husband was doing, trading his sexual services up and
down the Hudson Valley for a bag of chips from Marylou
at the 7-Eleven, a case of Dos Equis from Stacey at Bev-
erage World. Et cetera.

"It's not that he even asked for it, it was very touching.

These poor girls working for minimum wage were so moved by my millionaire husband they were ready to give him everything—every last thing they had."

Rosemary toasted this insight, then drained her glass. "I suppose this is a cue for the freshening of our drinks. I refuse to tell this sad tale to sober ears. *Salud! L'chaim!* Drink up!"

Simone thought about Geoffrey and about what had made these girls do this. It was how he let his eyes rest on you, how he looked at you when you spoke—with respect and real concern that could not be entirely faked, no more than he could deny the fact that he truly liked women. She could imagine the effect this had on young local girls who had never before and would never again see that look on a male face. Geoffrey knew that what women wanted was the simple attention a man might pay another man who was talking about his car.

"I would ask myself," Rosemary said, "what I minded most. Did I resent his being intimate with someone else? By then, intimate was way beyond *our* range, though we still had occasional sex, if you could call it that. I think what I really objected to was that it worked out so well for Geoffrey, like one of those perfect ecosystems where no energy gets wasted. I'd fall asleep in the middle of the videotape—and Geoffrey was home free. He didn't have to fuck me, and his slut of the week would give him another movie."

Simone watched a sip of bourbon work halfway down Rosemary's throat. Rosemary choked lightly for a few seconds until she gulped and swallowed.

"Whoa, big fella." She put down her glass and leaned toward Simone. "I don't want you to think for one minute that this is American love. I swear that at one time Geoffrey and I felt the WASP equivalent of passion.

"We met at a wedding at somebody's carriage house in Croton. Geoffrey was outside, leaning against a car, talking to my brother. When I came over a miracle happened—they stopped and talked to me. Geoffrey asked if there was a place to eat nearby. I mentioned the Tepee Diner, where now, I understand, he claims to have eaten as a child.

"What a fool I was to imagine that a grand passion could begin with restaurant conversation! Though this was before restaurant chat caught on—we were very avant-garde. But what stopped me cold was that when I spoke, Geoffrey actually listened. I'd had three or four regrettable affairs in my, I'm appalled to say, debutante career. And none of them had been what you would call an ego-building experience. In fact, I was never exactly a monster of sexual confidence. But then again what woman is ... well, secure about her charms?"

"I don't know," Simone answered, but she was thinking: Inez and Shelly. Women like that knew what to do, knew a way of acting, and it was always so disillusioning how well their act worked on men. It made men seem so predictable, so stupid and easily fooled, and it always disheartened Simone, probably more than it should have.

A silence elapsed, and Simone knew that Rosemary was also thinking of Shelly. It would have been cruel of Simone to bring up Shelly right then, though she recognized an impulse to make Rosemary suffer for her own feeling that she and Rosemary had this shameful thing in common: they were two out-to-pasture nanny goats no man would ever want. Emile hadn't looked at Simone—or worse, he had looked just once, long enough to judge that she wasn't worth the risk of complicating his business. In the cab Simone felt she'd ruined things by mentioning the corpse on the street, but really, it was decided by then; Emile had dismissed her, and Simone was getting back at him, saying: Look how we'll wind up. All this preening and strutting and flirting and, inside, bloody meat. But what precisely had she ruined and what did she want from Emile? A proposal of marriage? An expression of sexual interest that she could then deflect? Would Emile's indifference have hurt her if Joseph hadn't run off with Inez? Anything that happened twice seemed like a trend or a confirmation.

"I don't know either," Rosemary said, "but I'd bet on a

low percentage. Most women get the message when they
are very young that they are not the female perfection every
man thinks is his birthright. Most women get kind of
turtle-y, thick-shelled, and settle for less. They get used to
having their feelings trampled in a particular way. We all
learn sooner or later, it's species survival knowledge. I
mean, *pigeons* stop pecking the lever when the pellet
doesn't drop.

"But Geoffrey was, as they say, different. He had this
way of looking at you, you felt he *wanted* to be around
you. Who wouldn't want a man like that, to be with all the
time? Male attention is like a drug, it creates the need for
itself and punishes you when you don't have it—even
though you were perfectly okay before you knew that you
needed it. Well . . . not *okay*. Maintaining.

"Geoffrey and I and my brother went to the diner. I don't
remember what we ate. Geoffrey and I were talking. My
brother left, the diner emptied. I hardly registered any of
this, I was so focused on Geoffrey. The diner was closing,
the waitresses took turns glaring at us. You couldn't expect them to notice or care that Geoffrey and I were falling
in love. But I'd lost all touch with the so-called real world.
I simply couldn't have got up, I couldn't have left that ta
ble."

Rosemary went to the window and pressed her nose
against the glass. When she stepped back, a steamy patch
fogged the mullioned pane, on which she scribbled a little
fist with its middle finger raised.

"Geoffrey and I were children, children of twenty-five,
though the problem with being twenty-five is that you don't
know you're still children. But wait! How old are you,
Simone? I don't think I've ever asked."

"Twenty-five," Simone replied.

"Well!" said Rosemary. "Life makes some of us grow up
faster than others. How did you meet *your* husband?"

Simone, too, had first seen her husband leaning against a
car: specifically, the taxi in which Emile met her at Kennedy Airport. But if she told Rosemary this, the whole

story would have to come out. Why not confess that she
was an illegal immigrant, the on-paper wife of a cabdriver
living somewhere in Brooklyn? Rosemary wouldn't turn
her in, Rosemary might even help her. But Rosemary
wouldn't be able to take it seriously for very long. To her,
the truth that had the power to get Simone deported would
just be juicy gossip with which to entertain Shelly. Besides,
Simone had trouble remembering what exactly she'd said
so far, which had always seemed to her to be the major
problem with lying.

Anyway, the story Rosemary wanted was the story of
how Simone met Joseph. Simone had watched him for
months, for years, before he knew who she was. She had
watched him with one woman, then a second, then a third.
All that time Simone watched him, she felt she was waiting
in line. Joseph was a compulsive flirt, and you had that
sense about him: he was telling you to stay ready, keeping
you in reserve. This should have made Simone angry; what
angered her was that it didn't. Because finally it *was* Simone's turn, and Joseph took her to a café where he put his
arm around her in mirror after mirror. Of course, it was the
same café where she saw him later with Inez.

Simone had known two women who lived with Joseph
before her. Why hadn't she asked them what went wrong,
how the romance ended? She was less circumspect than she
would be standing in line for a movie, asking people who
came out: How did you like the film? Would this make
Rosemary think that Simone was a careless person? But
Americans, she'd noticed, liked seeming reckless, wild,
even foolish; they believed that admitting these qualities
made them seem sexy and brave.

"I bought six of his paintings," Simone said. "We had
just been friends before that, though once at a bar he asked
me to dance—but his girlfriend was with us. His girlfriend
was a friend of mine, and I tried to resist. But when I was
with him it was so strange: everything else just vanished."

"Didn't I just *say* that?" Rosemary said. "That's what I
meant about Geoffrey."

Simone said, "He took me to a café for a drink, his previous girlfriend found us." For a moment this seemed so real that Simone imagined the scene. But when she looked in the café's mirrors she saw Inez with Joseph. She was horrified at herself for appropriating Inez's story. One reason she'd always feared voodoo was the idea of possession—a state that always seemed so unsafe, so perilously out of control. Now she knew she had been right, you had to be clear about who was speaking or something might creep into you and force you to tell a lie and then a second lie and a third to cover the first and the second.

In Haiti she had stolen—just that once—but she had never lied, except at the very end. Miss McCaffrey was so upset about leaving and about being replaced by Bill Webb that she used to sit in her office and cry, and Simone had to protect her and say she was on the phone. But in this new life small lies came easily, you told them without blinking, with no more thought than it took to jump out of the path of a speeding car.

"Oh, I adore love stories," said Rosemary. "But I have a dopey question. I thought your *boyfriend* was the painter in Haiti—and your husband lived in Brooklyn. Didn't we go through this? I'm always getting them confused."

Simone looked at her in amazement. So Rosemary *had* been listening. So much of the time here, Simone felt she was talking to air. But how could you tell when people here heard you? They so rarely answered or expected you to respond. Simone had read that two Australian Aborigines meeting in an empty desert would stand for a while in silence and then continue on their way.

Simone frowned at the bourbon bottle. "I meant my fiancé. I've had a little to drink."

"Un petit peu," said Rosemary. "And we are about to have *un petit peu* more."

After that drink she asked Simone, "Why wasn't it enough? I let him have the video trollops, we had the house and children—a life! But he had to wreck even that. Slash and burn, take no prisoners. I refuse to believe that what motivated Geoffrey was some insane notion of honesty!

"He couldn't go on living this way, he said. That phrase sticks in my mind, perhaps because I'd already heard it in so many grade-Z movies. What strikes me is that it wasn't totally coincidental that it was around this exact same time that I was finding myself as a sculptor.

"I could tolerate Geoffrey seeking, shall we say, other outlets. But Geoffrey couldn't allow me the equivalent, even though you might think art would have been less of a threat than beer salesgirls and pizza slingers under the age of consent. I can still see the look he'd get on his face when I'd try to show him my work!

"So the man set out to destroy me. One night we sat in this very room and he just lasered my psyche. I can't remember how it began, I didn't know where it was leading. I assumed we were having the standard vicious exchange.

"But before long Geoffrey had shot past the usual boundaries and was working his way from a devastating critique of my art to a soul-destroying assessment of my very being. I can't tell you all he said that night. I've blocked most of it, thank God.

"He began with my work or, as he said, my delusional art pretensions. He said my Venus series was basically a celebration of cellulite and that I shouldn't be surprised if not many other celebrants joined me. He accused me of using my so-called art as a social gambit, torturing every conversation till it died an unnatural death and I could drag its corpse around to the subject of my work."

Rosemary was getting red in the face, hissing with righteous outrage. "From there, I believe, he went on to my talents as a mother, a role for which he said I had the gifts of a hamster, and if he'd been smarter earlier he would have removed George and Maisie from my cage. He said the children were fortunate I hardly knew they existed; every time I noted their presence, I did them permanent psychic harm. He said that in my dealings with George I was no better than a sadist and that George's tears and timidity were completely my fault.

"Then he finished me off with a neat *coup de grâce* about my hopelessness as a person, my general failure to notice any other human but myself as I dangled by my fingernails from the edge of reality. He went on to insult my scatty mind, my distractedness, my reasoning ability, the impossibility of following my illogic from one stupid idea to the next . . . Oh, Simone," Rosemary wailed. "Tell me it isn't true!"

"Of course it isn't," said Simone, though its truth was precisely what had made her feel such overpowering sympathy for Rosemary. The cruel accuracy of Geoffrey's analysis had left Simone slightly giddy.

Rosemary brightened a little. "After that, there was no going back. There's no unsaying things like that, no I'm sorry, no excuse me. Not that Geoffrey was apologizing. He'd got some important things off his chest for my benefit and edification. He just radiated a job well done as he went off to stay in his office. Couldn't he just have ditched me without the free character analysis? And the first time I saw him after that he—"

The phone rang and kept ringing till Rosemary answered. Simone knew who it was before Rosemary covered the mouthpiece and stage-whispered, "Speaking of the devil!"

Frantic writing motions signaled Simone to find a pencil and paper. "That noise?" she heard Rosemary say. "That's Simone bumping into the table."

Rosemary scribbled directions over several notebook pages. Finally she said, "I can't promise that. You know I can't promise that," and slammed down the phone. She read over the directions. "Oh, this is just unreadable dogshit! Take this down, Simone, please, before my short-term memory fails completely."

Simone's hand was unsteady, too, but she wrote what Rosemary dictated: "South on 9, left on Cold Brook, go two miles past a white barn, right at the fork, right at the next fork, then three miles straight ahead. So there! One

thing Geoffrey deconstructed that night was my power of
recall.

"Simone, you have to do me the most gigantic favor.
You know that I have been very conscious not to make you
feel like a servant. I never ask for overtime or any little ex-
tras. Actually, I have a problem asking for *anything* at all.
But now there's a kind of crisis, I guess, and I need you to
do this for me.

"Geoffrey's jeep is stuck on the road in the snow, and he
and the kids need to be rescued. So Geoffrey hiked to the
nearest house and, as he went out of his way to tell me,
phoned everywhere in the county before in desperation he
called me.

"I told him I couldn't promise that I could stand to see
him today. In fact, I feel certain that it would be positively
lethal to drive through this vile weather with him waiting
for me at the other end. But on the other hand, I cannot see
leaving my children out there to freeze and die. So if you
could do this for me, Simone—if you could drive over and
pick them up—I would be eternally grateful. I would never,
ever forget."

THE GLITTERY LATTICE of branches made the landscape unrecognizable, a monochrome, petrified, magical world, at once dangerous and narcoleptic. It would have been pretty, Simone thought, had someone else been driving. A new world required she take it slowly and on faith and not get discouraged by the sight of cars buried in snow, abandoned by far better drivers.

Suddenly a clump of snow broke and slid down the windshield. Simone thought she had struck something and for a moment couldn't breathe. She hit the brakes, and the car slid and fishtailed behind her. As she turned the wheel, with no effect, a high whimper of fear escaped her.

The car stopped when it wanted, by which point her heart was pounding so hard she had to put the car in park and rest her head on the wheel. It was safe to do this; no other vehicles were on the road. She could barely see the road or tell if she was on it.

Before leaving, Simone had asked Rosemary if there were any special tricks to driving in the snow. Rosemary said, "I cannot fathom my own depths of self-involvement. Do I think they have blizzards in Haiti? I suppose the special trick is not going out at all. But when you can't escape it, the best thing is to go two miles an hour, max. Everyone says steer into a skid, but no one ever does it. People say when you see a grizzly bear you should open your arms and walk toward it. Fortunately, the car is a Volvo, and I find it a comfort to know that it's made in a country where, if we're to believe Ingmar Bergman, people need to be able to drive through the snow in mid-hallucination. The car makers know that, believe me. It's built into the machine. But why am I assuming you know about Ingmar Bergman?"

It was hard, not trusting the brakes; they had always been Simone's friend. Only now did she wonder why Rosemary wasn't more worried about her children. Which was riskier—being stranded in the snow or being rescued by Simone? She felt like the fairy-tale character who must learn certain rules for the journey—Don't look back, don't drink from the stream, don't steal the crocodile's mango. But out here there were only two rules: Don't go fast. Don't stop. The pace gave Simone ample time to get watery-kneed with terror and calm down and collect herself and then get dizzy again.

And yet, it seemed, if one followed its rules, this snow-world kept its promises. The Cold Brook Road sign was legible. Trees marked crucial forks in the road.

Covered with such a thick layer of snow that it might have been buried all winter, Geoffrey's red Land Rover was parked, or abandoned, sticking out into the road. The engine wasn't running. Simone panicked. Where were the children?

Her arrival seem to wake the vehicle, which emitted a cough of exhaust. She pulled up in front and got out. A small part of the Land Rover's windshield was clear, and through it she could see Geoffrey watching her stagger through the snowdrift.

Geoffrey grinned and waved broadly, but with a certain chagrin, like a shipwreck victim signaling a boat that he knows would rather keep going. Then he jumped out of his car and ran over and took Simone's elbow. As he guided her forward he whispered, "Come sit in the car a minute while we reconnoiter. But please don't assume things are how they look. You should know better by now."

There was someone in the passenger seat, but that part of the windshield was iced over, so that it wasn't until

Geoffrey opened the back door that Simone saw that it was Shelly.

Simone slid into the back seat and got between the children. George and Maisie looked tense and drawn but otherwise unharmed. George pressed up against Simone; Maisie flung herself into Simone's lap and squirmed against her for solace and warmth.

For a long time no one spoke. Shelly and Geoffrey were lovers, that was entirely apparent. And they hadn't been lovers for long—that was obvious, too. A kind of sexual crackle popped in the air between them, and Simone didn't have to think too hard about where she had last felt that buzz: anywhere there was music, Joseph and Inez. And now it seemed so painfully clear—of course, the children had known.

Shelly twisted around in her seat. "Simone, I have never been happier to see you in my life." The tip of Shelly's nose was pink, enhancing her delicate beauty with the hint of a fever raising her body temperature to something approaching low normal. She wore jeans and a heavy tailored wool jacket in a muted pine-tree green. Simone thought of Rosemary and her sad mouton coat.

Geoffrey watched in his rearview mirror till he caught Simone's eye. Then he shrugged and grimaced at her, miming a clownish admission of guilt.

"What a killer," Geoffrey said. "It's not as if I haven't driven in weather like this all my life. I assume one hundred percent of the blame. I should have known better, suggesting we take this baby out to test its four-wheel drive.

"Simone, driving over here must have been a bitch! I never would have called Rosemary if I hadn't tried every towing service in this and three neighboring counties. The one poor hungry sucker working today said he'd put me on a list. I told him I had *kids* in the car. By then I'd hiked three miles to some old lady's house. She barely let me in the door. It was either the Long March for George and Maisie or leave them here to freeze. You may notice Rosemary didn't think to provide the kids with boots."

All five of them lapsed into silence. Then very softly George said, "Are we going to freeze?"

Shelly said, "Good God, George, you've asked that question every five minutes for the last two hours. The answer is: No, we are not going to freeze. Freezing was never an option."

"He couldn't have been asking for two hours," Geoffrey said. "We've only been here an hour." Even the way he corrected Shelly revealed their erotic attachment. He wouldn't have spoken like that to a friend he had just picked up for a drive. Didn't he care if Simone knew? Maybe that was what he wanted. Geoffrey's arm crept, as if on its own volition, around Shelly's shoulders.

How could he have telephoned Rosemary and asked her to pick them up? What if it had been Rosemary who came and found Shelly in the car? He must have assumed—correctly—that Rosemary would send Simone. Simone always forgot or could never believe that Rosemary and Geoffrey were once married.

The jeep was tropical inside. Breath flowered on the windows. Outside, a wet snow fell. No one made a move to leave or improve their situation. Possibly they all intuited that their situation could not be improved. Sitting here, suspended in time, was tolerable, even pleasant. After this something would change—even the children knew it. Simone's finding Shelly with Geoffrey would rearrange everything. A caregiver was nominally an adult, and when an adult knew something it was different from when a child did. You could go from month to month not worrying about what a child knew, but adult knowledge counted as a fact in the world. Perhaps if they sat here and never moved, the future could be forestalled, its damage contained and the safe static present indefinitely continued.

Geoffrey spun the wheels several times to prove he hadn't forgotten. Shelly, ever the hostess, raked up the embers of conversation. "Lord, Simone, I don't think I've seen you since that unspeakable wedding. Have you ever been subjected to more grotesque excesses? I have never seen such pretension, such false camaraderie. A woman I'd never met in my life said, 'We've got to have lunch and catch up.' The part I liked best was watching the Count during the service in the stable. Didn't you think he was eyeing the stallion and imagining the bride and groom and himself and the horse in a double-ring ceremony?"

George said, "In school our science teacher brought in a horse's heart, and we all took turns holding it in our hands and passing it around the room. It was rubbery and gross."

Shelly said, "I see Georgie has inherited his conversational style from his mother." She raised one petite leather-gloved hand for attention and said, "While we're on the subject of biological hearts—if that's what subject we're on—let me tell you children something that happened when I was your age.

"My dad was a doctor, and when I was—I don't know, ten or so—he brought a dead person's heart home from the autopsy room. He carried it in a fried-chicken bucket and dumped it out in the bathroom sink. I remember my sister and I crowding into the bathroom while he held up the heart and showed us how it functioned. I mean, how it *used* to function. It wasn't working so well right then."

They waited for the rest of the story, but it seemed to be over. Shelly had just wanted to mention the heart in her bathroom sink. Geoffrey was smiling and, Simone observed, regarding Shelly with admiration. Shelly's story had made her sound gutsy and unsqueamish, the way Inez sounded when she told intimate anecdotes about her lovers: the dangerous places they made love and what items of clothing she wasn't wearing. One old man had had a fatal heart attack lying on top of Inez, who repeated some very frank details about how she realized he was dead.

This was something else that women—certain women—knew how to do: to talk daringly about unpleasant things and make men think right away of sex. And yet when she, Simone, had told Emile about the body on the sidewalk, her story had been only about death and not at all about sex. She could not make that corpse work for her like flashy jewelry. It lay on the street with its organs out and refused to perform, refused to make her seem like a bad girl who would do bad things with men.

Geoffrey said, "From what I hear, Haiti offered daily opportunities to see the freshly dead human heart beating right in your own front yard."

Simone had to stop and tell herself: There was no way Geoffrey could know this. Emile was the only person Simone had told about the corpse since she'd left Port-au-Prince. Geoffrey must mean some body or bodies he'd seen in a news report. He meant it happened to everyone. It was a Haitian daily event.

"Poor Simone!" Shelly said. "She looks totally blown away. We can't expect her to sit here and discuss the tragedy of her homeland as if it were cocktail party chitchat."

Simone felt taken care of, grateful, almost safe. But seconds later she thought: Wasn't it Shelly who told Rosemary about Duvalier's testicle-eating dwarf? Shelly wasn't protecting her but establishing dominance, showing that she had the power to dole out loyalty and kindness, to guard Simone's tender feelings, to prove that she was sensitive and could watch out for someone else. Or perhaps it was Geoffrey whom Shelly was trying to shield—to safeguard from whatever engaging thing Simone might have been about to say.

Shelly turned and gave Simone a look of compassion and utter triumph, a look that reveled and gloried in female competition the way the facial expressions of certain athletes celebrate effort and strain.

Shelly said, "Isn't it wonderful how globally conscious Geoffrey is?" Her face told Simone: This is perpetual war. I am not to be trusted.

Simone recalled how Rosemary had warned her about Southern women, but now, now that she thought of it, she remembered that look on Inez. She had chosen not to see it, or had confused it with friendship. When Simone first starting going with Joseph, she told everything to Inez. Inez, they both acknowledged, was the expert on love, and inevitably she felt challenged to test her expertise on Simone's lover.

Shelly said, "You know, Simone, I've always felt that you and I were alike." Simone could only stare at her. Whatever did she mean? And what was Simone doing making small talk in a stranded car with Rosemary's husband, Rosemary's children, Rosemary's alleged best friend? If Rosemary died today, these were the people who would bury her.

A wave of sympathy and fellow feeling for Rosemary nearly bowled Simone over. When, at what point in these last months, had Rosemary become her friend?

"I think we should get going," Simone managed to say. The others turned and looked at her—accusingly, she thought, because the last to arrive had been the first to suggest they leave. She had not been stuck here, as they had, but already she was cracking. The children were desperate to get out—Simone felt it in their bodies. But they couldn't or wouldn't say so; besides, it was warm in the car. They had miles to go in Rosemary's Volvo, and there was always the danger that they might get stuck again, stranded in a smaller vehicle on a lonelier stretch of road.

Finally Shelly yawned and said, "I completely agree with Simone. If we've exhausted the subject of corpse hearts, we should take this zoo on the road."

That day the Volvo was Simone's car. She had claimed it by driving it ten miles through the snowstorm. But Geoffrey got in on the driver's side and Shelly sat beside him, and Simone and the children climbed into the back.

Simone had left the keys in the car, so Geoffrey didn't have to ask for them and risk making them self-conscious about what had been automatic—Geoffrey assuming command control with Shelly as his co-pilot. Simone felt she had joined the children in their private back-seat world, from which they eavesdropped on the adults making plans as if they weren't present.

Shelly repeatedly pointed out that Geoffrey's house was

much closer than hers, and at last Geoffrey took a gulping breath and said into the mirror, "I think the smartest thing, kids, would be to go over to my place so I can make some calls. You guys can wait out the worst of the storm. After that, I can either run you home, or Simone can drive you."

How easily he suggested this after all those months of overexplaining why it made no sense for Simone to ever go to his house. Now, of course, Simone realized what he'd been worried about, and it struck her that once again she'd gotten everything backward. She had envisioned the corpses of the pirates' wives stacked against the wall, when probably what Geoffrey was hiding was Shelly's toothbrush and shampoo.

As they pulled away from the Land Rover, Maisie waved good-bye at it out the window. "Stay warm, Land Rover," she said.

"How was your day?" asked Simone, and George answered, "Good," a word he had managed, with practice, to rid of any affect or meaning.

"We went to the mall," said Maisie. "We saw this stupid Christmas show. All the kids from this stupid tap-dancing school were dressed up as reindeer."

"I was stunned," said Geoffrey. "George liked it better than Maisie."

Shelly said, "Maybe Maisie might like to study tap."

Simone cringed at Shelly's crude attempt at seducing Maisie, and her heart sank when Maisie smiled and said, "Great!"

"That might be just what Maisie needs," Geoffrey told Simone.

"Yes," Simone agreed bleakly.

It was vital that Geoffrey stop talking so he could watch the road. Several times they skidded, and Shelly made a sound like bacon frying in a pan.

Geoffrey said, "Shelly, please don't hiss. I've told you it doesn't help." After that, Simone and the children were careful about how they breathed.

"Almost there!" Geoffrey said heartily, several times before they almost were.

Finally Geoffrey pulled the Volvo into a driveway and stopped and said, "Let's hike."

"I don't have the shoes for this," Shelly complained, but no one paid attention. Geoffrey got out and began to slog through the snow; Simone and the children followed. Shelly's short black boots had high heels on which she wobbled dangerously, and she soon lagged way behind the others.

"I haven't had this much fun since the Gulag!" Shelly's high-pitched, brittle cry sliced through the hush of the snow.

Geoffrey looked back at Shelly. You could see him torn between the desire to run and help her and some strange hesitance about seeming solicitous in front of his children and Simone. Or was he perversely enjoying seeing Shelly helpless? In the end, the forces of chivalry lost and Geoffrey plunged ahead.

"Take your time!" he called back to Shelly. "I'm bushwhacking us a path!"

Simone paused and watched Shelly struggle to catch up, her blond head plunging and rising. Simone couldn't even pretend to herself that Shelly's misery didn't please her. She had never wanted to feel this way about another human being. But if she and Shelly were in some sort of war, it was Shelly who had begun it.

Finally they reached a clearing surrounding a little shack. Surely Geoffrey didn't inhabit this run-down cabin covered with shredding tar paper and chipped asbestos shingle.

"Camouflage," Geoffrey told Simone as they neared the sagging front porch. "Clever, no? For me the fear of a break-in back here is just not a problem. This is exactly the sort of lesson my ancestors should have learned from the Indians, instead of which they went for the ostentation that's going to explode in their faces. I mean, when the revolution comes and the urban poor rise up and Rosemary's château gets sacked and burned, I'll be sitting pretty here in my Tobacco Road hovel. My God, I sound like that creepy groom at that awful wedding."

"Who's going to sack and burn Mom's house?" said George.

"No one," said Geoffrey. "Or at least not now. Not while you and Maisie are in it."

But only when Simone walked inside did she understand what camouflage meant in this case: the interior was so imposing, so unexpectedly grandiose, that she reflexively looked up to check the massive support beams. On the floor and folded over the rafters were exquisite Indian rugs; still others hung, like drying laundry, from a wooden rack. Rich woods and leathers were everywhere—some tanned, some still covered with hair.

Simone couldn't imagine a man creating this for himself. She thought of Joseph's bare studio—the Coleman stove, the camp bed, the Manet painting on the wall. She knew with the force of a revelation that Geoffrey had had help.

Then Simone understood the real reason he'd never let her come here. It was not about dead bodies, incest, or evil or, really, about sex, or anything so intimate as a woman's toothbrush and shampoo. It was a modern secret: interior decorating. Shelly had decorated Geoffrey's place and he must have thought that when Simone saw it she'd jump to the wrong—or right—conclusions.

Oh, the poor children! The implications struck Simone again, more forcibly than in the car. How long had they known their father was involved with their mother's best friend? Now Simone understood their melancholy preoccupation, their air of carrying some guilty secret, the burden she'd mistaken for the normal weight of family trouble and divorce.

Simone wondered how long Shelly and Geoffrey had been lovers. First, she suspected, he'd hired Shelly to decorate his house. Then their romance started—probably around Thanksgiving. It occurred to her that this was what she had seen from across the tent at the wedding when Shelly was supposedly making sure Geoffrey left Rosemary alone. Once again Simone had misread the situation, mistaken Shelly and Geoffrey for warring creatures when actually they were mating.

Poor Rosemary, Simone thought. Pitying Rosemary was simpler than facing the fact that Simone pitied herself. You would think she was in love with Geoffrey and had expected something to happen between them, when in fact he was only a man she'd liked thinking about from time to time. It was absurd that the loss of that should seem so serious and so painful. Only now, too late, did she wonder if she'd missed some vital cue. That day they'd danced to the jukebox—the memory made Simone want to weep. Was there something she could have said or done that would have made something happen between them? Probably, at some equivalent moment, Shelly had just snapped up Geoffrey, and now Simone had her principles while Shelly had Geoffrey—and Kenny! Once more another woman had proved to be less high-minded. You had to believe that look on their faces that warned you it was war.

From the children's point of view, of course, none of this made any difference. All that counted was that Geoffrey and Shelly had a long-standing connection. When interior decoration had turned to romance really didn't matter compared to the fact that the children knew, and knew that their mother did not. It was amazing and not surprising at all that children could keep such a secret. Because when Rosemary discovered it, their whole world would unravel.

At Geoffrey's door they turned and watched Shelly struggle up behind them, nearly slipping and catching herself and making grotesque faces. It was at once polite and cruel of Simone and the children to stop and wait and witness every misstep of Shelly's tortuous progress.

The minute her foot touched the doorstep, she was restored to her normal self. "Children! Take off your shoes and leave them outside—I had this floor redone twice! I spent days in some dump of a Santa Fe bed-and-breakfast talking one savvy Navajo squaw down on the price of those rugs. Give me your coats!"

As she took Simone's jacket, Shelly's mouth puckered with concern. "Simone, you look frozen! Let me get you some brandy!"

When Simone took the first sip from the snifter, she noticed that she was still slightly tipsy from drinking with Rosemary this afternoon. How could she have made that drive in this impaired condition? How could she have done it any other way?

When Geoffrey stepped out to get logs for the wood stove, Shelly drew Simone's attention to her decorating triumph.

"Isn't this place a gas?" she said. "Altogether the perfect spot for a wealthy cowpoke to lay his head. The basic design principle is that all these grown men are still little boys who still want to play Lone Ranger. Hi-yo, Silver. Giddy-up and away."

Shelly didn't feel obliged to make self-justifying excuses for betraying Rosemary and Kenny and in the process subjecting two children to considerable strain—though to be fair, this last was something she probably didn't suspect. How brave and confident Shelly seemed in comparison to Kenny, making Simone swear secrecy about how much sugar he put in his coffee. Obviously, Shelly believed no explanation was required. What you did with men, what you did to *get* men, was just not a moral issue.

Shelly said, "Wouldn't it be great to have a chance to do something with Rosemary's place? Don't you think that the Miss Havisham thing is getting a little old?"

Simone glanced across the room. Both children were watching and listening. She wanted to rush over and put her hands over their ears and promise to protect their home from Shelly's redecorating plans.

"Great Expectations," Shelly said. "Do they read that in Haiti? Suffice it to say that this batty old woman has been stood up at the altar and has preserved the wedding party, dress, cake, and all. I mean, has Rosemary showed you that *attic* . . . ?"

Just then Geoffrey announced his return by stamping the

snow off his boots. Simone fought an absurd desire to fling herself on his mercy and make him swear that he would never let Shelly have Rosemary's house. She looked at the children again and wondered if they were thinking this, too.

"Maybe we should call Mom," said George—a simple suggestion that was, for George, spectacularly brave and assertive. "We should tell her we're all right."

"All right?" said Shelly. "Hah!"

"That's a fine idea," Geoffrey said. "Very big boy, grown-up and considerate. Why don't you go into the kitchen and call your mother right now?"

When George ducked around a pillar into the kitchen area, Geoffrey stage-whispered to Simone and Shelly, "Would anyone like to bet on whether the mother duck is even aware that her ducklings are gone?"

The phone must have rung for a very long time. Then George said, "Hello, Mom?"

The rest of them fell silent and listened to George's soft voice. "Simone got there okay. We're at Dad's." George fell silent and listened, nodding from time to time. At last he said, "Okay, Good. Me, too. Okay. See you. Bye."

Only after he got off the phone did he notice that everyone was focused on him. He shrugged and forced a smile. "Mom says that Simone—not Dad—should drive us home."

"What are you smiling about, George?" Maisie said.

"I can drive, goddamn it," said Geoffrey.

Shelly said, "Simone, if it wasn't for you, these children would have perished like baby birds in the snow."

Perhaps Shelly imagined a life with Geoffrey that would also involve Simone—and was saving herself the trouble of finding a new *au pair*. Shelly would not be as careful as Rosemary was to always say "caregiver"—that classless, neutral, genderless word, so unaristocratic, suggesting that employer and employee were all working people together. Shelly was seeking Simone's complicity in her plans for Geoffrey and his children, and meanwhile subtly assuring Simone her job security was intact. But Simone knew better than to think that her life would improve under Shelly's regime, and what was meant to reassure made her extremely anxious. Shelly would not tell her to find her own personal bottom line about housework. Shelly would have definite plans involving white paint and track lighting. Sooner or later she would ask about Simone's immigration status, and Shelly would not be satisfied till she'd found out the truth. Then far too much of Simone's future would depend on her pleasing Shelly.

The phone call had exhausted the last of George's energy. "I'm tired," he announced, and his eyelids drooped to prove it.

"That's babyish," said Maisie. "It's the middle of the afternoon."

"I imagine they *would* be tired," Shelly said. "Getting stuck on the road is exhausting."

"Okay, pardners," said Geoffrey. "Maybe it's time for you guys to crawl up to the sleeping loft and catch a couple of z's."

Shelly said, "Geoffrey, I adore how your language changes to match your house."

Recognizing that their father's suggestion was a nonnegotiable demand, Maisie scampered up the corkscrew staircase and George followed, clutching the center pole. Simone found herself in the same paralyzed state she'd slipped into whenever Joseph got angry and flung bottles around his studio, slamming them against the walls but never too near his paintings. It was unthinkable to be left down here alone with Geoffrey and Shelly. George and Maisie had protected them, and now they were leaving, and it was beyond her to make any move at all.

Then, blessedly, Simone's duties showed her the right direction. She was the children's caregiver. She said, "I will go with the children." Geoffrey and Shelly smiled their agreement that this was a sensible plan, and Simone knew that if she worked for Shelly, she would often feel vaguely insulted.

At the top of the stairs Simone tried to stand and cracked

her skull on the ceiling. Tears blurred her eyes, and she had
to wait before she could see where she was.

One side of the wainscoted sleeping loft was open to the
room below and provided a hidden perch from which to
spy on the grownup world. But the children weren't spying.
They were already curled up on an elaborate antique bed.
The gray headboard was made from branches, twisted and
bound into curves; on the bed was a patchwork quilt in
cheerless shades of brown and charcoal.

Simone lay down between the children. They rested their
heads on her shoulders. First their heads grew heavy and
then Simone heard their light syncopated wheezing.

Downstairs Shelly and Geoffrey were doing a great deal
of walking. Simone heard the thud of Geoffrey's boots, the
tap of Shelly's high heels.

In the hills above Simone's grandmother's village there
had been a little church in which, if you whispered at the
rear wall, you could hear it up at the altar. So from the loft
Simone could hear the coffeepot bubbling downstairs. She
could almost hear Shelly and Geoffrey breathe; she wondered if they knew it. What else had the children
eavesdropped on during the nights they'd spent here? Or
had they learned to fall asleep fast so as not to have to listen?

Finally Geoffrey said, "It's quiet up there."

Shelly said, "That must mean they're unconscious. You
really do have weird children. You know that, don't you,
Geoffrey?"

"Meaning what?" Geoffrey didn't want to hear. Simone
heard in his voice the same edge of fear that Kenny had,
talking to Shelly. Why hadn't anyone taught Simone that
meanness gave you power? How stupid of her to think that
men liked you to be nice! Perhaps it would help Maisie to
grow up observing this.

Shelly went on. "George never picks up his feet and
Maisie's feet don't touch the ground. They're both such
morbid little freaks. Living with Rosemary can't be foster-
ing tiptop mental health. Geoffrey, I mean, for example:

there we were in your car stuck in the snow—and what were we talking about? Children all over the country are talking Batman and Robin. *Your* children were talking about horse hearts and hearts in fried-chicken buckets."

"Batman was three summers ago," Geoffrey said coolly. "If you're going to spend time with them you're going to have to keep current. Anyway, *you* were the one with the wholesome story about the hearts in the bathroom sink."

Shelly said, "*Heart*. Singular. The funny thing is, I got halfway through the story and realized that I couldn't finish it. There was an adult detail I had to quickly blue-pencil out. The R-rated part is that afterward my sister took me aside and told me: the whole time my dad was showing us that heart, she could see a humongous erection underneath his pants."

"Wow," Geoffrey said. "Was it true?"

"How should I know?" Shelly said. "I wouldn't have known what one looked like."

"You've since learned," said Geoffrey.

"So they tell me," Shelly said.

An unwelcome image arose before Simone: the corpse on the street in Haiti. The dead man was not just sliced open—he had been castrated, too. The crows briefly attended the hole in his groin before they moved up to his eyes. Simone shouted and waved her arms at the crows. They rose a few inches up in the air, then fluttered and landed again.

Downstairs it was quiet. Then Geoffrey thudded across the room. Simone heard him take down two cups and fill them with coffee. The legs of his chair scraped the floor as he sat. A spoon clinked against a cup.

"Ugh, sugar," said Shelly. "White death."

AFTER THAT, SIMONE was always uneasy when she was apart from the children. It was not unlike the way she'd felt when she'd first begun to drive. Now, too, she felt safer in George and Maisie's presence, perversely reassured by the fact that they all knew the same troubling thing. Not once did they mention the afternoon with Shelly and their father, a silence that permitted Simone the faint unreasonable hope that it had all been a hallucination induced by the white and the cold. Once more the children reminded her of Haitian children as they took on the bombed-out look of civilian noncombatants in a war that has dragged on so long that nothing more can shock them. Now that Simone knew their secrets, she wondered why she had wanted to—so they could all suffer together in this uncertain state?

Irrationally Simone let herself think that they could keep Rosemary safe, as if their knowing the truth would somehow give them control and they could protect her from having to learn it. Simone could hardly remember how Rosemary had looked to her that first day, the doyenne of the manor conducting her on a tour of the filthy attic, the dotty rich woman in the fur coat, the owner of eyeless paintings. More and more, Rosemary reminded Simone of a frazzled cartoon creature, blithely crossing a chasm on the ghost of the bridge that its nemesis has just exploded. Rosemary talked about Geoffrey evicting them—but not for a moment did she believe that it would actually happen.

Shelly wanted Geoffrey and the house. Their peaceful

life here was in danger. Each morning Simone woke up thinking catastrophe might occur before nightfall. But it didn't, Rosemary didn't find out, night came, and then the next morning.

The elements protected them. Snow fell every day. The pantry was stocked with plantains, rice and beans, frozen shrimp, carrots and celery, so there was no need to leave the house or ever go outside. In the mornings the school bus came on one-hour and two-hour delays, and the radio station that warned them of this became their link to the outside world.

The radio announcer called this a record-breaking early December snow. He remarked how bizarre the weather was—had anybody noticed?—in dire tones, as if in a code whose dark meaning his listeners would know. Simone had no trouble believing that nature was struggling and dying; there was hardly a tree left on the whole island of Haiti. But she had only his word for it that this was unusual weather here. For all she knew, it was a lie cooked up for foreigners to believe, and the truth was that their Decembers had always been like this. She had not seen a year here, she had not even been through a season. It was so often a mistake to think she knew what this place was like.

The radio announcer became a presence in the house, with his own personality and quirks, one of which was the inability to say something bad without immediately saying something good. So the fact of six inches of snow was the promise of a white Christmas. He was constantly reminding them of how many days were left till Christmas, announcing the number aggressively, as if he meant to scare them. And indeed the children's gloom deepened as the number decreased.

One evening the phone rang, and when Simone answered, Geoffrey said, "Is Rosemary home?"

Simone said, "She's in her studio."

Geoffrey said, "Could you get her?"

Rosemary had been in a sculpting frenzy ever since the day she'd got drunk and told Simone the story of her and

Geoffrey's last fight. Simone found her covered with plaster dust, her lips powdery and caked. When she took off her goggles, two raccoony circles remained. Her spattered fur coat seemed to have been rescued in mid-cremation. Rosemary was sanding a statue made of some kind of pumice that looked at once like a female nude and a cankerous growth on a tree.

Simone walked with Rosemary from the studio back to the phone. On the way Rosemary said, "I know this is awkward for you, Simone, it would have been very hard for you to refuse to disturb me. But if, when I am working, you could find some way to spare me these distracting interruptions . . ."

Rosemary picked up the phone and, without saying hello, said, "I know what this is about. This is going to be about Christmas."

It was the first indication that, unprompted, she knew what season it was. She took the phone in the pantry and closed the door behind her. Simone and the children could hear her rage like a madwoman in a cell. At last they heard the unmistakable crack of a phone slammed down on the hook, and Rosemary appeared at the pantry door, red-faced and streaked with tears.

"Well, it's settled!" she trilled. "George and Maisie will spend Christmas Eve at their father's. At precisely eleven on Christmas morning Geoffrey will bring them back as far as the end of the driveway. I will not have Simone driving all over creation on Christmas Day just because my children's father is being possessive and selfish. And George and Maisie will have *two* Christmases—the divorced children's compensation!"

George cranked his forearm in the air. Maisie clapped her hands. They were so relieved to be having any Christmas at all.

Rosemary said, "We'll have a real old-fashioned Christmas dinner. George and Maisie and me and Simone. And we'll invite Kenny and Shelly."

Rosemary's new resoluteness had sparked a flicker of

hope in the children that, at the mention of Shelly's name, instantly sputtered out. Simone and the children stared at the floor, to which they were suddenly rooted. People believed there were voodoo spells that could paralyze you like this: you were walking across your house and suddenly froze in position, and you stood there as your systems shut down and your heartbeat quit.

Rosemary, on the contrary, seemed galvanized into action. Perhaps her talk with Geoffrey had reminded her of reality, or at least infected her with the spirit of healthy competition.

Early one afternoon she called Simone to her studio to plan the children's Christmas. She said, "I feel like some Pentagon spokesman with bad news about the military budget. I've squirreled away two hundred dollars from Geoffrey's stingy allowance. So what we are looking at, basically, is poverty-level Christmas. Meanwhile, the woodchuck parents of my children's school friends are spending major bucks on remote-control high-tech junk that will break on Christmas morning."

What school friends? Simone wondered. This wasn't the time to ask. It was surprising, even impressive, to see Rosemary so focused, so in touch with the fact that she had children, and that a holiday was coming that they might want to observe. Had Rosemary done this every Christmas? Delayed till the last minute and then pulled everything together? However would Simone know? This was her first Christmas here. She couldn't even tell if this was a record-breaking snow.

Rosemary said, "This will be a test of our creativity. A real old-fashioned pre-MasterCard Christmas. Popcorn and cranberry wreaths for the tree—as if fresh cranberries weren't expensive! It's a lot like Halloween at the mall, another creativity tester: American women, including ourselves, using skills they don't think they possess. I just wish there were a wider range, that we got to do something artistic besides making dinosaur costumes from packing foam and big Christmases on small budgets."

But weren't they in a studio crammed with Rosemary's artistic life? It would have seemed mean-spirited for Simone to point this out while Rosemary was so generously making a wish on behalf of other women.

"Dress warmly," Rosemary cautioned Simone. They went out on the lawn. The brittle crust on top of the snow cracked beneath their feet. Rosemary carried pruning shears, Simone a two-handled straw basket. Rosemary clipped a few pine boughs, and they gathered the rest from the ground. The heavy basket rocked into their shins as they lugged it back to the house.

In Haiti Simone had seen *Macbeth* performed by a troupe from Puerto Rico. Palm fronds camouflaged Macduff's army, and the audience gasped when the jungle shuddered and glided across the stage. Now Simone wished that Rosemary could camouflage the mansion, cover it with pine boughs, and sneak it away past Shelly. But all Rosemary had in mind was some greenery over the doorways. Simone held the ladder while Rosemary tacked up the boughs and flecks of paint and wallboard showered down on their heads.

The next day Rosemary took Simone shopping to the grocery and the mall. She practiced the driving advice she'd preached—two miles an hour in bad weather. The errands took even longer because Rosemary had heard of a market in Fishkill giving away free Christmas turkeys with every thirty-dollar purchase.

En route they considered the question of why the turkeys were free. Were they the victims of some toxic spill or pernicious turkey disease? Rosemary said, "If this is what Geoffrey wants, I guess he's going to get it. His beloved children eating turkeys from Chernobyl, the poisonous food of the poor. Or maybe they truck these turkeys in from voodoo temples in the Bronx. Do you think you could tell, Simone—identify secret ritual markings?"

The turkeys were crammed in a cooler just inside the supermarket door. Floating in pinkish fluid in amniotic plastic sacks, they resembled specimens preserved in cloudy jars, medical anomalies: adults dead in the womb. Rosemary deliberated as if they were puppies she was trying to pick from a litter, as if each one had a living soul that might beg her to take it home. Finally she chose one, apparently at random, and raced off after cranberries, popping corn, broccoli, and yams.

The turkey beeped as the cashier whisked it over the sensor. She said, "You should have seen the guys that brought these in on the truck."

"Did they glow in the dark?" Rosemary asked.

"I'm not kidding you," the woman said. "Dust masks and space suits and goggles."

Rosemary and Simone loaded the car, and as they drove to the mall, Rosemary outlined her plans to divide and conquer. They would split up and shop for the children and meet in time to leave. Attacking the problem this way would let them cover more ground and not oblige them to be an audience for one another's choices. It would spare them competitive jostling if they both found the same perfect gift.

Rosemary never considered that Simone might not have money. She must have assumed that Simone was cashing the checks she infrequently gave her—one more happy consequence of refusing to balance her checking account. In fact, Simone had thirty dollars skimmed from grocery money and another thirty still left over from the original sixty she'd got to pay Kenny. Even touching the uncashed checks in her drawer felt dangerous and risky, while not cashing them seemed like a sacrifice, a ritual offering: paying money to the drawer so her life here would not have to change.

In the mall, before they separated, Rosemary said, "Look around you. Everyone is either on the edge of tears or on the edge of murder. To not keep this constantly in mind is to ask for a chilling surprise."

Simone found the toy store with its maze of burrows, more like tunnels than aisles between high walls of cardboard boxes. Many of the boxes showed gleeful, shiny-faced children enjoying the games inside, aiming missile-like plastic bees at vibrating electric hives and bouncing on the kind of sports equipment that George and Maisie would most despise. The tiny hassocklike trampoline would humiliate George and demean Maisie's power to leave the ground on her own.

Parents staggered through the store weighed down by bulky objects; their faces were contorted gargoyles of frustration and rage. Many searched frantically for some unfindable special offer. A young woman told Simone, "My girl friend warned me they'd be sold out by October. You would not believe how many people do their Christmas shopping on Labor Day weekend. Each year I swear I'll be like that. But we can never get it together till the last minute. Am I right?"

Simone bristled at being included in this fellowship of the slow, and hurried off past the models of fighter planes designed to make George seem unhandy, the sewing sets created to make Maisie feel clumsy, exiled from female life. She floated out into the mall, where in the bright light every face suggested an arrested scream, except for the mothers of small children who were actually screaming. Two teenage girls in jeans walked by with a little boy on a leash.

Simone was suddenly conscious that no one here looked like her—for the moment, anyway, there were no other black faces around, and people either stared at her like naturalists at a weird bird or saw her coming and averted their eyes, as from a wreck by the side of the road. She couldn't remember feeling this way since she'd come to Hudson Landing, not at the supermarket or on the street or here at the mall on Halloween; but then she had been with a white family and everyone had been in costume.

The only ones who paid no attention to her were the children standing in line, waiting to see Santa. Simone's first year at the embassy, they'd had a Christmas party at which the embassy children lined up to see Santa with the

same poleaxed looks of horror as the children here. By the
next year, the escalating violence had sent the children back
to the States, and the Christmas party had no Santa Claus,
only very drunk adults.

Now, as she drifted past the children, past a store special-
izing in neon-framed photos of movie stars, Simone, like
Rosemary among the turkeys, was listening for some private communication—in this case from some shop or toy
that was right for George or Maisie. At last she caught a
faint signal from a stall of odd lamps that resembled ghost
acquariums from which all the fish had decamped, leaving
fantastic plant forms waving sinuously in a lit-up neon sea.
The water in the smallest lamp was a maraschino red. Simone's instinct, that Maisie would love it, was confirmed
by its costing ten dollars.

The wrapped-up lamp felt like ballast, anchoring her to
the world and making her somewhat more confident as she
entered a store devoted to gadgets made of steel and
chrome. Huge blown-up photos showed men fishing in
streams and rafting through foaming rivers. A compass that
told the time and gave the positions of the stars was much
too expensive, but the Junior Jacknife cost twenty dollars
and seemed perfect for George.

The ponytailed salesman agreed. "It's never too early,"
he said. "If I had a kid I would get him a knife as soon as
he could hold it. The shit kids have to deal with in their
neighborhoods these days—I'd get my kid an assault rifle
to bring along to first grade."

Simone wondered if he would have said that if she
weren't black. The photos around them suggested that
knives were for freeing trout from hooks rather than for
self-defense in outbreaks of bloody street violence. Probably she should reconsider what she was doing—buying a
knife for an unhappy, morbid ten-year-old boy. Now, of
course, she remembered how terrifying it was when George
borrowed Rosemary's X-Acto knife to work on his science
projects. And yet Simone felt sure that George wouldn't

hurt himself and would greatly value the knife as a talisman and a vote of faith in him as a miniature man.

But the minute both gifts were in her possession all her happy conviction vanished, and she realized that they were wrong, misguided, pointless wastes of money. She didn't know these children, really, didn't know what would make them happy, and had got them demoralizing, insulting objects they would hate.

How primitive it all was, she thought, like some voodoo sacrifice in which everything depended on finding the right offering for the right god. But in this ritual the spirits were those of your family and friends, and you knew in advance that no gift would suffice and everything would be rejected.

Simone spotted Rosemary on a bench by the chocolate-chip-cookie wagon. She dreaded the prospect of Rosemary asking what she'd bought. She sat down beside her, by the artificial trees that dappled the shafts of colorless sun filtering down through the skylight.

"Let's see." Rosemary rummaged among Simone's parcels. Unlit, Maisie's lamp looked putrified and stagnant.

"Nice," Rosemary said.

She reacted more positively to George's pocketknife. After a minute of speechless horror she said, "No, I get it. I get it! This is a genius present for George. It will make him feel more like a male—what a revolting prospect."

Rosemary reached into her own bag and pulled out two boxes of crayons, two jars of rubber cement, and two packs of colored construction paper. "I got the children art supplies," she said. "We really must do something to supplement their art education. It has just struck me that my children are six and ten and I personally have never once seen either of them pick up a pencil to draw. Does this mean that yet another natural impulse has been stomped out of them already? First generosity, then their *joie de vivre*, and now the urge to create!"

"And speaking of generosity . . ." Rosemary rewrapped the presents and stuffed them in the wrong bags. "Simone, I have to tell you: I *forbid* you to get me a gift. But I also want to confess that I've got something for you. Straight-forwardness is the only way to prevent an etiquette disaster. What we do or don't do matters less than being clear about it. Eyes front and center as we march toward the nightmare of Christmas morning!"

The next afternoon Simone went out to buy a Christmas present for Rosemary. Incapable of facing the mall again, she thought of Glenda's store.

Good Witch of the East smelled of bayberry, a fire roared in the wood stove; the marble tombstone cherub wore a rakishly tilted Santa hat. Glenda greeted Simone with a thimble-sized glass of eggnog. She said, "Non-alcoholic holiday cheer. Everyone's got to drive. Shopping for the kiddies?"

"No." Simone was embarrassed that she'd bought their presents elsewhere. Perhaps it was discomfort that made her say, "For Mrs. Porter," though she hadn't called Rosemary that since her first days in the house.

"Rosemary," Glenda corrected her. "What a wonderful person. Of all the people to work for . . . you are truly lucky. She's a deeply good human, and the sad thing is: so is Geoffrey."

Simone made a stiff, unsuccessful attempt to smile con-curringly. Glenda said, "Kenny says the meanest things about Rosemary, but I always defend her." On the face of it, Glenda was taking credit for her loyalty to Rosemary, but actually she was boasting about being someone with whom Kenny gossiped meanly. Knowing Kenny, Simone imagined that many could claim this same intimate connec-tion.

Glenda said, "Let's work on this. Let's give it some thought. Rosemary deserves something beautiful at this point in her life."

Glenda sashayed through her store, pausing and picking up objects, as if seeing each one with a fresh shock of dis-covery and pleasure. "Rosemary is so dramatic. Almost theatrical. Also, she's an artist. That requires something special."

Disappointed that Simone didn't know Rosemary's astrological sign, Glenda finally settled on a long, colorful chiffon scarf and flung it around her neck with a brittle, stagy gesture so reminiscent of Rosemary that Simone had to buy it.

"Ikat," said Glenda. "From Bali. The most romantic place on the planet."

Counting out the money, Simone discovered that she had only one more dollar than the scarf cost, with tax. What would she have done if it was more and she couldn't afford it? At least then she would still have had money left—instead of only a dollar. Simone felt light-headed, as one might after a haircut, except that this sudden weightlessness spread all the way to her feet.

While she gift-boxed the scarf, Glenda asked Simone how they celebrated Christmas in Haiti. Simone couldn't remember telling Glenda that she was from Haiti. Kenny must have told her. She wondered what else he'd said. Could it be that Kenny said mean things about her, too?

"I was wondering," Glenda said, "if you had any friends back in Haiti who could maybe send us some paintings or those incredible sequined voodoo flags. We could work something out. I used to carry these darling decal-covered metal briefcases, but when things got rough down there, the supply completely dried up."

Simone said, "People in Haiti are poor. They don't give so many presents. No one has time there now to make beautiful things."

Glenda said, "People continue to make beautiful things in unbelievable circumstances. You would not believe the stuff I'm seeing from Afghan refugees. Though I guess Afghanistan and Haiti are totally different cultures."

Glenda took a deep breath. "Simone, Kenny is a totally changed person since he's known you. He is always talking about what a good influence you are. What a lot of people don't realize about Kenny is how lonely the man is. He doesn't let anyone see it, but he's told me in private that he would really like to settle down with a wife and kids, the whole enchilada. Instead of which he's got Shelly."

"Thank you." Simone took her present and left, leaving it unclear if she meant for the information, the compliment, or Glenda's help in the shop.

"Merry Christmas," Glenda called as Simone closed the door.

Simone's legs felt a little rubbery as she walked along the mini-mall toward Kenny's salon. She thought of Kenny's story about lingering near his Spanish teacher's apartment. Would he spot that nervousness in Simone if she ran into him here? Would he be sympathetic? What did he mean about feeling that way when he drove past his own house now?

Standing to one side so she couldn't be seen, Simone looked in Kenny's window. Kenny was cutting a little girl's hair. Tears streamed down the child's face. Simone watched Kenny talking to her, trying to charm her into not crying. Finally his charm must have worked; the little girl grudgingly smiled. Up above, on the ceiling, a hundred monkeys looked away, each contemplating the luminous Christmas light clutched in its sticky paw.

On the ride home Simone pulled up behind a yellow New York City taxi. When she appeared in its mirror, the cab sped up and took off. A black man was driving the taxi and naturally Simone thought of Emile, especially when he took curves on two wheels—the driving style of Haiti. Simone gripped the wheel and took a deep breath and hit the gas and followed.

It was intoxicating to do something so unlike herself, thrilling to take this winding road at this suicidal speed. Who would have predicted that, in only three months, Simone would have learned to drive like a maniac? An image filtered into her mind: that steamy morning in Port-au-Prince when she'd gone to the travel agency with Inez's money. For the first time she could admit to herself how excited she had been. Hadn't Geoffrey said that sometimes you had to smash through the roadblock?

Several times she got close enough to see the back of the cabdriver's head, and at one point she thought, teasing herself: What if it is Emile? She knew it probably wasn't Emile, and anyway, if it was, Emile's presence in Hudson Landing would not be a happy sign. Emile had his life in Brooklyn, perhaps an illegal-alien harem; he had no reason to pay Simone a friendly social call, seventy miles into the country in the dead of winter. Emile coming to find her here could only mean serious trouble.

She counted slowly backward from ten and told herself: It isn't Emile. But that was fleeting comfort; in fact, no comfort at all, like waking from a troubling dream to the real troubles of the morning. Her life here was like a stack of chairs in an acrobat's routine, and with or without a push from Emile, the pyramid was bound to topple. Shelly would take Rosemary's house; Rosemary would let it happen. Though Shelly might want Simone to stay, Simone knew she couldn't, no more than she could have stayed in Haiti and watched Joseph romancing Inez and gone from working for Miss McCaffrey to working for Bill Webb. Losing her job would send her reeling out into America, or at least as far as Brooklyn, the only place she knew to go. Would Emile's cousin remember her and be willing to help again?

A jittery rumba the car did while pulling out of a turn chased all this from her mind—emptied it of everything but fear and pride that she could go this fast without crashing. She had never driven or wanted to drive anywhere near this speed before. Simone was so admiring her competence that it almost seemed she willed it when every turn the cab took was the correct turn toward Rosemary's house. It felt nervy and dangerous, trailing a strange man alone on the road, but the cabdriver wanted the road to himself, he clearly wanted to shake her, so that keeping up with him seemed like harmless entertainment. She was sorry when she reached the driveway and the cab continued on.

Within moments she heard the screech of brakes, and the yellow cab came up in her mirror. Adrenaline surged through her in discreet little bursts. A cab following in her driveway was a whole different matter from the game she'd thought she was playing on the country road, and Simone was scared and annoyed at herself for having let this happen.

Simone checked her mirror again. And now she saw that it *was* Emile. And because she'd envisioned this, it was somehow more of a shock. She found herself unable to stop, fleeing him down the lane, driving on out of inertia and fright and some instinct for postponement.

Emile flashed his lights and gestured out his window as if bouncing a ball on the road, but Simone pretended not to notice, even as she had to swerve to keep from falling off the slippery driveway; she was mortified that Emile was behind her, watching her oversteer. She parked in her usual spot, a short distance from the house, then realized how unwise she'd been; she should have stopped up the drive, where at least they might have been able to talk without Rosemary seeing.

Immediately Emile jumped out and ran across the frozen rutted driveway. He was wearing jeans and a puffy denim jacket appliquéd with patches of fawn-colored vinyl. He opened Simone's door and took Simone's elbow and hustled her across the snowy fields. He pushed her lightly ahead of him, at once bullying and uncertain; she could tell he was unaccustomed to walking through deep snow. She led him in the footprints she and Rosemary had made when they'd gone for branches. Emile wore canvas sneakers. Simone thought, His socks must be soaked. And this made her think, as she often did: she was spending too much time with the children. It was not her job to worry about the dryness of everyone's feet.

At the edge of the woods Emile stopped. Speaking rapidly, breathlessly, he said in Creole, "The travel agent who arranged your trip has been arrested in Port-au-Prince.

Their files have been confiscated. There is an INS investigation."

Emile waited for this to sink in, then said, "Probably they stopped paying protection to the CIA. Now the U.S. government has enough evidence to deport or imprison many Haitian people. Hearings have been scheduled. Official letters have been sent. I expect any minute a letter for you—of course, at my address. There will be a hearing. You will not mention me or any of the people who helped you get to this country. You will not remember anyone's names and the white man will believe you: he understands that Haitian names are easy to forget."

A weird mix of exhaustion and relief ebbed and flooded through Simone. She had the strangest desire to get in Emile's cab and put her head on his shoulder and sleep. She felt as you do in a dream when a car is hurtling toward you and you just sit there in the road and wait for it to hit.

Emile said. "The mail and telephone are not safe. Just as it was in Haiti. So I have driven here to warn you. And all the way from New York I am afraid that someone is following, and I drive very cagey and excellently to shake pursuers off my trail. Many Haitians like myself will suffer for helping innocent Haitian people."

Simone couldn't believe how quickly exhaustion flamed into rage. How incredible that, in the midst of this, Emilie was boasting about his driving! And if his purpose was to help innocent Haitian people, why did he charge so much? He had made her feel like a package he'd been hired to pick up at the airport. She so wanted to say all this, she was so irritated at Emile—she and Emile could have been veterans of a very long, bad marriage. She had a mean desire to point out that it was she who'd followed him here from Hudson Landing and he had not driven so excellently in shaking her off his trail.

Or maybe this was just what one felt for the messenger bringing bad news. Simone gazed past Emile into the woods, where she'd seen the dead sheep. And all at once the anger and worry drained out of her, just disappeared, and left her on the verge of tears from wanting so badly to talk to Emile.

Once more she imagined getting in his cab, this time not to sleep but to tell him, in a rush of Creole, French, and English, everything she'd experienced since coming to this country, all about George and Maisie, how she'd come to love them and what it was like, watching these people to whom she was invisible except as a mirror they preened before in the hope she'd reflect an acceptable view of their lives. The Emile she imagined listening was not the real Emile, but Emile transformed, her countryman, her long-lost Haitian brother. Why should the pleasure of seeing Emile suddenly seem so sweet—was Simone just homesick for someone from her own country? Her desire to talk to him now felt almost like love: not love for Emile, precisely, but the stinging love you might feel for a bright warm room you passed, walking alone on a dark night.

She would have given anything to tell Emile about the morning she'd seen the sheep. It seemed to her that this incident contained in it everything else, all the terror and strangeness of being in a new place. No matter how many magazines you read, how quickly you caught on, there would always be terrible things you would never understand. And Simone had so wanted to think that she was smarter than the tourists who fooled themselves into believing the voodoo dances were real, that the dancers were being possessed on cue by the appropriate loas.

In Haiti you tripped on dead animals in unexpected places—chickens hanging from branches in the city park, a cow skull in a crowded street—and you knew they were there for a reason; everything had been arranged. But here how were you supposed to know what something like that meant? And the most disturbing thing was that no one around you knew, either. No one knew what to sacrifice, they made it up on the spot, and the sheep in the woods had an air of the totally private, the shameful, and the furtive.

But what good would it do her to say this to Emile? She

remembered his response to her telling him about the dead body in Port-au-Prince. He would think her only subject was disemboweled corpses. Was there something about him that brought such thoughts to mind?

If Emile replied at all, she knew what he would say: Dead man, dead sheep. Haiti and the United States. Everywhere was the same. There was no point asking Emile if she and the children had been shot at on purpose. And what did any of this have to do with the crisis before them—the possibility of an investigation that might end in their both being deported or sent to freeze in a hellish camp on the Canadian border?

"What should we do?" Simone said. She could hardly hear her own voice. She sounded as if she'd do anything: move to Brooklyn, be Emile's wife.

Emile's response was a rakish smile meant to convey his regret that Simone was hardly the only woman now turning to him for assistance. And though she might suppose that this fact was immigration-connected, actually it was the consequence of his incredible sexual allure.

"Unfortunately . . ." Emile looked at the ground. "Your name is one of the names I will have to say I don't remember. Married? That is ridiculous! I have never heard of this woman. And if by some chance they find you, I expect you to say the same."

Emile shrugged. "Alternatively . . . I can give you the names of several of my cousins, unmarried U.S. citizens, bona fide citizens, who for a small fee you could marry now. But I cannot guarantee that this will fool the INS. The safest thing would be for you to go back to Haiti. Fortunately, I have a cousin who is a travel agent in Brooklyn."

Simone glanced back at the house; there was no one at the windows. "Would you like a cup of coffee?" she said.

Some insane, hospitable instinct was asserting itself against Simone's common sense. What would she do if Emile said yes? How would she explain him to Rosemary?

"Better not to," said Emile. "Good luck to you now. Okay, now. Goodbye. We will not be in touch, I hope."

Emile stumbled back to his cab; he got in and turned it around and waved as he pulled away. Watching him, Simone felt a sinking sensation down inside in her chest, as if a tiny elevator had plummeted from her neck to her stomach.

Just then Rosemary came hurrying outside. "Simone, who was that? Who was that man in the cab?"

"That was my husband," answered Simone.

"Your husband?" Rosemary repeated. "Why didn't he stay for lunch? Why didn't you invite him in?" Then she laughed. "Oh well. Who am *I* to talk? I am hardly a shining example of wifely hospitality. God knows what I would do or say if Geoffrey treated me like I treat him."

SIMONE LAY AWAKE all night, puzzling out a plan. Alternatives rose before her and popped and dissolved in air. Nothing seemed more practical or likely than anything else. She buried her head in the pillow to keep from hearing Maisie's soft snoring. She would not let herself be fooled into going to watch the children sleep.

Just before daybreak she found herself thinking of her trip to Connecticut and in particular of Kenny's little speech about wanting the little house and the little wife. And as the dawn performed its daily trick of making the hopeless seem almost possible, Simone wondered if perhaps she couldn't marry Kenny. Kenny needed a house and a wife, Simone needed citizenship. It would certainly be a toehold from which to fight deportation. What could she lose by trying, and wasn't it worth the attempt?

Of course Simone knew perfectly well that it wasn't a viable plan. Even if she carried it off, something would go wrong. She didn't believe in marrying for anything but love, but that might be one of those principles that had never proved very useful. Nor did she have the faintest idea how to get Kenny to marry her—she didn't even know if he was attracted to her or not. How many women did he drive to Connecticut, dropping hints along the way that he would like to be with them if he wasn't with Shelly? It was never a hopeful sign when a man said you were too good for him, but surely she could show him that she could be bad, too. Maybe *Kenny* was the virtuous one, loyal and faithful to Shelly, camouflaging it jokingly as paranoia and

fear. When the truth came out about Shelly deceiving him
with Geoffrey, Kenny would be thankful that he had de-
ceived her with Simone.

Simone's feelings for Kenny were for the moment beside
the point. The whole thing was less frightening if she ig-
nored that part completely. First she had to get through the
intermediate phases. She saw the path in front of her like
the steps in a cookbook. Kenny was a romantic and would
balk at a match of convenience. Kenny would only marry
for love, or at least desire, and Simone's job was to inspire
in him one or the other or both. Other girls knew how to
manipulate men, to make men do what they wanted. These
girls had learned to give signals. Had Simone missed that
lesson? She had never needed to show Joseph she was
available; it was always so painfully clear he could have
her if he wanted.

Simone got out of bed, then stopped and covered her
face with her hands. She was extremely conscious of how
theatrical she must look, of how odd it was for her to strike
a pose like a woman in a painting. If she stood there a minute more, she felt she might never move. She would never
get the courage to do what had to be done; it would be simpler in Kenny's house than in his salon. She had to go to
Kenny's before she lost her nerve. She had time to get
there. He never went to work until noon.

She took a long shower and put on clean underwear,
stockings, perfume, the dress she'd worn to the wedding.
Hadn't Kenny said she'd looked like a high-class Caribbean
whore? Perhaps she could rely on the dress to make her in-
tentions clear. Unhelpful, morale-sapping images kept
creeping into her consciousness, descriptions and illustra-
tions from the human sacrifice book: brave girls bejeweled
and anointed en route to the pyramids and the pits.

It was not yet nine when Simone drove to Kenny's
house. How far she had come since that first day the children had steered her to Short Eyes! Now she bought a map
at a gas station and thought about directions and located the
route they'd taken back from Connecticut. Her fear of los-

ing the children forever enabled her to do this without them, to simply drive to Kenny's without getting lost.

Kenny's car was in his driveway. Simone sat in Rosemary's Volvo, thinking of Kenny waiting outside his Spanish teacher's apartment. And this time what she told herself was: Kenny will understand.

Simone knocked softly on the door, then louder. After a long time Kenny answered: yawning, unshaven, sallow. He wore only a wrinkled white T-shirt and baggy white Jockey shorts. In the frosty morning light his arms and legs looked blue.

Simone's eyes fixed on Kenny's. There was nowhere else to look. Yet even with her staring at him it took Kenny ages to focus. Finally he said, "Simone! Jesus Christ! What the fuck are you doing here in the middle of the night? Well, come in." He turned his back, and she followed him into the house.

The interior was wildly at odds with the house's façade. For if the neat vinyl siding suggested a tidy elderly couple, inside the couple's teenage son had stuffed his parents in a closet and gone hog-wild according to the lights of his bad-boy aesthetic. The dividing walls had been removed to make one room. On the floor in a corner was the giant rumpled mattress from which Kenny had just risen. Above it a large poster matched each astrological sign with the silhouette of a man and woman in a different sexual position. Nearby was a wall of bubbling lava lamps and an immense TV. Zebra rugs and neon-colored pillows were artfully scattered about.

Even in his stupefied state Kenny couldn't stifle the urge to explain how the look of his house expressed him. "Shelly did it, needless to say. But I have to admit I dig it. The sixties astrology fuck poster is a period classic. We spent a fortune making this place look like some sleazo bachelor pad. Rock Hudson meets Jimmy Dean—if both of them were straight. Isn't it weird how many popular sex symbols turn out to be fags? Doesn't this seem to indicate that chicks don't really like guys?"

How disheartening, thought Simone, to see Shelly's hand in every male habitation. How many men were installed somewhere amid Shelly's fantasies?

Kenny went into the kitchen and took down a can of espresso and then—very violently, shockingly—slammed the cabinet door. Almost at once he seemed to forget whatever had made him do it and began to whistle a meandering, genial tune.

"Want some java?" he asked Simone, who was still resonating with the slammed cupboard and could barely shake her head yes.

Kenny filled the automatic coffeepot and flipped on the switch and glared as if to intimidate it into bubbling and perking. But the coffee machine would not be bullied and showed no signs of life. Finally Kenny ripped off the brown plastic strainer and flung it into the sink, spraying tarry coffee grounds all over the counter and floor.

"I cannot handle this," he said. "I cannot fake being the kind of hospitable asshole who gets up at the crack of dawn and makes breakfast for the guests."

"I'm sorry," Simone said. "I thought you would be awake. I would never have come here if—"

Something about this must have touched Kenny, because he turned and gently laid his palm along the side of Simone's face. When he let go, he regarded her strangely.

"Jesus." He swabbed at her temple. "I got coffee grounds on your cheek."

While Simone was rubbing her face Kenny said, "I need a shower and shave. Then I'll be back on line. You can keep me company while I perform my morning toilette."

Beckoning for Simone to follow, Kenny walked into the bathroom. Simone took several deep breaths to steady herself and then took a couple more. Well, this would make things easier. This was going according to plan. Kenny was taking off his clothes, saying: Go ahead. Seduce me.

But Simone stayed in the living room, pacing and stopping and pacing, decorously avoiding the astrology poster on which twelve couples contorted themselves into pretzels of bliss. By the time she got to the bathroom Kenny was out of the shower and was shaving at the mirror, with a towel around his waist.

Simone hesitated in the doorway; it required an enormous effort of will to get farther into the room. Instead of sitting on the closed toilet lid that Kenny graciously offered, she went and stood behind Kenny, between Kenny and the tub. The bathroom was tiled in rough pumice squares of a subdued sooty gray that despite the warm steam gave the room a cool wintry aura.

Kenny wiped the foggy mirror, which clouded over again. "Go fuck yourself," he told it. He cleared a circle in which he and Simone appeared, her face behind his shoulder.

Even covered with shaving foam, Kenny was recognizably Kenny, but the face behind him only faintly resembled Simone's. She saw herself grown older, her flesh pouched, hanging from the bone, gums shrunk from her grinning teeth. She thought of George in the bathroom in the dark, saying Bloody Mary Bloody Mary Bloody Mary. The children thought it was magic to make something bad appear in the mirror, but adults knew it was ordinary: your own face in a bad light.

Simone couldn't imagine what was going through Kenny's mind. It seemed to her that they both understood that this was a critical juncture. Unless something happened now, the moment would pass and never return. Simone would sit down on the edge of the tub and prattle about something casual, and Kenny would dress and they would talk and just go on being friendly.

What was needed was some gesture, impossible to mistake. There was a physical but invisible line Simone must cross toward Kenny's back, and once she was on the other side, it could only mean sex. Why couldn't Kenny cross that line, why couldn't he turn and embrace her? She had been crazy to imagine that this was a practical plan; that sex, if they had it, would lead to marriage and to her staying in the United States.

In convent school the sisters had skipped the story of Samson and Delilah, glossed over those chapters and verses and gone on to something else. The girls had believed that the fuss about Samson's hair embarrassed the bald nuns. Now Simone wished she had studied the story as a possible source of directions to follow at awkward moments like this, when seduction was required.

Simone put her hand on Kenny's shoulder. His skin was dewy and soft. Kenny gave no sign of noticing. He looked in the mirror and went on shaving. Simone's hand weighed heavier on him, like a paw or some kind of chop. Why couldn't he reach back and take it?

They couldn't remain like this very long, some action would have to be taken. Simone would have to give up or take the next step. Really, she should let it go. Kenny had had his chance. If he was attracted to her he would already have responded.

Simone leaned forward from the waist, her breasts almost brushing Kenny. The front of her dress was wet with blotches of water from Kenny's back. The skin of their shoulders stuck and made a sucking noise when she moved.

Soon her dress was uncomfortably damp. It was better to ignore it. She was glad she couldn't see herself. How ashamed she would be—an alley cat in a party dress rubbing up against a man in a towel.

Finally Kenny took her hand. Simone waited to see what he would do next. He turned and, still holding Simone's hand, steered her around to face him.

Smiling crookedly, Kenny said, "I make it a matter of policy never to be in a small enclosed space with a chick and an open razor blade." He meant for Simone to laugh with him, and she made a sincere attempt.

"Come on." Kenny rinsed his face and went into the other room.

Simone felt very awkward, all alone in the bathroom, but still she delayed a moment, as Kenny assumed she would. By the time she walked into the main room he'd put on a

pair of blue jeans. To Simone the sight of them was a re-
proach and a humiliation.

This time Simone sat obediently where Kenny indicated
she should—perched awkwardly, her knees to her chin, on
the edge of the mattress. The sheets matched the bathroom,
charcoal gray with a thin white pinstripe; the bottom of the
sheet had pulled away, revealing a black leather pad.

"My biker futon," Kenny explained. "Cultural contradic-
tion."

Kenny was busy at the mirror, lovingly slicking back his
hair with an antique mother-of-pearl comb-and-brush set.
"Check out the grooming equipment. Straight from the
dressertop of Al Capone or some other dapper kingpin of
twenties organized crime."

Kenny frowned into the mirror. "Getting my hair cut
drives me nuts! I go to this chick named Vicky in New-
burgh, I know her from the city. Every time I look in the
mirror I see what she didn't get right, and I keep going
back and making her fix it. I tell her it's not a haircut, it's
a three-day ordeal. What's frustrating is, I wish I could do
it myself. Lots of guys are like that. If we could give ourselves blowjobs it might be the end of our social life."

Simone thought of Kenny's story about getting a hard-on
passing his house. How stupid she'd been not to realize that
he was warning her. He'd said it for the same reason that
a married man might mention his wife. Once again she'd
gotten it wrong, misinterpreted completely. She'd selec-
tively heard the part about his high-school Spanish teacher
and had thought that he would have sympathy for her having the nerve to come here. In fact, he had only contempt
for her pitiable attempt to seduce him into cheating on the
important thing—his love affair with himself.

Simone's spirit ebbed so dramatically that Kenny must
have sensed it. He came over and sat on the edge of the
bed and kissed her on the mouth.

That was a relief, of sorts. Kissing was like hiding. At
least Simone knew what to do and did not have to decide
every minute. She could move her lips against Kenny's and

not be expected to talk. Comfort overwhelmed her, so liquid and accommodating it felt very much like desire.

Kenny said, "I just put gel on my hair. Do you know what it'll do to these sheets?"

Even now, even after this, Simone was ready to keep on kissing, but Kenny drew back and touched her shoulder and lightly pushed her away. He said, "This is blowing me away. I mean: I am a shithead, but not enough of a shithead to be pulling something like this on you."

The gathering weight of their kisses had angled them toward the horizontal, but now they sprang up and sat side by side as if they were watching TV. Kenny took Simone's hand and turned her toward him again and, hugging her warmly, said, "You *know* not to take this personally. It is not a personal thing. I like you as a person, Simone. And it's not an AIDS thing, either. I mean, I don't even know: is AIDS still a Haitian thing?"

How was Simone supposed to answer? Many Haitian people were sick, though she had read in a magazine that Haitians in this country were once again allowed to give blood. But none of this would exactly rekindle—or kindle—Kenny's desire.

Kenny said, "Babe, I *meant* it when I said that women who aren't bitches don't turn me on. I need women to see what I see, how fucking horrible everything is, and when I see them trying to be nice and maintain a positive attitude, I just want to be out of there. I know most guys are the opposite, they *like* their bimbos happy. It's part of how totally dishonest things are between guys and women. Guys dig brain-dead chicks telling them life's great. But girls like that just turn me off—I'm not saying *you're* one.

"Oh, you know what I mean, Simone. You're just not a total cunt. And to tell the truth, I don't understand how you can be wasting yourself on this fucked-up Hudson Landing scene. If I were you, if I looked like you, I would be history.

"What amazes me is how many chicks actually *have* that good attitude—when you stop and consider the shit they go through daily. I myself used to be really bad. Sometimes things would happen like today, I'd be fooling around with a woman and I would let it get so far that the chick and I would be naked, and I would tell her I couldn't do it, it wasn't happening between us. That was really lousy—I'm much better about that now."

Simone was struck by how often men tried to comfort you by making you feel part of a group of women they had personally tormented. Relax, they said, you had company—it wasn't only you. The women Kenny stopped kissing, the women Geoffrey had sworn off, the wives whom Emile had parked all over Brooklyn and upstate New York. How could anyone think it consoled you—membership in this group?

Kenny got up and went to the bureau and pulled a white T-shirt over his head. His face reappeared with the guileless, washed-clean grin of a kid. He said, "Let's just erase what happened today. We can rewind the tape and rerecord over what went down."

He put on his socks and high-top black sneakers. He got his jacket and car keys: Simone's signal to leave.

He said, "Christmas dinner at Rosemary's could be a fairly insane proposition."

EVERYONE SEEMED TO understand that this was a dangerous season. In one magazine a panel of ministers and psychologists sagely advised their readers on how to prevent holiday dynamite from detonating in their lives. A psychiatrist described past grievances and hurts as destructive presents family members bring to family occasions. The secret, he said, was learning to leave those explosive packages home.

Every culture, thought Simone, had its unhealthy times. Haitians feared certain saints' eves and nights of the full moon and, more recently, election eves and days after demonstrations. The Mayas, she'd read, had periods when no one left the house. How safe it would be to live like that, everyone knowing the risks. If you forgot and started out the door, someone was sure to stop you.

Despite the magazines that Simone left scattered around to warn her, Rosemary blithely insisted that, for Maisie and George, Christmas Eve at their father's and Christmas Day at home would simply double their portion of holiday joy. But perhaps she, too, secretly realized that Christmas was mined for disaster. Why else did she keep complaining about how the Holy Nativity provided no preparation or guidance for this era of child support and split-custody arrangements? She said, "Maybe the myth would still apply if the Church acknowledged its complications—as a parenting situation, Mary and Joseph and God were genuinely avant-garde. But instead of admitting this, they keep trying to convince us that Mary, Joseph, and Jesus were the parthenogenetic *Father Knows Best.*"

As she ransacked the attic for the Christmas decorations that she was becoming increasingly, hysterically certain Geoffrey must have taken, Rosemary seemed more than ever like a newly hatched creature, a feathery duckling emerging from the sticky fur of her mouton coat. It was painful to watch her ripping open boxes, searching for lights and baubles that had been in the family for ages. Each year, she said, Geoffrey had supervised the children in the hanging of the ornaments with an anal-compulsive methodicalness that precluded creativity or fun and so reminded Rosemary of Geoffrey's mother that there were several Christmas Eves when she'd run screaming from the house.

Near the eyeless colonial paintings was a large portrait of a matronly woman in long gloves and an evening gown. Could she have been Geoffrey's mother? It was hard to tell—the portrait had been turned upside down and its eyes had been cut out. Simone could hardly believe that only one short season had passed since that hot afternoon she first came up here with Rosemary. Those few months seemed longer than her whole life up until now.

Puffs of mildew wafted up as Rosemary tore through a steamer trunk. She said, "I paid my dues in this attic. When the children were little and they'd nap, I'd come up here and look through the stuff. That is how I got to know how sick these people were. The unspeakable things they stashed for someone to find after they were gone—human-hair wreaths, slices of wedding cake under glass, the handkerchief that Uncle Ebenezer spit up into on his deathbed. Of course they never imagined they'd ever die—otherwise, how could they have kept it?

"I was fascinated, I'd spend hours here, very voyeuristic. I see now that it was the closest I came to a creative state. Then one day I woke up and realized that seven years had gone by.

"My first idea was to make junk sculpture from the

things in the house. But I knew that getting Geoffrey to part with one tiny scrap would be like convincing him to donate a testicle to science. I can't imagine who I was before I did my art, when my entire existence was this house and the children, and I hunkered here like a monkey, pawing through someone else's stuff."

As always, it surprised Simone that Rosemary had a past here, that she and the children were not parachuted in to coincide with Simone's arrival. It was so hard to even imagine the life they led before she came. And yet now she heard, in Rosemary's voice, nostalgia, even grief, a longing for those seven years she claimed to have spent in this attic. She was mourning the person she used to be when George and Maisie were little; she wanted back her life and the layer of skin we shed in every house we spend time in.

Only now did Simone understand that Rosemary's taking her here that first day had not been some casual *pro forma* house tour. Rosemary was showing her where she lived, territory staked out by those years. But the mood in which she had shown her around was nothing, nothing like now. Then she had been rattled, dithery, falsely efficient, and brittle. Now she seemed at once mushy, irresolute, and driven, and when she gave up searching for the Christmas ornaments, she hid her face and wept.

Simone looked on helplessly, wanting to tell Rosemary how sad and beautiful everything seemed on her last day in Port-au-Prince, the vigilance it took not to fall in love with everything she was leaving: goodbye bougainvillea, goodbye desk, goodbye bed, goodbye street, goodbye café where Joseph took Simone and later took Inez. Then somehow she might gently hint that Rosemary might be leaving here, too. Simone could still hear Shelly asking, "Have you seen that attic?"

For days Simone had been fighting the urge to warn Rosemary about Shelly, to shock her out of the ignorance that struck her as willed and a little maddening. At moments it seemed possible that if Rosemary knew what was coming, together she and Simone and the children might somehow forestall it. But as Simone watched Rosemary weep helplessly over the misplaced Christmas ornaments she understood that telling her would only hasten the inevitable.

"Ho ho ho, Merry Christmas," Geoffrey said in a rolling baritone. He looked very different in the cottony white stick-on eyebrows and beard, but Simone peered through the Santa disguise to the familiar unreadable Geoffrey. This was the first time they had been face to face since that day in the jeep with Shelly, and it went without saying, it was understood: they would never discuss it.

Maisie giggled appreciatively. George said, "Oh, outstanding," then reconsidered and smirked and blushed, embarrassed for his father.

"How was the traffic?" asked Geoffrey. "Mobs of Christmas Eve partygoers hitting the road after their seventeenth eggnog?"

"It was all right," said Simone.

Geoffrey said, "In a couple of hours those roads will be demo derby."

Simone didn't reply. She was remembering how Kenny had described Geoffrey's face as working in two halves, the half that felt entitled to tell you what was real and what wasn't, and the other half always checking to see whether you believed him. But Simone hadn't met Geoffrey yet, so Kenny's description made no sense; the face she had pictured when he'd said that was, she realized now, Joseph's.

Now at least she could stop resisting what everyone said about Geoffrey. He was not, after all, a nice man at a difficult point in his life. He was a man who could sleep with his wife's best friend and make his children keep it secret. It was always a mistake to ignore such a wide range of warnings, when everything you saw or heard advised you to watch out. Hadn't there been signs everywhere that she should never have trusted Joseph?

"Hang on," Geoffrey told Simone. From his desk he took a small rectangular package wrapped in olive-green paper.

"Merry Christmas." Geoffrey kissed Simone clumsily on the cheek.

Inside the box was a necklace of delicate silver ovals, each containing a miniature sunset—an iridescent pink-and-blue sky behind black silhouetted palm trees. Light winked off the pearly clouds so they appeared to be shifting. Simone felt sad and inadequate, as she often did at sunset: the compulsion to keep looking, the sense of not taking in enough, the pressure of knowing how quickly it would all disappear.

"Like it?" said Geoffrey. "It's 1940s, I think. I hope it isn't tourist crap you used to see all over Haiti."

Simone was amazingly pleased that Geoffrey had got her a present. What moved her was that he'd gone to a shop, to a case of jewelry, and that—who cared how obvious it was?—the tropical scene made him think of her. That she had been on Geoffrey's mind was evidence she existed. It made her catch her breath to imagine him picking up the necklace and picturing it against the skin at the base of her throat. Even now, despite everything, she was gratified and deeply happy that his thoughts had, however briefly, lingered on her.

"Thank you," Simone said. "I'm sorry. I didn't get you—"

Geoffrey said, "No problem."

A certain wariness in his voice made Simone pause and wonder if what he'd been thinking about was not the necklace against her throat but the appropriate gift for someone who knew he was sleeping with Shelly. Was it affection and concern—or bribery, buying her silence? One depressing possibility was that Shelly had bought the necklace, which, Simone suddenly noted, repeated the tropical motif of the asparagus plates at Shelly's dinner. Her face prickled astringently with shame at how flattered she'd been. She knew she would feel even worse if she allowed herself to remember how she used to imagine asking Geoffrey to help solve her problems with Immigration. Anything she asked Geoffrey now would necessarily involve Shelly; she might as well have stayed in Haiti and put her fate in the tiny hands of Bill Webb.

Geoffrey said, "Shelly's in Memphis this week."

"I know," said Simone. "Rosemary invited her for Christmas dinner." Once more Simone had the sense of having blurted out too much, that the smallest detail of Rosemary's life was classified information. Simone had been glad to hear that Shelly would be away, even though it meant Kenny would be Rosemary's only guest.

Geoffrey was reassuring her that Shelly was out of town—the children wouldn't be spending Christmas Eve in the adulterous snake pit he shared with their mother's best friend. But given their unspoken agreement that nothing untoward had happened, it was just peculiar for him to bring up Shelly's holiday plans.

Geoffrey said, "Jesus Christ, why am I telling you this? You're not a judge, Simone. You're not my mother."

He hesitated momentarily, which was in itself endearing, that a man would stop and consider what he was about to say to her next. He said, "You can't imagine what it's like to be a male. Every little temptation is an invitation to redesign our whole lives and a huge chance to disappoint ourselves by not having the guts to do it. Every choice feels like a crossroads with cops and barbed wire and barricades, a cop with a grinning skull for a face, the face of your own death, and it's always a question of whether to stop or crash on through . . ."

Simone let Geoffrey ramble on. This was not the time to point out that he had told her this before. It was more or less what he'd said that first day at the Tepee Diner. She had to admit that now, as then, it was touching and seductive. But this time it saddened her—and it wasn't just hearing it twice. Though Geoffrey seemed to be stating a fact, in fact he was making a request, asking her to save him from something that no one could be saved from. He was asking her a question without any answer, but still he expected her to know and would blame her for not knowing. Geoffrey was so much like George, bringing Simone his

nightmares and wanting her to promise that they would
never come true.

Geoffrey sighed. "Speaking of cops and crossroads, be
careful on the drive home. You do not want to know what's
out on those roads tonight. Will you listen to me, for God's
sake? I've been drinking since lunch, or whatever that meal
was, and I'm scaring you about drunk drivers. Don't
women get sick of men telling them to watch out for men
just like them?"

In fact, the roads on the drive back home were curiously
deserted. Simone felt like a surfer riding a quiet swell between crashing waves of partygoers separating from their
friends. She could tell from the clumps of parked cars that
there were only a couple of parties. Even so, many houses
were brightly lit, and Simone slowed down and looked
through the windows at the silver Christmas trees and electric candelabra that told her so much, but only so much,
about the lives lived inside.

But what could a stranger tell from looking in Rosemary's windows this evening and seeing Simone and Rosemary drinking eggnog and watching TV? Rosemary had
promised that they would consume tons of eggnog and trim
the Christmas tree and watch Alastair Sim in *A Christmas
Carol* on a videotape they would rent from the store where
Geoffrey was so well known.

Rosemary had said, "*A Christmas Carol*'s the trade-off
for not having George and Maisie. You can never get children to watch anything good or old or uncolorized black-
and-white. I'm sure there'll be no problem with it being
rented. The big demand is for *Slasher Santa* and *Rambo
Saves Christmas, Part Three*."

Now, turning into the driveway, Simone could only hope
that Rosemary would not be hitting some new crescendo of
disaster. She was thinking about the time she had danced
with Geoffrey and come home to find Rosemary gasping
for breath, and though she knew the two things weren't
causally related, she was very aware of Geoffrey's necklace

hidden in her purse. It was almost as if she could hear it ticking away · like a bomb. If a dance had wrought that much havoc—who knew what a necklace could do? She could never tell Rosemary that she had got a present from Geoffrey. If she ever wore it, she would have to lie.

Simone had a vision of Christmas Eve in a hospital waiting room, observing firsthand the carnage created by holiday dynamite detonating in American lives. She knew this fear was just disguised guilt for her pleasure in Geoffrey's gift, but in Haiti, voodoo proved daily the wonders that guilt and fear could accomplish. She had gone back to being happy for having got the present; at this distance the fact of it was more real than any potential connection with Shelly.

Prepared for all manner of hellish scenes, Simone gingerly entered the house. In one corner of the living room a small, rather lopsided fir tree grew from a foil-covered pot. In the kitchen Rosemary, perfectly in control, was separating eggs for eggnog and holding forth about salmonella.

"Every egg a health threat! What's truly sick is this culture." Rosemary juggled the yolk between shells, letting the slimy gel loop down and catching it at the last moment. "This could be a pleasure, a very Zen thing to do, but I keep thinking that I should be able to look at the eggs and see the teensy spirochetes wriggling around or whatever. You can't even have Christmas Eve without wondering which doctor's on call. I'm proceeding on the theory that enough rum will kill anything bad."

Rosemary vigorously whipped the cream with an old-fashioned rotary beater that shot shrapnel flecks of red paint into the stiffening peaks. "You'll like this, Simone. It's the New England piña colada. Like something I imagine being served in Port-au-Prince. If only we'd gone there instead of trying to tough out Christmas up here. I realize that Haiti is no longer the vacation paradise it was. The other day, in the bookstore, I was skimming a travel guide to the Caribbean, reading about all the idyllic places the children and I aren't going. I noticed that the Haiti entry was three-quarters of a page. They reprinted the state department advisory and let that speak for itself."

Rosemary talked about Haiti just as she had when Simone first came to work here. She had learned nothing, nothing at all about Simone's country. But Simone couldn't blame her; she had never tried to teach her. Miss McCaffrey used to quiz Simone about every aspect of Haitian life, and Simone tried to provide thoughtful answers to even the silliest questions. With Rosemary it was different—you gave up on her before you started. Only Geoffrey had tried to tell Rosemary a lot of truth very fast, but he had only hate in his heart, and he had gone way too far.

As Rosemary mixed the eggs and rum and cream in a huge cut-glass punch bowl, Simone thought uneasily of the necklace in its box. Rosemary said, "It looks like this recipe was for a hard-drinking party of twenty. We've got our work cut out for us, Simone. I suppose we'd better get started."

She ladled Simone's glass full of lumpy liquid that separated into a cloudy brownish fluid with pods of yellow cream floating on top. Simone held the cream back with her teeth and strained the rum from underneath it.

"Drink the eggnog part," ordered Rosemary. "It's a Christmas present for your arteries. Though Christmas isn't the time for dreary subjects like arterial circulation. Come into the living room and see my brilliant idea—the remarkable *objet* I found for decorating the tree."

On the living-room floor was a crystal chandelier that appeared to have crashed there. Nervously Simone looked up; the old chandelier was still there.

"I found it in the attic," Rosemary said. "It was a stroke of genius. We unhook the crystals and fasten them on the tree, and when this baby catches the light, we get dazzled by the full megaforce of High Victorian Christmas glitter."

Lots of jangling and cursing ensued as Rosemary untangled the chandelier and unhooked the teardrop pendants.

She wielded the pliers so carelessly that she kept nipping her hand. Eventually she had a pile of crystals and tied them onto the tree. But gravity was against her; the weight of just one crystal dragged down a branch till it hung perpendicular to the ground. Under the pull of a dozen or so, the tree closed up like an umbrella. Rosemary experimented, attaching the wires at different points on the branches, but at last she removed all the crystals and the tree limbs sprang up as if the winter had ended and it had shed its great load of snow.

Rosemary said, "Well, it was a good idea. Thank heaven, we've got the chains." She went into the kitchen and came back with red-and-white ropes over her forearms: skeins for someone planning to knit a popcorn-and-cranberry sweater. "I strung the cranberries last night," she said. "From racial memory."

Rosemary looped and cast the ropes with a singular lack of direction, and the tree looked unhappy again—an evergreen in bondage with a few glass teardrops still weeping from its limbs. She said, "George and Maisie will go nuts with joy when they see this tree. Next Christmas you're going to read about this in some decorating magazine. You'll be in line at the supermarket, paging through some piece of trash, and you'll see a photo of this tree of ours, the latest tree-trimming sensation."

After they had tortured the tree to the limits of its endurance, Rosemary directed Simone's attention to how much eggnog remained. They brought the level in the punchbowl down a couple of inches. Rosemary put on *A Christmas Carol* and tossed Simone a blanket and cuddled up on the facing couch.

The screen was frosted with static from the old videotape. No amount of tracking could clear the fog from those London streets. Rosemary said, "My favorite part is the ghost of Christmas Past. Our Anglo-Protestant zombie droning on with his little lesson in business ethics . . ."

* * *

Simone must have fallen asleep. She awoke curled up on the couch. Snow drifted past the windows and on the screen of the buzzing TV.

She took one shallow breath and was on her feet and running for the bathroom. Whatever was inside her, her system wanted it out and ejected it in a series of convulsions so violent that, even in mid-attack, Simone had to admire her body's power of refusal. It was strange how little she had to do for her stomach to empty—just lean down over the toilet and brace herself against each new assault. In between spasms she observed that she was frothing at the mouth. She thought of rabies, then of epilepsy, then of Rosemary's warnings about the eggnog. Burning liquid rose up behind her nose and she choked and cried out.

Simone stayed on the bathroom floor until she thought she could stand, then washed her face and rinsed her mouth and returned to the living room. On the way she was nearly knocked down by Rosemary running past her.

By the time Rosemary got back from the bathroom Simone was sitting up, wrapped in a blanket. She had tried lying down again, but that had made her feel worse. Rosemary sat on the opposite couch, shivering in her fur coat.

"It's probably not salmonella," Rosemary said. "If it were salmonella we'd be hospitalized by now. It's probably something less serious—God knows what sort of microorganisms were living in that old punchbowl."

Simone remembered the chips of red paint that had sprinkled from the eggbeater. "Merry Christmas," said Rosemary. "In fact, it's a perfect merry Christmas. How very much in the holiday spirit to start the day off barfing."

The digital clock on the VCR was flashing 5:45. Rosemary said, "I read somewhere about digital clocks wrecking our sense of time. Digital shows us only the present minute and not the past or future. I must say, though, there are times when I *like* not seeing a clock face and confronting how far the hands must travel to get through Christmas Day."

Eleven, when the children were due home, did seem a

long time away. A bubble of nausea rose in Simone's throat but subsided on its own.

Rosemary said, "Not to worry. You are now experiencing a real American Christmas, families all over America freaking—how are they going to survive the day? The vomiting is an extra, but it's essentially the same story. I suppose we could exchange presents. That's always good for ten minutes of bliss."

Simone said, "Don't you think we should wait for George and Maisie?" She was afraid she sounded guilty, as if she were stalling for time in which to run out and buy Rosemary a last-minute present. Even though Rosemary had forbidden Simone to buy her a gift, Simone had distinctly just heard her say "exchange."

Simone went to her room and got Rosemary's present from the same drawer in which she kept her uncashed checks. When she got back, the living room was empty. Some time later she heard the toilet flush, and Rosemary returned, looking pale.

Rosemary gave Simone two presents. One seemed to be a heavy book, the other a large stone basketball, which, to judge from the crumpled gift paper, had been a challenge to wrap. Simone unwrapped it and found, as she'd feared, not a basketball at all but one of Rosemary's sculptures. Two flat breasts and a globular belly were carved into a rough pumice sphere that gently abraded Simone's fingers as she turned it over.

"*Swamp Witch Number 1,*" Rosemary said. "The first of my new series. Supposedly there is a tribe of swamp dwellers outside Damascus, I think, who believe in a race of female djinns who can roll themselves into balls and skim like phosphorescent missiles on the surface of the marshes. The phosphorescence is a problem. I've been considering neon."

"Thank you," Simone said.

"This is the first time I've given away work. I thought it would be therapeutic for me to learn to let things go." Rosemary sounded like a child shamed into sharing a favor-

ite toy, but instead of feeling irritated, Simone thought once
more of Shelly and of how much Rosemary might soon be
required to let go. Unexpected, affectionate tears welled up
in Simone's eyes.

Mistaking them, apparently, for tears of gratitude, Rosemary modestly averted her gaze and attended to Simone's
present. She gave a little cry of pleasure and wound the
scarf around her neck. But now the floral pinks and oranges
that were so pretty in Glenda's store seemed instead cruel
and mocking; they made Rosemary look like a woman who
had been vomiting since dawn.

Rosemary cried, "I'll never take it off." Simone imagined she saw a shudder disturb the fur of Rosemary's coat,
as if it knew how literally Rosemary might mean this.

"I feel so Isadora Duncan," Rosemary said. "A model
for us all. Raising those children on her own and living her
life in art. I just learned the most amazing fact. Did you
know that the woman who gave Isadora Duncan the fatal
scarf was Preston Sturges's mother? Isadora Duncan? Preston Sturges? I can never tell for certain, Simone, how much
of this cultural stuff you are getting. I assume you catch everything. Stop me if I'm wrong. But speaking of art—
Simone, you haven't opened your other present."

Simone unwrapped the heavy book. She looked at it for
a while, and before she could blink them back, more tears
came to her eyes. "My, my," she heard Rosemary say.
"What an emotional morning we're having."

The naked young woman stared out at Simone, as did
her black maid and black cat, almost as if they recognized
her, remembered watching her from Joseph's wall. Simone
struggled to recall how much she had told Rosemary. Was
it possible that in a drunken, unguarded moment she could
have mentioned this painting and what Joseph had done to
it? She'd had a few drunken moments here but none, she
believed, that unguarded.

"This book had your name on it," Rosemary said,
"though I know it says Manet. For years I've been intend-
ing to buy it for myself. But in the store, when I looked

through it, I knew it was meant for you. I assume you realize I don't mean the *Olympia*. That would be just too insulting and humiliating to *consider*."

Rosemary took the book from Simone and leafed through the pages until she found a large color reproduction of a portrait of a woman. The woman had on an ermine hat and cloak, a white gown trimmed with black lace. She wore one glove and held the other and seemed on the verge of weeping. It sent shivers up and down Simone's spine—the woman could have been her twin.

"Isn't she gorgeous?" Rosemary said. "Manet's portrait of Madame Brunet. The story is, she hated it and went storming out of his studio. She didn't think it made her look pretty, compared, I guess, to those simpy cherubs everyone was painting. But I always thought that maybe no one until then had realized that she was—wouldn't you say?—part black or Latino. And when she saw the painting she suddenly thought: Now everyone will know. Isn't she the most beautiful woman practically anyone ever painted? This feeling I'd had since I met you that I'd seen you before—I was thinking of this painting. Isn't that amazing!"

Shouldn't it have pleased Simone that a great and famous artist had thought it worth his while to paint a woman who looked like her? In fact, it made her feel diminished, robbed of herself, reduced to one of many: it was how she'd felt when Kenny tried to comfort her by mentioning all the other women he'd hurt.

Rosemary said, "Isn't it fascinating to know that people just like us existed before?"

Simone shut the book and turned its cover to face Rosemary. She said, "My fiancé had a copy of this painting on his studio wall." It was the one true detail she had revealed about her past since she had come to this country. She caught herself and with a sharp intake of breath sank down on the couch.

"I'm not surprised," Rosemary said. "*Olympia* is the most famous naked girl in the history of art. One can hardly imagine the scandal this innocent creature created—

more than you could generate these days with public live sex with a donkey. Then the feminists got hold of it with all that blather about female self-determination, when you only have to look at it to see that poor girl's scared to death."

"He mutilated it," said Simone. "He painted slashes and blood and dirt all over the woman's body. He made it look as if she'd had her throat cut and her breasts sliced off."

"My goodness!" exclaimed Rosemary. "Why did he do that?"

"He hates white people," Simone said. "Especially white women. Especially colonial white girls with black mammies and black cats." She simply wanted Rosemary to know that there were people who had such feelings. It was a little like wanting to warn Rosemary about Shelly, the urge to protect combined with the urge to shake her and force her to look. Willed innocence did that to you, it made you want to stomp it, or maybe it was real innocence and what you wanted was to corrupt.

Rosemary said, "That's ridiculous. I mean, I can see his point. But it would have scared the hell out of me. If I'd caught my fiancé defacing a painting of, I don't know, a *black* woman, a green woman, I don't care what color woman, I would have been out of there in two seconds flat. Though I'm not exactly the expert on self-protection or survival, or even on jumping ship before the whole thing goes down in flames. But I would rather have had a husband fucking the entire video store than a fiancé slashing master paintings of reclining female nudes."

Simone noted how neatly Rosemary had transformed this into a contest over which of them had had to put up with the most terrible man. But if it were a contest, how easily Simone could win, stunning Rosemary into surrender with the truth about Geoffrey and Shelly. *Then* she and Rosemary could decide who had chosen the worse man. Which was crueler: a man who slept with your best friend and let your children know or a man who defaced a painting . . . Or a man who defaced a painting *and* slept with your best

friend? There was no reason to tell Rosemary the part about
Inez. It would not console Simone that she and Rosemary
had this in common, that they had both lost their men to
their so-called good friends.

"But listen," Rosemary was saying. "Listen to the way
women talk to each other. Always in competition over who
has the best man. Or the worst man. Trying to sound as if
we have a good deal and are luckier than our friends, or alternatively as if we have a bad deal and are suffering more.
It drives me crazy when Shelly does it, but I know I'm just
as bad."

After that there was nothing that either of them felt like
saying. Simone lay down and rolled over and must have
fallen asleep again. Because the next thing she knew, Rosemary was waking her and asking if she felt capable of
meeting the children at the end of the driveway.

Rosemary said, "In the highly unlikely event that their
father brings them on schedule, we should be seeing their
bright little faces in about fifteen minutes."

THE CHILDREN WERE walking up the driveway by the time Simone reached them. She was struck by a sharp, humbling pang of loss at having missed seeing Geoffrey. The children looked like two little tots in one of Maisie's fairy-tale books, bravely trudging toward the hut of the witch with the recipe for baked children. George was focused on his boots. Maisie squinted up at the trees. Neither of them saw Simone till they had almost run into her. Then they seemed to make a point of not smiling or wishing her Merry Christmas, of calculatedly pouting and sulking and making sure she noticed. "How was Christmas Eve?" Simone asked.

Maisie said, "Fine."

"What did you eat?" said Simone.

George and Maisie glanced at each other as if to confirm some vow of silence or pact that George, predictably, would have more trouble keeping. "Roast beef," he said.

"At the diner?" Simone asked.

"No," George said. "At Dad's. We had sweet potato timbales."

Simone had only the dimmest idea of what timbales were, except for an absolute certainty that they were code for "Shelly." Did George know she would know this? Was he trying to tell her? It was not beyond Geoffrey or Shelly to pretend that Shelly was in Memphis. Perhaps this was the reason for the children's grim reserve. They couldn't even tell Simone that Shelly had cooked Christmas Eve dinner. But why were they blaming her for what they couldn't say?

"If you had been home," Simone said, "we could have had carrot sticks and frozen fried shrimp." She had reached the point of being able to tease the children about their peculiar food tastes. But now the children were miles away, unreachable through charm. Maisie narrowed her eyes at Simone.

Each child carried a shopping bag full of toys and scraps of wrapping. "What did you get?" Simone said.

"Stuff," said George. "We left most of it at my dad's."

Simone put her arm around Maisie's shoulders. Maisie wrenched away.

"What's wrong?" Simone asked.

"Nothing," said Maisie.

"Nothing," echoed George.

They continued in silence, and as the house loomed up before them, Simone felt progressively more gloomy. Once they were inside, she felt, there would be no hope of resolution, of discovering the trouble and even perhaps the cure.

They were still a good distance from the house when Rosemary ran out of the door and knelt in the driveway and gathered George and Maisie in her arms. Simone watched the hem of her mouton coat sopping up the wet snow.

"Merry Christmas! Merry Christmas!" Rosemary cried, squeezing Maisie around the waist. Maisie went limp and drooped her head and dangled her hands in the air.

In the entrance hall Rosemary again threw herself on the children, chafing their little bodies while trying to help them with their coats. George and Maisie gently fended her off; she was making undressing harder. At one point there was a brief tug-of-war over who would remove George's boots.

The warm house smelled invitingly of cinnamon and turkey. Rosemary must have been cooking while Simone was asleep.

Rosemary said, "I am afraid to ask what George and Maisie got for Christmas—what expensive and dangerous items their father is seducing them with now. Wait, let me guess. State-of-the-art computers, murderous off-road vehicles last seen on *60 Minutes*, matching snowmobiles, and a week in a private suite at the best hotel in Disneyland."

George took a book from his shopping bag.

"People of the Igloo." Rosemary read the title and pretended to stagger under the weight of the massive book. "I love it. An over-produced coffee-table extravaganza full of photogenic starving people. No doubt it omits the part about the alcoholism and the gonorrhea that were never a problem until we went up and showed them how. I hate to think what evil agenda is being signaled here. Is Geoffrey planning to kidnap the children and spirit them off to Anchorage? Why can't I imagine him in a place with twenty-four hours of winter darkness? Perhaps he thinks that lending house-guests your wife is still a popular Eskimo custom."

All this floated past George and Simone, who were focused on each other; she could tell he held her accountable for the appropriateness of his present. Keeping secret his Eskimo inner life had been his test for Simone, and once more she had failed it. After this, his expression said, there would not be another chance.

What excuse could Simone make that would smooth everything over? She hadn't told Geoffrey that George compulsively watched a videotape about drinking fresh seal blood and eating raw animal blubber. She had just said that George was interested in Eskimos. Of the secrets being concealed, it seemed so unimportant. But it was the one that, from the start, George had made clear he wanted kept. Who cared if he was angry at her, this spoiled American child? Now she was hearing Joseph's voice, and she shook her head to dislodge it.

Maisie reached into her shopping bag and eased out a toy—a bright plastic daisy with sunglasses and a saxophone growing out of a plastic pot.

"Oh, I've seen those in the mall! They're fabulous,"

Rosemary said. "George, quick, get the radio! Tune it to one of those stations that play disco Christmas songs!"

George fiddled with the radio dial until he found the right station and soon the plastic flower was wailing on its sax and gyrating to the bass.

"Magic!" pronounced Rosemary. "Goddamn Geoffrey. He always had a great eye."

While Simone and George and Rosemary watched the flower dance, Maisie glared at Simone. George said, "Dad said he heard Maisie was burying light bulbs. He said this could be a flower dancing on a light bulb's grave or, if you believed in it, a light bulb reincarnated as a flower."

"Fascinating," sneered Rosemary. "Fascinating and poetic. Needless to say"—breaking off in mid-sentence, she went into the living room, obliging the others to follow—"your presents from your mother are by comparison pitifully tedious."

When they saw the tree, the children slumped, their faces slack with grief and defeat.

"I know it's not many presents," Rosemary said. "I know it's a giant letdown after your dad's materialist extravaganza. But at least I tried to get you stuff to carry with you all your life."

Maisie opened her presents from Rosemary. "Art supplies," she murmured.

"Good," said George. "Thank you."

Rosemary said, "I know it's hard for you to understand, but it's the greatest gift I can give you. My hope for the both of you is that you do become artists. It gives you a kind of pleasure that nothing else comes near. I also hope it will someday cause you to look back and understand and in retrospect feel more sympathy for your poor old brain-damaged mother."

Simone felt a mean, competitive pleasure: they'd opened Rosemary's gifts first. Now hers might seem, by comparison, marginally more exciting. George examined the knife suspiciously. "Is this for me?" he said, and when Simone

nodded, a grin lit up his face. Maisie seemed bewildered by
the hideous aqueous lamp.

"Plug Simone's lamp in," Rosemary said.

Maisie said, "I will. Later."

Silently they watched George struggle to pry the blade
out of his knife, rotating it and picking at it and making impatient, frustrated faces. Humiliated, he gave up and asked
Rosemary to open it for him. Rosemary got the blade out
and gave a little scream. She said, "God in heaven, be careful! You could cut your hand off with this!" She pushed the
blade in and gave it to George, who hastily put it aside.

"Say thank you," Rosemary prompted.

"Thank you," the children chorused.

"We have presents for you," George said.

Maisie said, "No, we don't." George shot Maisie an anxious, questioning glance, looking for direction.

Finally Rosemary said, "I can see there's an issue here I
wouldn't touch on Christmas Day at the end of a ten-foot
pole. God knows, the occasion is loaded enough without
pursuing the question of whether or not you got me and
Simone presents. If you *do* have gifts for us, and we're not
expecting you to, you can give them to us any time all day,
when the spirit moves you, or tomorrow or later in the
week, next year, we don't care. Gift-giving should be like
that, spontaneous and unscheduled.

"Speaking of which . . . I hear a car outside. Oh, goody!
Kenny's here!"

They listened for the car door to slam. In a while they
heard stamping on the porch and Kenny walked in, stamping.

"Oh, look everyone!" Rosemary said. "Kenny's wearing
a tie. A black tie and a black shirt. Godfather Santa. I love
it."

This was a moment for which Simone was not exactly
unprepared. In the past days she had spent considerable
times reassuring herself that it was possible to get through
Christmas dinner with Kenny as if nothing had happened
between them, as if she had not gone to his house and tried

and failed to seduce him. It should also be humanly possible not to let Rosemary and the children know. If she and Kenny hardly looked at each other, even *they* might not have to face it.

"Merry Christmas, big fella." Kenny gravely pumped George's hand. "Ho ho ho," he said to Maisie, and lifted her in the air.

"Merry Christmas, guys," Kenny said, and hugged and kissed Rosemary.

Embracing Simone, he whispered, "I could fucking kill someone. I can't cope with this holiday shit."

It was instantly, blessedly obvious how easy this would be, a day with old familiar Kenny, to whom nothing special had occurred, an experience no more intense than one she might have had if she'd gone to his salon and asked him to cut her hair. He was always accusing the people around him of having convenient memory lapses, a fault, Simone saw now, that he was sensitive to because he suffered from it himself.

Already Kenny was dealing out presents: an oddly shaped package for George, a middle-sized box for Maisie, a smaller one for Simone, and the smallest for Rosemary.

George and Maisie tore theirs open first. "Yesss!" hissed George, holding up a complicated digital watch.

Kenny said, "What every man wants on his wrist when the submarine goes down. It tells you everything—time, date, phases of the moon, longitude and latitude, Tokyo stock market closings. You can program in chicks' telephone numbers, your fucking name if you forget it, though I guess a guy your age doesn't need that feature yet."

Rosemary said, "With that watch and Simone's knife, George is equipped to guide us through the end of Western civilization."

Maisie had already set up a circular mirrored lake on which a tiny magnetized ice skater was maniacally skimming and twirling. Looking down in the mirror Simone saw: Maisie's mouth was open.

"A little girl's classic," Kenny said. "Always in good taste."

"One thing about Kenny," Rosemary said. "He knows what children want."

Kenny said, "Hey man, it should be obvious. I'm really an eleven-year-old."

Simone opened the small white box on which a little silver oval bore the logo of Glenda's shop. Inside, she found two button-shaped earrings. On each button an iridescent tropical sunset matched the necklace from Geoffrey. Coincidence was impossible, as was collaboration, as was any chance that these objects had spontaneously moved these men to think of Simone.

Perhaps Shelly bought both presents: her little private joke. Or maybe Kenny and Geoffrey went separately to Glenda's shop and Glenda arranged the match. Glenda would have imagined she was doing Simone a favor. Once again Simone felt pathetic and foolish for ever having imagined that Geoffrey had bought the necklace because it reminded him of her. At least she would know better than to think that about Kenny.

"Try them on!" said Rosemary.

It would have taken too much effort for Simone to refuse, though screwing on the earrings demanded heroic coordination. "Pull your hair back," Rosemary said.

"Gorgeous!" pronounced Kenny, and kissed Simone on the cheek so naturally that no one watching would ever suspect how recently they had enacted a scene of sexual humiliation.

"Rosemary gets two presents," Kenny said. "A hostess present and a Christmas."

The presents were wrapped together, and when Rosemary untied them, a plastic toy fell to the floor: a wind-up jaw with white teeth and shiny bright pink gums. Rosemary bent to pick it up and, with the resigned air of someone submitting to an inescapable punishment, wound the key and skittered the chattering toy across the table.

Rosemary said, "Why do I perceive this as personal criticism?"

Kenny said, "I thought you would go for it, man. I thought it would relax you. Anyway, come on now. Check out your *real* present."

"Oh, a tape!" Rosemary said. "I love music! I play it when I work. *Neon by Starlight*. Fabulous name. It looks somehow . . . homemade . . ."

"Home*grown*," Kenny said. He retrieved the tape from Rosemary and tucked it into the stereo, hit the power button, and white noise blared from the speakers.

Abruptly the static resolved itself into Kenny singing, "Embraceable You." In the background a tinkly cocktail piano and a quavering sax kept falling behind the melody and rushing to catch up. Kenny's voice slid smoothly over the quicker runs but wobbled and cracked on the longer notes so that, listening, you came to dread them.

"Pay attention," Kenny said. "The sound of my new life."

"Kenny!" Rosemary said. "That's fantastic!"

Simone caught the bored, disappointed looks on the children's faces. They'd tired of Kenny's presents. The ice skater's spin seemed more frantic, grabbing dizzily for attention. The digital watch sat on the table next to the pocketknife. How small, thought Simone, that she should be pleased by yet another competitive thought, by the children's not valuing Kenny's gift any more than hers.

Kenny and Rosemary were discussing the fact that Kenny's band would be playing New Year's Eve at the Villa Anita Motel.

"This year when the clock strikes twelve," Kenny said, "I'll be kissing the microphone."

Rosemary waved irritably at the stereo, as if enjoining it to be quiet. When it refused to obey she went over and silenced it herself. She said, "Kenny, we got you a collective present—from Simone, the children, and me."

Kenny unwrapped the box and, piece by piece, lifted out

an inlaid mother-of-pearl comb, a matching shaving brush
and mirror.

Simone thought, It's a perfect gift, then realized why
she'd thought so. Kenny already had one almost identically
like it. His combing his hair while she'd sat on his bed was
forever engraved on her mind. That he already had such a
comb and brush was another unwelcome secret that bound
them, though it was hard to be certain if Kenny would
know she knew; he had been so much more focused on
grooming himself than on Simone's presence. Still, he had
made a special point about his gangster hairbrush.

"Hey, thanks," Kenny said. "Very Al Capone. It's me."
Kenny looked into the mirror and twisted his face into a
mask of shock. "Jesus Lord in heaven, help me! A fat mirror! Adds twenty pounds to your face. A mirror from an era
when fat was cool and hip. Check it out, Simone. You'll
look like Ethel Waters."

"A fat mirror!" Rosemary flapped at the mirror and
turned away with a shriek.

Simone looked in Kenny's mirror. She didn't resemble
herself, not even the haggard version of herself she'd seen
in Kenny's bathroom. And it wasn't that she looked fat. She
looked somehow transparent, as if she could see through
her skin to the tangled nerves inside. Something had come
disconnected. A wire had jiggled loose. She recalled the air-
plane lavatory in which she'd surprised the CIA man. She'd
glimpsed her face in the mirror and seen there the face of
a woman whom a stranger had meant to find his urine.

Rosemary said, "Everybody play with your toys! I've got
serious cooking to do!"

Simone followed Rosemary into the kitchen, where a
large, attractive turkey sat in a pool of its own juices. There
were bowls of yams and mashed potatoes, broccoli and a
green salad.

Rosemary said, "You were sleeping, Simone. I know it's
hard to believe. It's a miracle what one can accomplish in
the throes of salmonella!"

Through the kitchen door Simone saw the dining-room

table set with a dark green cloth, red napkins, heavy silverware, and white plates. Rosemary said, "I want it to go on record that I am capable of approximating the housewifely Christmas virtues if I think it might add significantly to my children's happiness."

It was astonishing, really, what Rosemary was capable of. Watching her whip up a glossy, smooth flour gravy, Simone couldn't have been more shocked had she levitated off the ground.

"You look mind-blown," Rosemary said. "You must have thought that the way I've been these last months is how I've always been. Please, Simone, even Dracula had his day among the living! Within the past twenty-four hours I have begun to feel as if I, too, am rising from the tomb." And indeed Rosemary did look a shade less pale; she was flushed and slightly mottled from the heat of the oven.

"Maybe it was the solstice passing," she said. "The darkest day is behind us. But I honestly sense a thin ray of light breaking through the gloom. I feel that I am ready to make a change for the better. How strange that you can sleep for years and one morning just wake up. Isn't this Rip Van Winkle land? It must be a geographical thing. Gracious, this turkey is perfection! But who in the world's going to carve it? Are you up to it, Simone? Don't answer. I feel the same. That is: maybe I could, maybe I couldn't, but please, please don't ask me. Kenny carving our Christmas turkey—how sexist and degraded. Isn't that the very definition of *reduced circumstances*?"

The turkey fell away from the bone under Kenny's knife. He said, "Cutting is what I do. Still, I can't believe these chicks, trusting me with a carving knife, alone with women and children."

"Kenny the serial killer." Rosemary swigged from the bottle of port she had just splashed on the yams. "Isn't he adorable?"

At last the table was covered with food, and the children were summoned. George sat down before the feast and said quietly, "I'm not hungry."

"I'm not either," said Maisie.

"That's ridiculous." Rosemary poured wine for Kenny and Simone and herself, and drank hers and poured more. Kenny drained his glass almost as fast, and Rosemary refilled it.

Rosemary said, "I refuse to consider what your father probably fed you. Marshmallows with candy-bar sauce and a Pepsi chaser. Anything to feed your sugar jones and turn you into total junkies clawing your way back to his house."

Maisie munched a celery stalk. "We had Christmas Eve dinner," she said.

"I'm sure you did," said Rosemary, "in some diner somewhere where your father happens to know the waitress."

"No," George said. "At Dad's house . . ."

Rosemary said, "Well then, I can imagine. Your father sees food, like everything else, as an occasion for manipulation, a way to keep you coming back for more. For children it's white sugar with Red Dye #2 and everything deep-fried in tropical oils and doused in ketchup or honey mustard."

She finished off another glass of wine. "Really, the hardest thing for children to comprehend is that simple actions can have symbolic and metaphoric significance not directly affecting themselves. This dinner, for example, is not just food. It would *mean* something not to eat it. I was just telling Simone that this meal has meant something to me. I was saying that it dawned on me while I was pulling this together that if I could do this, I was capable of getting my life back on track.

"Of course I have no idea yet what precisely this means for me and the children. But having the will and desire to act is certainly the first step. Actually I guess the first step is admitting you have a problem; having the will to change is the second. In which case I have taken two at once and we should toast the occasion." Rosemary lifted her glass and clinked it with Simone's and Kenny's. "Of course you're hungry, goddamn it, kids. Not to eat this meal would

be a cruel mistake. This is not food but evidence of your
mother's spiritual regeneration."

"Which means we're eating the evidence," said Kenny.
"Like in that Alfred Hitchcock show where the woman
killed her husband with a leg of lamb and cooked and
served it to the cops, and they could never find the murder
weapon."

Rosemary's sniffy silence made it eloquently clear that
Kenny's reply was inadequate to her expression of faith in
the future. Tension piqued everyone's appetite. The children
even tried the yams. They each took a bite and proceeded
instantly to the mashed potatoes, with which they contrived
to be busy when the broccoli came around.

"You'd like the broccoli, Maisie," said Rosemary. "I left
it nearly raw. Think of it as green carrots with a flower on
top."

Kenny said, "This is total bullshit."

"Excuse me?" Rosemary said.

Kenny said, "I never trust those flashes that tell you your
life's going to be okay. Those are the very moments when
we are being most grievously bullshitted by the cosmos.
Your life is never going to be okay and whatever's coming
is *worse* than whatever was. All those things we took for
granted and lost, they're never coming back. Being a kid,
running around on the street after dinner. The first chick
you imagined you loved and actually let you fuck her. All
that's finished. History. Gone. You won't see that in this
life again. You're losing the whole thing, day by day: your
parents, your kids, your own body. Every minute is taking
you closer to death and you're never going back, and the
dead aren't returning to start out again as babies. Every second, your cells are getting slacker and weaker and your
muscle is losing its tone and things are growing on your
skin. If you're even halfway awake there's not a minute
you can't feel it. What's the purpose of doing *anything* is
what I want to know. I cut hair and the hair grows back. It
fucking grows after you're dead.

"I'm sorry to have to give you kids the bad news on

Christmas Day. But the earlier you're prepared for it, the less of a shock it'll be. Not that you're ever prepared for it. When you're young you don't believe it. The ability to blow it off is one of the first things you lose. This is just the dark side, guys. It's something that's always there. Lots of times I could kill myself just to escape from knowing about it."

George said, "Can I have a biscuit?"

"I thought you weren't hungry," said Maisie, and puffed out her cheeks.

"Are you saying your brother's fat?" said Rosemary. "Is that what you're doing with your cheeks? Saying your brother's fat?"

"Not listening," said Kenny. "You kids aren't listening. Species survival technique."

Simone, too, was doing her best not to dwell on what Kenny had just said. She was just not in the mood to feel sorry for Kenny right now. Why was it that everyone here wound up winning your sympathy—first George and Maisie, then Rosemary, and now, it seemed, even Kenny. At the same time she had to admit that Kenny's speech cheered her a little in that it offered a reason not to take his rejection personally. She had read a magazine article about how worries and problems can sap male sexual interest. Was this true of all men or only American men? Trouble hadn't sapped Joseph's interest, but rather deflected it elsewhere.

Everyone reached for their drinks. Rosemary said, "Except for the suicidal overlay, Kenny, that sounds like something Geoffrey would say. I know you mean it, I do. But I am sick of men sharing the secrets from the wrenching depths of their soul, the screaming cries of pain that have just at that moment bubbled up from their hearts—and later I discover they've been saying it to every woman they meet. Geoffrey had the most fabulous speech about a death's-head traffic cop and feeling his life depended on breaking through this roadblock. It was just so moving, you fell in love with him the minute that you heard it, until you realized he'd been telling every underage twit in the Hudson Valley."

Simone felt as if something cold had been dragged lightly over her shoulders. Really, she should have suspected that. Oh, poor Geoffrey, she thought.

Another silence fell, longer even than the last, so thick the children cut their turkey just to have something to do. Finally Kenny said, "Speaking of old TV . . . last week I saw this killer old show. Some creep horror thing, pre-*Twilight Zone*, black-and-white, Golden Age of Television. Very experimental. It was based on Edgar Allan Poe's 'The Telltale Heart.' This guy was lying awake in bed freaking out with guilt. On the sound track a heartbeat got louder and louder and louder, until by the final commercial it was bouncing off your skull."

"What's 'The Telltale Heart'?" asked George.

Kenny said, "It's a story about a guy who kills someone and buries him under the floor and he goes nuts thinking he can hear the guy's heart still beating. I read that story as a kid, I had to read it for school. I remember I stayed up all night—it was the most terrifying thing ever. But I can't recall why he killed the guy, if it was love or money or plain psychotic hate. Hey, listen to me. Christmas dinner and I'm talking about a heart beating under the floor. I'm starting to sound like Shelly. Worse. I sound like Shelly in drag. Shelly's always telling this perverted story about her father bringing home a human heart and getting a giant hard-on dissecting it in the bathroom sink."

Simone and the children looked down at their plates.

Before they heard or saw it, they all knew George was crying; they sensed it, like a sudden drop in barometric pressure. An abyss had opened up at the table, and at the bottom was George. Helpless tears ran down George's face. His eyes kept filling and overflowing.

Rosemary walked around the table and put her arm around him. "What's the matter?" she said.

"I hate Shelly," George said.

"Get in line, Georgie boy," said Kenny. "Join the club."

"Shelly?" said Rosemary. "Why Shelly? What did poor Shelly do?"

George began to blubber. Words stuck gummily in his mouth and broke loose in ragged pieces. Two clear words kept emerging. One was Shelly. The other was Dad.

At last even Rosemary understood. She let go of George and stood up very straight. She said, "Was Shelly at your father's today? I mean last night. Christmas Eve."

Maisie had been staring at George, but now she quickly recovered and looked slightly fevered and glassy-eyed with energy and excitement, with the thrill of finally saying what was most crucial and most forbidden. She took a deep theatrical breath and self-consciously held it till the air leaked out of her in a high, breathy whistle. Using her rib cage for emphasis was something Rosemary would do, and as always, it startled Simone to see Rosemary in her children. Maisie filled her lungs again and this time said, "Shelly was at Dad's last night and this morning. Shelly said that next Christmas we would all be having Christmas here at this house."

It was how George talked about grisly murders and bloody auto wrecks, how Geoffrey talked about temptation and getting old and regret, how Kenny talked about losing your life and nothing coming back. So Maisie, too, waited for Rosemary to promise it wouldn't happen.

"Not *all* of us," George said. "Not Mom."

But Maisie already knew that. She was looking at Rosemary, more or less as she'd looked at Simone when they'd been shot at in the forest. In danger the children took their cue from the nearest adult.

Rosemary said, "And what did your father say?" But she didn't wait for an answer. She turned and walked out of the room.

George called after her, "We said we wanted to live with *you*, Mom!"

They all heard the bathroom door close. No one moved or said a word. The whole kitchen seemed to hum softly, some hum from the depths of the house, to which the refrigerator added a ratlike squeal Simone couldn't remember hearing.

Kenny said, "Fuck Shelly, that lying motherfucking bitch." He stood up and grabbed his jacket and stormed out of the house.

Simone and the children remained at the table. Maisie twisted a coil of hair and ran her finger along the dry ends. George poked at his chewed-over turkey with such concentration you would have thought the solution to their dilemma lay beneath that gristle and skin. Simone fought the urge to tell him not to play with his food. It was Rosemary's voice she imagined, coming from her mouth, and this seemed the clearest sign yet of how mixed up everything was.

Maisie said, "Kenny forgot his present. We'll have to save it and give it to him."

Out of some reflex, Simone said, "That's very nice of you, Maisie." George looked stricken, as he had since Rosemary left the table. Simone thought: He will feel better if he washes his face. But selfishly, she didn't want him getting up from the table. Neither Simone nor Maisie nor George wanted the others to leave. This was what they had learned in the forest: Keep together. Keep quiet. Don't move.

In the chalky winter light the children's faces were tense. They had reverted completely to what they were when Simone arrived. There was no sign of her having been here, of her having helped the children. They were Rosemary and Geoffrey's children, that was the story of their lives, and in a short time their Haitian caregiver would come to seem like a minor character. Simone saw the children's lives as cold clear oily water that would rush in and fill the empty space created by her absence.

Simone said, "I want to tell you something. You are thinking this is your life, but your life will change. You are thinking you will always be children, but you will grow up. You can decide how late to stay up and what you want for dinner. You will not always live with your parents. You can go to another country—"

Simone stopped, appalled at herself. Now she *did* sound like Rosemary, lecturing the children on the subject of their own childhood. And what was she telling them? They had already decided what they would eat and when they would go to sleep. These were not their problems. Their problem was that they would soon be propelled into a whole other life and there was no way they could stop it, nothing they could do.

No one spoke for a long time. Somewhere, far off in the house, chimes struck. Rosemary did not return. From where they sat, they would have heard if she had come out of the bathroom.

Finally George said, "Hadn't you better go check on Mom?"

They all knew too much time had passed; something had to be done. Simone got up and walked slowly down the hall. She stopped and listened at the bathroom door.

"Rosemary?" she said. "Mrs. Porter?" There was no reply. She hesitated, then knocked on the door with a light tap in which anyone could have heard how alarmed she was.

"Come in," Rosemary said.

Simone opened the door too fast. A hot cloud of steam wet her face.

Rosemary was standing by the sink. She was naked and dripping wet. She turned and held out her palms to Simone. Blood ran down her forearms and in watery rivulets down her pale belly. There was blood all over the bathroom. Bright scarlet marbled the veiny tiles and blotched the dirty towels. It was stunning what a spectacular mess a little blood could make. The light tube over the mirror buzzed, a dying-insect hum. Rosemary showed Simone her wrists and studied them with diagnostic scrutiny, as if the two of them were doctors consulting on an emergency case.

She had made a cut across each of her wrists, a surface scratch with a razor. She seemed understandably awestruck by how much blood had flowed. But Rosemary wasn't in mortal danger; one wrist had almost stopped bleeding. Simone had to watch the other before she saw blood well up. Rosemary's cutting her wrists had not been serious, just a raging, impotent gesture—like Joseph's throwing beer bottles, but more like throwing them at yourself. If you intend to kill yourself, you don't do it during Christmas dinner and leave the bathroom door unlocked and say "Come in" when someone knocks.

"I meant to do it in the shower," Rosemary said, "but the shower felt so wonderful I could almost find a reason to go on living." The towel she'd wrapped around herself was bloodstained, wet, too small. "Of course, the second I got out of the shower, things got a little more urgent and suddenly it felt like an—I don't know—a now-or-never situation. They always say that cutting your wrists isn't the way to do it, but of course you never believe them until you try it yourself."

Rosemary was not in danger, and it was good that Simone knew that and knew that what she had to do was get Rosemary cleaned up and the place in some kind of order before George and Maisie saw it. There was blood on the unscrewed tube of the children's bubble-gum toothpaste. Simone should go to the children—they would be very worried. She should tell them some reassuring half-truth, then come back and help Rosemary.

Rosemary held out her hands to Simone. There was no way for Simone to refuse them. She braced herself not to mind the clammy wetness or Rosemary's blood. Rosemary's hands rested lightly in Simone's upturned palms. They stood like that for a very long time, looking past each other, not moving. Simone felt that to remove her hands would hurt Rosemary severely, and for one giddy moment feared they would stay like that forever.

At last they heard footsteps and a knock on the door. Simone used the distraction to disengage her hands. Another knock followed. Rosemary wrapped her arms around herself and looked, terrified, at Simone.

"Mom, are you okay in there?" George's high voice trembled on the other side of the door.

Rosemary said, "Mommy's got a touch of stomach flu. We'll be out in a minute."

There was a moment of hesitation while George weighed this information. Then he said, "Kenny said to tell you that he had a terrific time, and he was sorry he had to split."

It took Simone a moment to realize this hadn't happened. She had been there when Kenny left, and he had said no such thing. George must have wanted to console his mother about the Christmas being ruined. George must have thought he caused it, blurting out the truth about Shelly. It was a good little lie, a commendable lie—but a lie nonetheless. Simone had never heard George lie, but clearly he had the knack, he had picked it up automatically, grown it, like adult teeth. It was the longest, most extroverted sentence she had ever heard him utter, and its being a lie disturbed her as much as Rosemary's blood.

Neither Simone nor Rosemary breathed till they heard George leave. Then Rosemary clasped her hands and said, "Thank you, Lord, for not letting George walk in. It would have blown the poor child's mind forever and ever and ever."

Rosemary cleared a space in the mirror and regarded herself through the smeary haze of blood and water. She said, "We look like a couple of neo-Satanist hippies or Aztec priestesses participating in some vile primitive blood ritual. We could be Sumerian goddesses, those shiny gold ones without eyes. Sacrificial spirits so scary you hit the ground when you see them, and the first things you reach for are a knife and someone else's beating heart . . . Oh, God, whatever fluids I've lost, alcohol isn't among them."

Simone looked in the mirror. She watched Rosemary talking. And suddenly she had the oddest sense of having always expected to see this. She had seen this scene, or dreamed it: Rosemary naked, the tiles, the blood.

Simone caught herself and ran the hot water so she could wash the blood off her hands. But strangely, she couldn't

do it, and she stared blankly at the water. Hot water continued to spatter and cough, filling the room with more steam.

Then suddenly she remembered where she had seen all
this before. Of course. It was Manet's *Olympia*, annotated
by Joseph. The naked bloody white woman, the black
woman servant: differently positioned but otherwise the
same.

Yet anyone who looked closer would see that it wasn't
the same. Even with Joseph's additions, the painting was
comforting compared to this. The girl in the painting was
saucy and firm, reclining on her bed. Rosemary's white
flesh puckered with age as she grabbed at her slipping
towel. The girl in the painting half smiled at you; Rosemary's eyes bulged with fear. The wounds Joseph painted
were elegant, like jewelry or tattoos, compared to the
smeary red fingerprints turning brown on the children's
towels. A black cat sat in the painting, placid and impas-
sive, but the pets of this house had died one by one and
been buried outside by the children: shards of bone and
scraps of fur decomposing under the snow. The servant in
the painting was as unreadable as the cat, but Simone
looked like someone having a vision of a sea of blood.

There would be more bodies, more blood. Simone understood that now. She knew what sacrificial spirits Rosemary
had meant. They had followed her here from Haiti. They
were giant carrion-eating crows, flying around the earth and
from time to time alighting and pecking every living thing
to shreds. They were everywhere, could find you anywhere;
they were brutal, violent, and greedy, and every little cru-
elty was an offering on their altar. They were blind and evil
and merciless, a sea of blood wouldn't quench their thirst.

Staring fixedly at the bathroom floor, Rosemary said,
"Dear Heloise. Perhaps you can give me some helpful advice on this embarrassing home repair problem. After my
last suicide attempt we've had these terrible stubborn
bloodstains in the grout between the bathroom tiles."

Rosemary smiled weakly at Simone. The blood on her
face looked like war paint.

"Dear God," she said. "Who knows? My blood in the tile grout may turn out to be Shelly's headache. Let her write the goddamn letter, get the bathroom cleaned. Let her have the problems, Geoffrey included. I will be somewhere else."

Rosemary sat down on the edge of the tub and buried her face in her hands. "I'm thinking about the future," she said. "That must be a positive sign."